Wonders Never Cease
Debra Salonen

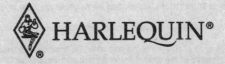

HARLEQUIN®

TORONTO • NEW YORK • LONDON
AMSTERDAM • PARIS • SYDNEY • HAMBURG
STOCKHOLM • ATHENS • TOKYO • MILAN • MADRID
PRAGUE • WARSAW • BUDAPEST • AUCKLAND

ISBN 0-373-71061-5

WONDERS NEVER CEASE

This edition published by arrangement with Harlequin Books S.A.

® and TM are trademarks of the publisher. Trademarks indicated with ® are registered in the United States Patent and Trademark Office, the Canadian Trade Marks Office and in other countries.

Visit us at www.eHarlequin.com

Printed in U.S.A.

To Paula—thank you for taking the leap.
And in memory of Chelsey—my very own Czar.

CHAPTER ONE

"PERMISSION TO ENTER with dog, sir."

The formal request was accompanied by a discreet knock on the jamb of the door. Amos didn't need to look up to know who was standing in his doorway. The vast majority of officers in his department didn't know the meaning of the word *polite* unless they were on the witness stand, and even that was questionable.

Sergeant Amos Simms had headed the detective division of the Bullion, California, police department for twelve of his twenty-five years on the force. It was enough. He was ready to stay home and write his novel, but his dream was to establish a canine unit before he retired.

He'd lobbied the city council for six years for permission and funds. The politicians had come up with an abundance of creative excuses, but Amos had finally worn them down and had gone hunting for the right dog and handler. Two months ago, he'd found the perfect combination: Ben Jacobs and Czar.

Now Amos just had to sell the public on the newest members of the Bullion P.D.

"Come in, Jacobs. We're not terribly formal here. Although I must say, it's a welcome change." Amos was fifty-six but most days felt eighty-six. He rubbed at the perpetual kink in his neck. "Have a seat. And try not to get too much hair on the carpet." He was joking, but the serious young man didn't smile. Amos had yet to see him smile.

Ben Jacobs was thirty-six, unmarried, a twelve-year veteran with the Santa Ignacio Police Force. Before that—according to his file—he'd served in the Navy and had been discharged with honors. At their first interview, Amos had discerned a strength of character and inherent intelligence that clearly made him the right choice.

Amos had liked Ben instantly, but he wasn't sure whether or not Jacobs liked him—or anyone else for that matter, except his dog.

"We're staging a demonstration today at two," Amos said, getting straight to the heart of the matter. Jacobs wasn't going to like this news.

The man nodded—a scant lowering of the chin. His serious brown eyes never left Amos.

A quick glance downward showed a second pair of serious brown eyes watching him as well. Amos repressed a shiver. He liked animals and had the greatest respect for police dogs, but he knew they were an extension of the person training them. And there was something shadowy, unapproachable, about Ben Jacobs. Something that kept him apart from the others in the department.

"The mayor will be there. And the *Sentinel*'s sending a reporter and a photographer. We'll meet at Founder's Park at two o'clock."

"Yes, sir."

Jacobs rose. He was a big man, but not bulky. At six foot one, he weighed a lean one hundred ninety pounds, but his fitness reports proved it was all muscle. His uniform differed from the ones the rest of Amos's officers wore. His black pants had extra pockets to carry dog-related gear, and he wore a black baseball cap with a canine patch framed by the words *Bullion Police*.

Amos couldn't look at the man standing before him without some sense of pride. His years of political wrangling had finally paid off. So far, Bullion P.D. had one handler, one dog and a slick new squad car, a four-wheel-drive Chevrolet Blazer with the back compartment fitted with a sliding window to keep the dog in touch with his handler. Amos hoped this would be the first of four units.

While Bullion itself boasted a modest population of just over 25,000 residents, the county was poised for growth. A new university being built in the Central Valley town of Merced, just forty-five miles away, would surely send home buyers Bullion's way. And Amos believed that in law enforcement, it paid to plan ahead. Ben and Czar were part of that plan but first they would have to prove themselves. This was the part Jacobs wasn't going to like.

"And bring along the bite suit."

Jacobs's movements were slow and deliberate. He didn't look at Amos when he asked softly, "Who will be wearing the suit, sir?"

"The reporter."

Jacobs inhaled sharply. Czar, who had risen to stand at his master's knee, pricked up his big, sharply pointed ears. He looked at Amos accusingly, as if knowing the chief was to blame for his master's disquiet; his unblinking stare seemed to pin Amos to his chair.

Amos didn't like being put on the spot by a dog, so he piled on the rest of the bad news. "The reporter's name is Jill Martin."

"A woman?" Jacobs took one step closer; so did the dog. Both were staring at Amos with dark, unreadable looks. "I strongly protest, sir. Did you explain to her that this is not a game? She could get hurt."

"She's got a reputation of being…spunky."

"Spunky?" Jacobs repeated. "This sounds like P.R.B.S. to me."

"Like what?"

"Public relations bullshit, sir."

Amos snorted, which made Czar cock his head. His brown eyes watched Amos as though he expected him to explode.

Amos knew that Czar, a ten-year-old German shepherd, was the only reason he'd gotten someone of Ben Jacobs's caliber to move to a Podunk town in the central Sierras. In most departments, mandatory retirement age for a canine is ten, but Jacobs felt Czar had at least two more good years left. Amos knew from talking to other canine handlers, retirement for a police dog meant imminent death. Most dogs went home with their handlers to live out the rest of their days, but those days usually amounted to only a few weeks once the dog realized he wasn't going back to the job he loved. Jacobs wasn't ready to let Czar go, and Amos felt lucky to have a couple of years with a dog of Czar's quality and experience. Within the next two years, Amos hoped to have his other canine units in place. *Unless some "spunky" wild-card reporter screwed things up.*

"P.R.B.S. I like that. And I agree. But this is at the mayor's request and there's no getting out of it." Amos glanced at the pile of papers weighing down one corner of his desk. "I'll meet you out there. Just suit her up, give her all the standard warnings and let the chips fall where they may. Maybe, just this once, we'll get lucky."

"DORRY FISHBANK, you're amazing," Jill Martin exclaimed, her gaze feasting on the two-inch-thick sheaf of papers clasped in the clerk's ink-stained fingers. "If you weren't a woman, I'd kiss you."

Dorry took a step back, whether from Jill's ebullience or

to protect her bundle, Jill wasn't sure. But it didn't matter. Here finally, within arm's reach, was pay dirt. Proof positive that Land Barons—the huge corporation her ex-husband worked for—was poised to exploit the citizens and environment of Bullion, California, with a new housing development called Excelsior Estates. Which, if Jill's investigation proved true, would break ground next week upon the contaminated tailings from the old Excelsior mine.

"This is it, Dorry," Jill said, trying to rein in her excitement. "We're talking jugular. If the documentation in those files is as solid as it looks, there's no way the planning commission could have approved that development without turning a blind eye to the pollution problem. I bet half the commissioners will be up on charges before this is over."

"Shh," Dorry hissed, the sound blending with the overhead racket of water pipes and muffled foot traffic. Jill hadn't known a basement level existed in the Bullion County Courthouse until Dorry showed her the vanguard of dusty file cabinets tucked in one remote corner. With surprisingly little effort, Dorry had managed to produce half a dozen legal-size folders stuffed with the documentation of land sales and property transfers dating back a hundred years. Folders she now held—white-knuckled—in her hand.

Jill tried to stifle her exuberance. Her mother always warned Jill about coming on too strong, "That kind of intensity is most unattractive, Jillian." Mathilda "Mattie" Jensen had a rule for every social situation and wasn't shy about imposing them on Jill.

"Don't worry, Dorry," Jill said, heeding Mattie's criticism. "Nobody knows about this but you and me. And I'm a reporter. You're my source. You're protected, like a lawyer-client kind of thing."

Behind the teal rims of her oversize bifocals, Dorry's eyes widened. "Really?"

"I'd never give up my source. I'd fry first." Jill crossed a big X from shoulder to waist. "But don't worry, it won't come to that. Where's the copier?" Jill squinted into the gloom; she supposed it was too much to hope the county kept a copy machine in the basement.

"A what?"

"Copier. I don't want to take the originals."

"Oh my gosh, no," Dorry peeped. "These are official documents. You can't have them, and I can't make copies without permission."

Jill swallowed hard to hide her impatience. "It's just a copy. Who's gonna care?"

"My boss for one," Dorry said stubbornly.

Up to this point, Dorry had been as docile as a puppy and eager to help Jill on her quest—especially when Jill hinted that her boss, Will Ogden, the Bullion *Sentinel*'s rather hunky city editor, might be interested in their discoveries. Apparently unrequited love had its limits.

"I'm not about to lose my job over this, Jill. I went looking for these because I was curious. I wouldn't have even thought to look here if you hadn't asked. I don't think anyone remembers about that old law."

When Betty Jean Fenway, the current Republican Woman of the Year and former loan officer of the Bullion County Savings and Loan, mentioned that at one time all loans in the county had been required to have a well test before escrow could close, Jill had kissed her God of Serendipity. Or rather, the small onyx carving of a smiling male figure her mother had sent from Bali.

"Dorry," Jill said soberly, trying to impart the gravity of this development, "think how important this could be.

We didn't read all the reports just now, but you could see a pattern developing, couldn't you?''

Dorry half shrugged one shoulder; the strap of her navy jumper slid over the polyester print blouse as far as her thickened biceps.

"Think about it, Dorry," Jill pleaded. "Some of the wells on those parcels near the mine were showing contaminants thirty years back. I'm no chemist and I didn't understand exactly what kind of stuff is in them or how bad it is, but I saw the word *arsenic.* You did, too. Didn't you?''

Dorry's sigh sent a halo of dust motes mushrooming upward into the light.

"We can't just let that slide and hope it all went away in the course of the last few years, can we?''

Dorry wavered visibly. Jill held her breath.

The dim light of the overhead fluorescent bulbs made Dorry appear sad and uncertain…and a lot older than thirty-three or thirty-four. Jill didn't know Dorry's exact age, but she remembered seeing her around school. Jill had moved to Bullion in her sophomore year of high school, and she recalled that kids had called Dorry "dumb Dorry." No one—not even the teachers, it seemed—thought Dorry would amount to much. But she'd gone to work for the County Recorder the day after graduation and hadn't missed a day in seventeen years. Jill knew that for a fact; she'd even written a feature story on Dorry Fishbank.

"I need to think about this, Jill.''

"What's to think about?" Jill felt her patience slipping. "If there's pollution, the public deserves to know. If Land Barons knew about it and tried to cover it up or worse, paid someone in Planning to hush it up, they deserve to face the music. What else is there?''

"My job for one thing," Dorry said in a tight voice.

Having grown up with a bossy mother as a role model,

Jill had vowed to work on her people skills when she was an adult. She tried for a plucky smile.

"Dorry, please," Jill wheedled. "Just gimme one. The oldest. Or the newest. I don't care. Just the hint of ground-water pollution might be enough to invoke public scrutiny and get someone to put the brakes on this project. I'll never mention your name. I swear to the God of Truth and Light. I'll even *give* you the God of Truth and Light in exchange for one of those reports."

"No," Dorry said firmly. She wrapped her pudgy arms around the manila files like a mother protecting her first-born. "*If—*" she emphasized the word with a stern, old-maid schoolteacher finality "—I decide to give you any-thing, it will be a copy, and I will pick which one and when. I have to think about this. I can't put my job on the line, Jill. I've got a family to support." Her eyes narrowed and her lips formed a hard line. "My brothers wouldn't much appreciate you getting me in trouble and them having to go to work for a living."

The threat was subtle but understood. Jill had been away from Bullion for nearly nine years—four years of college then a stint as a corporate vagabond following Peter around the country but one never forgot people like the Fishbank brothers. Surly. Ugly. And Mean. Jill couldn't remember their real names but those nicknames pretty well summed up their dispositions.

"Here," Jill said, fishing in the hip pocket of her jeans for a business card. "Call me anytime. I know you're wor-ried, but this is vital, Dorry. You can't let them get away with this. Bullion's future may rest on your shoulders."

A little thick, Jill thought, but then she'd never shied away from hyperbole—even in her obits.

A sudden buzzing sound made Dorry flinch as though she'd taken a bullet; the color drained from her rounded cheeks, making the artificial swatches of rose below each eye stand out like war paint. Jill clawed at the vibration tickling her waist. "My beeper," she choked out, trying to maintain her cool. Today was her first day with her new toy, and she hadn't experienced its "call" before.

She held the small violet device to the light and squinted at the numerical message. "Is there a phone around here?"

Dorry pointed to an old black model attached to a block wall near the stairs. "I have to put these back," she said, slinking away like a sinner who'd been given a reprieve at hell's less-than-pearly gates.

Jill tapped her foot impatiently, waiting for the rotary dial to complete its individual numbers. *If the Time God had meant for us to waste time dialing, he wouldn't have invented push-button phones.*

She gave her name to the person on the other end of the line and listened attentively. "Oh, he did, did he?" she growled before slamming the phone back in place. "The nerve of that man!"

Jill snagged the leather satchel she used as a briefcase off the top of a dusty cabinet. "I gotta fly. Mondo Cop's trying to pull a fast one."

"Mondo Cop?" Dorry questioned, locking the metal fire door behind them.

Jill paused, one foot on the stairway. "You know—the hunky new cop with the dog. That's what the she-cops are calling him because he's supposed to be the ultimate in cool, but, cool or not, you don't move up your appointment with no notice so the reporter won't be there on time and you can weasel out of the interview."

Jill dashed up three steps then turned around and ran back down two. "Dorry, I'll call you later. I appreciate this. I mean it. You're my one true lead, and I'll protect you with everything I've got. Okay?" She thought—hoped—

that tiny dipping of Dorry's head was an affirmative. "Okay. Gotta run."

As she sped out of the parking lot, Jill glanced at the oversized watch on her wrist. The Time God kept track of one's little indiscretions, and Jill was in enough trouble with him already. Hadn't she neglected to write to her mother for six months—failing to share such trivial matters as her final divorce decree and Peter's subsequent marriage to Jill's supposed best friend and former colleague, Clarice Asher?

Jill downshifted and stepped on the gas. Her little red MR2 shot forward. A gust of pure September, heavy with the pungent aroma of tarweed, channeled in through the open T-top. The smell reminded her of her sophomore year of high school when she and Penny had called themselves the "Two Misfiteers" and explored their alien—and sometimes hostile—environment via horseback. Jill remembered it as one of those rare, benign eras when the Time God had been magnanimous.

Three hours earlier, over a bag of powdered doughnuts—granted, an iffy choice to share with twin toddlers—Jill and Penny had discussed Jill's impending meeting with the city's newest hire.

"So tell me about this cop. I hear he's gorgeous and single."

"I haven't met him," Jill had said, licking white residue from her fingers. Normally, she would have found it hard to believe that in a town the size of Bullion, she hadn't bumped into the celebrated dog handler by now. But her on-the-sly investigation into Land Barons's exploits in Bullion was really eating into her time. Plus, she had a deadline to get the last of Peter's crap out of her garage. Her "ex" and his "new" were scheduled back in town this coming weekend for the big Land Barons gala.

"You can't tell much by his official picture. All hat, no-nonsense frown. But the dog is handsome. Classic Rin-Tin-Tin look. Tan with a black saddle and black muzzle. Keenly intelligent gaze. Awesome."

"You know, Jill," her friend had said with a maternal sigh, "it says something about your lack of social life when you're more impressed by the dog than the man. Why are you interviewing him? I thought the paper already ran the story."

Knowing Penny's tendency to worry, Jill had no intention of mentioning her impending rendezvous with a bite suit. "Just the press release from the Bullion P.D. The bureaucracy gives one side—all praise and accomplishment, triumphs and commendations. But when you talk to the regular uniforms, you sometimes get a different story."

"What do they say?"

"That he's smart, gorgeous and a real loner."

Jill could identify with the latter. Until her mother had put her foot down and declared that Jill would attend Bullion High for her final three—uninterrupted—years, Jill had never felt connected to one place. But now Bullion was home, and Jill took her job seriously. She intended to write a fair and accurate account of the canine patrol—even though she knew she'd been set up to fail courtesy of Bullion's mayor, Bud Francis.

The man had never forgiven her for painting an honest, but unflattering, picture of him two months ago after the last city council meeting she'd covered. After the series of irate calls to her publisher, Everett Davenport, Jill had been taken off the city beat.

This article was Jill's ticket out of Obituary Land, and she wasn't about to be late.

BEN JACOBS STUDIED the high-tech chronometer on his wrist. One twenty-seven. *Three more minutes and I'm outta here.* Jill Martin would have to get her interview over the telephone. The photographer, Jamal Mosely, an enthusiastic young African-American, had already snapped a few shots of Ben and Czar as they were unloading gear from the back of the Blazer.

Ben appreciated the new vehicle. In Santa Ignacio, he and Czar had been number eight on the totem pole for a new car, and even then it wouldn't have been as well equipped as the one he had here in Bullion. The Blazer helped reinforce in Ben's mind the validity of his move. Joely, his sister, thought he was crazy. "You'd sacrifice your seniority for a dog?"

Even after all these years, she didn't have a clue what Czar meant to him. They were a team. Twenty-four seven. They ate together, slept together and worked together. They were brothers, friends, partners and in a way—parent and child. Czar was intelligent, and Ben sometimes joked that his dog was smarter than any of his friends. In truth, Czar was his only true friend. It hadn't been hard to choose Czar over seniority.

In Bullion, they might have a chance to make a difference again. Santa Ignacio's murder toll was approaching the level of bigger cities like Oakland and L.A. Drugs were rampant. It was easy for a cop to feel overwhelmed, outnumbered and burnt out. Here, Ben hoped to create a legacy that would honor Czar.

And he wasn't about to see his new beginning screwed up by a story hound. He didn't trust the press. He didn't know any reporters personally, but he'd heard plenty of horror stories—all of which ended with the cop getting screwed. He hoped his obvious little ploy of moving up the interview time worked. He'd avoid this interview for as long as possible.

He was just reaching down for the canvas duffel bag containing the bite suit when a little, where's-the-fire, red sports car sped into the parking lot. Its tires coughed up a cloud of dust as the driver slammed on the brakes. A woman dressed in formfitting, indigo-blue jeans, white leather tennis shoes and a long-sleeve denim shirt decorated with embroidered American flags leaped from the car as though the seat cushion was on fire. She paused to lean over the side left open by the T-top, and grabbed a small leather backpack that looked like something his fifteen-year-old niece might carry; then she dashed toward him.

Obviously, she was worried about being late and didn't want him to bail, and understandably, she couldn't know how dangerous it was to run up to a canine officer when his dog was standing beside him, ready to defend him to the death. Blood and lawsuits flashed before his eyes, but for the life of him, he couldn't react. His mouth dropped open as though he might give Czar a command, but all that came out was a sharp little puff of air.

"Hi. You must be Mondo…I mean, Officer Jacobs. I'm Jill Martin." Her words tumbled over him like kernels of candy corn at Halloween, sweet and yummy, but lacking in substance. When he didn't shake the outstretched hand she offered, she dropped to both knees on the grass—throat level for Czar—and held out the same hand. "And you must be Czar."

Finally, Ben got back some element of control. He reached for Czar's leash at the same moment Czar went for the slim, pale limb offered up so innocently. Ben was about to throw a body block, when he saw the hand pet his dog's head. Czar's broomlike tail swished back and forth sonorously.

Czar was behaving as though he'd just found an old friend. Ben wasn't sure who to be mad at: her for running up to a police dog, Czar for being uncharacteristically friendly or himself for acting like a mute idiot.

Her. She was the reporter.

"Never run up to a police dog," he ordered in his very best I-am-the-law-and-you-will-do-what-I-say voice.

"Why? Will he lick me to death?" she joked, looking up at him. Ben couldn't see her eyes, which were hidden by dark glasses, squarish in design with a tie-dyed croaky, but he had no trouble interpreting her grin.

He held back a sigh. The cocky ones were the very worst. They had no idea what they were getting into when they pitted themselves against a trained police dog. He'd seen grown men try to take down a dog and come away with a bloody arm to show for all their bravado.

Ben gave a low command to Czar. The dog backed off from his newfound friend and took his place at Ben's side. The reporter pulled her glasses down on her nose, winked at Czar, then rose.

She was tall, but not as tall as Ben had first thought. She just carried herself with natural grace and straight posture as though she might have been a model. She was pretty enough to model, with fresh, sort of Scandinavian features and reddish-blond hair scraped back into a thick ponytail. Little wind wisps curled about her face. She looked young.

Without intending to, he asked, "Are you old enough to do this?"

"How old do you *have* to be?" she returned, her tone filled with mirth. "I'm five years younger than you."

"How do you know how old I am?"

She grinned and crossed her arms, drawing Ben's gaze to the gentle swell of her bosom. "I do my homework. You're thirty-six. Czar is ten. You arrived here eight days ago, although you were officially hired in August. You had to finish out your commitment to the Santa Ignacio force.

You bought the old Turner house, which before it was the Turner house was the Mobrick house. I know a lot about the house. More, in fact, than I know about you. What would you like to tell me?''

Ben was getting that tongue-tied feeling again. He couldn't explain it. He felt as stupid as a schoolboy on his first day at a new school talking to the homecoming queen.

"Were you homecoming queen?" *Who is running my mouth?*

She laughed. A bright, happy sound that caught at his chest somewhere under his flack vest. "Lord, no. Much as my mother prayed for that glorious honor, it wasn't meant to be. I was far too radical. I was busy reading *The Women's Room* and rallying support for the Equal Rights Amendment and writing scathing editorials for the school paper. Real geek stuff.

"I did try out for cheerleader in eighth grade because my mother begged me to, but thank God, they found six other willing sacrificial lambs who could yell without screeching. Don't ever ask me to yell. It's ugly, isn't it, Jamal?" She shuddered theatrically and looked toward the photographer who was just lowering his camera.

"Yep. Don't ask her to sing, either."

She stuck out her pretty, pink tongue at him.

Whipping off her sunglasses so they hung by the colorful strap just below the V of her open neckline, she gave Ben a serious look. Her eyes were greenish-brown with maybe a little gray thrown in. "So, what's the agenda? Why'd you move up the time? Hoping I'd be late?"

Ben didn't embarrass easily and he knew his face wasn't showing any change of color, still he had a feeling she knew that had been his intent. "I have an early roster call to meet everyone. My schedule's been hit and miss this week."

"I can imagine. New town, new problems. You'll settle in real fast, though. Bullion is gonna be a piece of cake compared to Santa Ignacio."

Ben weighed his words, knowing they could be used against him. "Czar and I are looking forward to the challenge."

"What challenge?"

"It's always a challenge getting adjusted to a new area and learning what kind of crime to be on the lookout for, where a city's strong points lie and where its weaknesses are." She'd extracted a slim, wire-bound notebook from her purse, along with a mustard-colored pencil. Cupping the cardboard-backed notepad in her palm, she scribbled something, glancing around while she wrote.

"Sergeant Simms says you will be the founding pair in what he hopes will grow to be a four-unit canine division." She paused and looked at him, then at Czar. "Every time he says that, I have this picture of you two spawning little baby dogs and cops. Not a pretty picture."

Ben tried not to laugh. It wasn't something that came easily to him and he usually had no trouble controlling it, but when she gave him an impish grin, he hooted.

He was saved from having to reply by the arrival of another police car and a huge, yellow, boatlike Cadillac.

"Oh look, Jamal. The mayor's here. Hide the liquor."

Ben bit down on the inside of his lower lip. That seemed to do the trick. He automatically reached down to stroke Czar's head and reassure him the people approaching were friends not potential suspects. He whispered a soothing word of encouragement.

"Are you speaking Dog?" Jill Martin whispered, leaning toward him.

"German. The dogs are imported from Germany and are initially trained in German. It seemed easier to retrain the cops than the dogs. And by using German commands, the average citizen can't give a dog a command.''

"Would he follow my command if I knew any German?''

"Probably not, but it might be enough to throw him off stride or distract him. Most dogs are attuned to their handler's voice and respond only to him.''

"If you were wounded or incapacitated, who would he respond to?''

"I can answer that,'' Sergeant Simms said, joining them. "When I was scouting the market for our canine unit, I took part in several training sessions and a couple of patrols. One dog and handler that looked particularly promising were involved in a gang fracas. The officer was wounded and unconscious. The dog wouldn't let the paramedics near, they had to shoot the dog to get to the officer.''

Ben was watching her. Her eyes filled with moisture, turning the ambivalent color into a limpid shade of green. Her chin lifted; she blinked rapidly and looked away.

"Didn't kill him, did they? Damn dogs cost a frickin' fortune,'' Mayor Bud Francis said, sauntering up to join the group. He was a small man, under five foot seven even with his built-up shoes. To make up for his size, he talked in a loud, booming voice.

Ben liked to make up his own mind about people and usually gave himself time to assess a person but he didn't need a second glance to peg Bud Francis. Family name, inherited wealth and a serious drinking problem. A combination Ben knew all too well—thanks to his father—a functional alcoholic who could hide his addiction from the world, but not his family.

Czar—apparently sensing Ben's disquiet—flattened his ears and pressed close to Ben's leg.

Jill Martin suddenly did that dropping-to-her-knees-thing again and pressed her face close to Czar's. "He looks like a bear when he does that. Look how cute he is, Jamal. Did you get a picture of that?"

This was Ben's worst nightmare. Czar was totally trust-worthy in public unless he was picking up on Ben's feel-ings, which at the moment were slightly askew.

"I think we'd better get this show on the road." He jerked on Czar's leash and gave him the one-word com-mand to jump into the back of the Blazer. Czar cleared the tailgate gracefully, and plopped down, apparently sensing his master's need to have him out of the way.

Ben faced his commanding officer. "I would like to go on record protesting the idea of using Ms. Martin in the bite suit. It's always best to use someone who is familiar with the dogs and knows how to react defensively. And the best defense—the *only* defense—is to lie still once you're down."

Ben talked loud enough for everyone to hear. He used his most official tone. He didn't want to take the fall for what most likely would happen. She'd get hurt, and the department would blame him and Czar.

Jill Martin approached him slowly—the exact opposite of how she'd approached his ferocious police dog. "Would you go over each step of the training procedure and tell me what to expect and what to do? I don't want to get hurt nor do I want to do anything that could compromise the de-partment or reflect badly on your program."

That was a very generous and unexpected sentiment on her part, but Ben didn't believe her. She might not want to be the cause of any problems, but she'd sure as hell write about them if they came up.

He pulled the forty-pound suit from the bag and de-scribed what she could expect to feel. "The most important thing to remember is to lie still once he has apprehended you. The dogs are taught to apprehend and guard. He will circle you until I get there, but if you move he'll pounce on you. So you don't get up and run again.''

She never looked directly at him; she was taking notes and examining the padded suit. ''Will he attack from behind?''

''He doesn't *attack*. People have this distorted Hollywood image of trained killers who go for the jugular. Sort of lethal weapons with fur. These dogs use their speed, their bite power and their looks to intimidate and hold a suspect until the foot patrol can make the arrest. If a suspect is fleeing and the dog has made visual contact, he will chase that suspect, pulling him down to stop him if necessary but it's not a random attack.''

She was still taking notes, so he continued. ''I'd honestly prefer you to do your story with the two of us on patrol. You could see Czar bully his way through a gang of thugs with his sheer presence then play with a group of schoolkids. He's gentle and respectful and playful with people, but he knows his job and how to do it.''

Ben took a deep breath and waited for someone to say something.

''I'll take those kind of pictures, too, but couldn't we get at least one shot of Jill being tackled?'' the photographer said, a wry grin on his face. ''You don't know how happy it would make some of the people back at the paper. I already have requests for four eight-by-tens.''

Jill swatted him with her notepad. ''You just wait, Mosely. My next batch of cookies will have a special treasure in one, just for you. Won't they, Czar?''

For a moment, Ben thought he might have talked his way out of this fiasco. They might have gone for it, but then the mayor spoke.

"Oh, we're here now," the man said. "Let's just do it. I haven't gotten to see a practice session, and Jill's the one who insisted on being the dummy. No pun intended." He laughed at his own joke.

Ben liked the shape of Jill's face, but he'd overlooked the strength of her jaw until he saw her eyes narrow and jaw clench. There was no love lost between her and the mayor. Ben was curious, but he didn't have a chance to do more than wonder.

"Let's do it." Jill yanked the suit out of his hands.

Ben grudgingly lowered the tailgate of the Blazer so she could lean against it to tug on the equipment.

Czar looked up but didn't move.

The actual dressing took a good ten minutes with Jill's constant inquiry about what went where and why things were the way they were. She reminded Ben of his nephew. Only she smelled better. A lot better. There was the smell of fresh air in her hair and a light perfume laced with citrus.

Before rolling up the extra-long sleeves, she made them flap in the air. "Are you sure these don't tie around the back until the guys in the white suits show up?"

"We all know you're crazy, Jill. Just look where you work," Mosely said, pulling a telephoto lens from the camera pack around his waist. He was a tall, lanky man who seemed to move even while standing still. His hair was cropped close to his head and a small gold hoop glittered in the lobe of his left ear.

"Too true, dear. Too true." She used the endearment casually, but Ben noticed a gold band on Mosely's ring finger and none on hers.

She put on the heavily padded gloves then turned to face Ben. "Is there a helmet?"

He dug it out of the bag. When he was squarely in front of her, close enough to smell the mint flavor on her breath, he gave her his most serious, I-mean-business look. "Don't move."

"I'm not," she replied, giving him a look that seemed to hold a slightly flirtatious challenge. Ben felt a familiar tingle surf across his nerve endings; it happened sometimes when he was involved in a dangerous situation. He called it his sixth sense, his early-warning alert.

"When he gets you down, don't move."

Her lips quivered as if they were going to break into a smile, but she managed to resist and gave him an equally serious look. "Okay." She made it sound like two words.

He stifled a sigh, knowing it was useless to try to explain to someone who has never been tackled by an eighty-five pound missile with teeth just how scary an experience it is.

As he fastened the last of the buckles, he noticed how still she was when his hands were touching her. She seemed to stop breathing. He wondered if she was intimidated by him or reacting to him as a man. He hoped the former; he had no room in his life at the moment for a romantic interest, even one as interesting as the inimitable Jill Martin.

"Okay." He put his hands on either side of her padded shoulders and turned her around to face the wide-open expanse of green. Part of what Ben liked most about Bullion was its clean, well-tended parks. So far, unmarred by graffiti and drug transactions.

"Run straight out. No fancy stuff. Don't look back and don't resist when he grabs you. Don't fight. Don't move. You got it?"

Her murmured affirmation was barely audible through the mask. He gave her a gentle shove, and she stumbled forward, getting used to the feel of the cumbersome gear. Ben often played the bite dummy because he felt comfortable working with the dogs in the training situation, where, unfortunately, most injuries occurred. Roll the wrong way and a dog's muscle could tear or discs become compromised.

He wasn't worried about Czar's well-being this time. Even if Jill Martin lost her head and put up a fight, she didn't have the upper-body strength to toss Czar. She might roll on him, but Czar was faster than most dogs.

Resembling a mummy, she toddled away in plodding steps. Ben almost smiled. Almost. After taking a deep breath, he ordered Czar to his side. He checked to be sure there were no innocent bystanders who might distract Czar or try to get into the picture. Mosely was perched in the wooden jungle gym not far from where Jill was trotting about. The mayor and Sergeant Simms waited off to one side, out of the line of contact.

"Czar," Ben said, his heart speeding up. He pointed in Jill's direction and gave the command. "Forward."

Czar sprang forward like a panther on the loose. He barely worked up to full stride before he was on her. Ben was running by then, too. For some reason his heart was beating out of sync and his throat was too tight to swallow.

His gaze was glued to the scene, and he didn't like what he was seeing. Czar had her down and wouldn't release. As soon as he'd start to back off, she would move, then he'd pounce again. *Why is she moving? Was she dazed by the fall?*

By the time Ben reached her, Jill was curled into a defensive ball, still enough to have been dead. Barking, Czar circled her, the hair on his back honed to a razor's edge. Ben snapped his fingers and the dog relaxed his guard, running to his master's side.

"Good boy," he praised the animal for a job well done. The exercise was textbook—except for the choice of dummy; if she was hurt, it was her own fault for moving. *Don't let her be hurt.*

Simms reached her before Ben could; she sat up, a bit wobbly. He knelt in front of her to remove the headgear. When it was off, she shook her head as if checking to see if it was still attached to her body.

"Wow, what a rush. My heart was going through my skull. I could hear him behind me, even with this stupid head thing on. My God, he's unbelievable." She looked at Czar with true awe, then glanced up at Ben.

Suddenly, he wanted to shake her. She had no business being excited by this. She should have been scared—worried about whether or not she'd wet her pants. "You moved." He heard the accusing tone, like a little boy whose friend had broken one of his toys.

"Did I move, Jamal?"

"Like a fresh maggot."

She made a face. "You need help, Mosely. Professional help. How does that sweet little wife of yours put up with you?"

Ben ignored the banter. He was getting madder by the second. She wasn't taking this seriously. She was joking about something he wanted the citizens of this community to understand and respect. If she wrote as flippantly as she acted, he was screwed.

"Are you okay, Jill?" Simms extended a hand to help her rise.

"Yes, fine. Except for my tongue." She stuck out her tongue looking cross-eyed at the deeply pink appendage. "I bit it when I fell."

Ben had to bite his own tongue to keep from putting his foot in his mouth. This was the worst thing about the press; you couldn't say anything without it being used against you. The police had to read a suspect his Miranda rights before they could question him. The press had no such rules governing their actions. Just journalistic ethics, which everyone knew was an oxymoron.

"It would help if you took this a bit more seriously," Ben said, fighting to keep his anger from getting the better of his common sense.

"I *am* serious. My tongue hurts. Honest." She was grinning. She didn't look serious or penitent; she looked like a bright flower in a weed patch, and Ben wanted to reach out and pluck her.

Amos steadied her as she patted herself in a couple of spots. "I bet I hurt tomorrow. I'd better write this story while I can still move."

Mosely joined them, tapping his camera. "Got some good ones, Jill. Looked damn scary. I wouldn't want that dog after me."

"Then you'd better give up that side job of yours, sweetie." She looked at Ben and whispered theatrically, "Designer drugs. Very fashionable."

"Ha. Ha. Very funny," Mosely said, giving Jill a dirty look. Then he looked at Ben. "She's kidding. She does that a lot."

"So I've noticed."

Jill seemed to pick up on the seriousness in Ben's tone because she faced him and said, "I take my writing seriously, Officer Jacobs. If you're worried this will come off as a fluff piece, don't be. I'm glad you and Czar are here. Bullion needs to play catch-up with the rest of the state's law enforcement agencies, and I think you two will advance that cause. I plan to write about the who and the why of the program, but I want potential criminals—there are so many of them who take the paper, you know—to understand Czar is a force to be reckoned with. Are we together on this?"

Ben found himself fascinated by this side of her. She had

more colors than a chameleon, and he wasn't sure which was the true Jill Martin. For the first time in a long time, he felt interested enough to investigate.

"May I read the story before it's released?"

"Sure...if you tie me down and torture my computer password out of me." She grinned and wiggled her light-reddish eyebrows. "I have to warn you, though, I'll never give it up. But it might be interesting to try."

Mosely groaned. "A simple no would have sufficed, Jill. You always go for the theatrical. Why is that?"

"I don't know, Jamal. I think it's because we moved around a lot when I was a kid and I never got to be in the class play. What do you think?"

The two shuffled off toward the Blazer, bantering like a couple of good friends who knew how to kid each other. Ben watched them go and felt a strange emptiness tug at his belly. Lately, he'd been feeling that gnawing sensation quite often. At first, he'd assumed he was hungry and had stopped at fast-food restaurants, but the feeling hadn't gone away. Nope. The emptiness was deeper and more basic. And he didn't like it.

"Well, sir," he said, turning to face the mayor and his commander, "I guess the rest is in her hands."

"Damn shame she didn't fall and break her neck," the mayor muttered as he walked away.

Simms watched him a few seconds then spoke in a low voice, "Watch your back, son. Jill's the least of our worries. The pen may be mightier than the sword, but nothing's as lethal as a politician with a hidden agenda."

Ben reached down and stroked Czar's back. Warmed by the afternoon sun, the silky texture was comforting. In the distance, Jill Martin was sitting on the tailgate of the Blazer stripping off the protective clothing. The sun glinted off her

hair, creating a halo effect. Ben snickered at the incongru-
ent symbol. Czar would watch for the demons at Ben's
back, but who would protect him from the *angels* in his
face?

CHAPTER TWO

NO DORRY.

Jill's heart pounded turbulently inside her rib cage; sweat tingled under her arms. She leaned one shoulder against the cool marble wall outside the office of the County Recorder trying to make sense of this development. Ten-thirty on a Friday morning and Dorry Fishbank, Employee of the Century, wasn't at work. And, her irritated supervisor had added, Dorry hadn't called in sick and no one answered at her house.

Where are you, Dorry?

A trillion answers—none of them good—cascaded into Jill's mind, courtesy of her fruitful imagination. Land Barons's new development was worth millions—Jill knew that because Peter had been bragging about it back when they were still married. Big business didn't like nosy reporters—especially reporters with an ax to grind—screwing around with its projects. What would stop someone from plugging leaks—particularly when the main leak was a lowly records clerk.

Jill took a deep breath to stifle her thoughts. She could practically hear her mother *tsking*. "The world doesn't revolve around you alone, Jillian," Mattie had often told her.

Just because Dorry's taking her first day off in seventeen years doesn't mean I'm to blame, she thought, pushing off from the wall. But as she walked down the near-empty hall, her legs felt shaky, and the gunshot snap of her pumps on the marble floor unnerved her.

Her initial impulse was to tell somebody, but whom?

Her editor, Will Ogden?

A shiver coursed through her. It didn't take a meteorologist to figure out which way the wind was blowing inside the Bullion *Sentinel.* The paper was pro-growth, pro-government. Will's effusive opinion pieces favoring the new development had swayed the public from hesitation to enthusiasm. While Jill's truthful article on the mayor had earned her a humiliating dressing-down from *Sentinel* publisher Everett Davenport and landed her at the obit desk.

If anybody finds out about this investigation, I'll probably wind up taking calls in classifieds, she thought.

Besides, there was something about Will that made her anxious to avoid scrutiny. Despite his nifty goatee and single status, Jill had once commented to Penny that she'd sooner date Stephen King—whose books scared the pants off her—than go out with Will Ogden.

Trotting down the wide marble steps to the first floor as fast as her footwear allowed, Jill considered another option.

The cops.

One, in particular, came to mind—which wasn't surprising since he'd been hovering around the surface of her consciousness ever since their Wednesday-afternoon bite-suit escapade.

But if something *had* happened to scare Dorry off, Jill would call Amos Simms, not Bullion's newest enigmatic, drop-dead-handsome cop.

"Keep your fingers on your pencil, girl," Penny had advised when Jill had called her from work after the interview. "You need to get over Peter before you get involved with someone else."

This decree had come after Jill mentioned how her fingers had itched to brush off Ben Jacobs's K-9 Patrol cap to see if his ebony hair was as wavy as the one or two stray locks suggested.

"Penny, you are my oldest and truest friend—emphasis on *old* since you seem to have forgotten one key fact—Peter and I are divorced."

"Pooh. We're the same age. And you're being obtuse. As long as you still have Peter's *physical* crapola in your garage and his *mental* crapola in your head, you won't be free to pursue someone else—world-class body or not. And if you were truly over Peter, you'd have told your mother about your divorce by now."

In a way Penny was right. But Jill's reluctance to inform her mother had less to do with love than failure. Mattie Jensen had a rule for everything. Rule Number Two: Never give up.

I gave up on my marriage, Mom.

Nope. Jill couldn't picture herself saying those words to her mother. Fortunately, Mattie's most recent postcard indicated she was still on a cruise in the Bahamas.

Jill put her shoulder to the revolving glass door with enough force to propel her into the bright sunlight and halfway down the sweeping approach. Blinking to refocus, she paused to dig for her sunglasses in her bulging leather backpack.

As she fretted over how to either find Dorry or confirm her disappearance, Jill tried to calm herself. *"Don't panic. Dorry's probably just avoiding you...like everyone else."*

A deep *woof*—close enough to sound like cannon fire— made her jump sideways. Her sunglasses slipped out of her fingers and clattered to the tile replica of the Great Seal of California.

Ben Jacobs retrieved them in one swift, fluid motion and offered them to her in as courtly a manner as she'd ever seen. She gazed at Bullion's newest cop in civvies. No stiff black uniform, reflective sunglasses and formal demeanor to keep her at arm's length.

Peter would kill for those pecs, she thought, her gaze lingering on the well-defined contours emphasized by his smoke-gray turtleneck.

"Hello, again," he said in an even, almost-friendly tone that made her still-sore tongue stick to the roof of her mouth.

Her gaze skimmed downward. Pressed denim jeans. An unadorned leather belt and cowboy boots—broken in but polished. There was something so neat and appealing about him, she almost forgot how to speak.

"Oh" was the only word her brain could come up with as she accepted the proffered eyewear.

A dog sound, sort of a cross between a growl and a whine, made her look down. If dogs could smile, this one was grinning. Jill suddenly realized that despite his reserved greeting, Ben Jacobs's dog was happier to see her than the man was. Low growling snatches of German and a stiff jerk on the dog's harness said a mouthful.

"Good morning, Officer Jacobs. Hello, Czar, how are you today?"

Czar's big cool nose checked out her fingers with intense attention to detail. The tickling sensation made her laugh. "Fancy meeting you here. A parking ticket already? Tsk. Tsk."

Jill's teasing words died on her lips when Ben turned to her. Since he wasn't wearing his sunglasses, she got a good look at his eyes. Brown. Plain brown. Until a tiny twinkle of humor turned them to café mocha—a sure fix for a chocolate junky.

"Not a parking ticket. Property taxes."

His voice revealed frustration and impatience. Jill had

felt the same way after agreeing to buy Peter's share of their home. She hadn't known how much paperwork would be involved.

"Let me guess. Your first Supplemental Tax bill?"

"My *first?*" he barked.

She stepped close enough to see the mangled piece of paper he produced from the hip pocket of his jeans.

"Yup." She recognized the print. "Been there, done that. Because of the lag time between the sale of a house and its yearly assessment, the tax collector sneaks these in to be sure the county gets its due."

He frowned. "I thought this was taken care of through escrow."

"I assumed my ex-husband had somehow managed to shaft me, and since he was long gone, I focused my rage on the tax collector." She motioned toward the building behind them. "I blew in like Patton, but ended up lunching on crow."

Jill shook her head, remembering the humiliation. "To make matters worse, they told me my mother had done the same thing twenty years earlier—only she took the tax collector to court."

"Did she win?"

"You would have thought so. Mattie Jensen never backs down, but I guess she met her match that time." Jill grinned. "Guess that explains why I never heard about it from her."

He smiled, which triggered the memory of his intriguing *accidental* laughter the day of their interview. For a guy with such a stern demeanor, his smiles were truly something.

But it's not *just* his lips, she thought. It's the way they fit his face. And his nose is very nice, too. *Have I ever noticed a man's nose before?*

"What about you?" he asked. "Trouble with the tax man, too? You seemed a bit upset just now."

Jill knew he was speaking to her, but her mind—stuck on cataloging facial features—couldn't quite make the connection. *Upset? Oh yeah, Dorry.*

"Who's Dorry?"

The name penetrated her fog. Her nervous tingle started anew, making her hope she'd remembered to use antiperspirant that morning. "Dorry? Dorry who?"

His neatly arched eyebrows came together.

Ooo…nice.

"I don't know. You said, 'Dorry.' "

"I did? Oh!" Jill blinked, trying to come up with a believable ruse. She was sorely tempted to share her worries with him, but what if she was blowing this totally out of proportion? She'd look like a fool. Better to check it out more thoroughly before calling in reinforcements. "Of course I did. She's my sourc…sore, I mean, sick…friend. I came to see her, well not her, specifically. Today's Friday—my life-and-death day. Then I stopped by to see Dorry, and she wasn't there. That's it."

Her babbling nonsense didn't seem to faze the serious frown scrutinizing her. *Did my face give me away?* Peter insisted she couldn't lie worth a hill of beans, and since he was an authority on the subject she took his word on it.

"Why is this Dorry person's absence a matter of life and death?"

For a second, Jill thought he'd somehow read her mind, but then she realized he'd misunderstood her. "No," she explained. "Friday is *my* life-and-death day. Once a week I collect folk data from the Hall of Records—marriages, deaths, births, divorces. I enter it all on my laptop, then rush back to the paper to make deadline." Jill patted the thick black case at her side.

"I see," he said evenly, still looking at her with a shade of that all-too-familiar cop look. "And Dorry is…"

Jill shrugged—the weight on her left shoulder making her feel like Quasimodo. "Probably sick at home. That's what upset me. She's never sick, so it must be serious. In fact, I'd better go call her."

She leaned over to give Czar a quick pat. She loved the way her fingers sank into the thick, soft fur. If only Ben Jacobs was as approachable as his dog.

"You are such a sweetie," she told Czar, planting a kiss on his large, wet, black nose. "I wish I'd had a dog like you when I was growing up."

"You never had a dog?"

Jill knew instinctively the word *either* deserved to be attached to the question. "Nope," she said. "No pets. Not even a goldfish. My family moved around a lot."

"Really? Why did I get the impression you're a Bullion native?" His eyes didn't reveal anything beyond mild curiosity. Most people were intrigued by her roving childhood.

"We lived here from my sophomore year on—the longest we ever stayed put, so I call Bullion home. Then I went away to college, got married, moved around some more, and finally ended up here, again. Which is kind of ironic, but cool. This is a good place to live." She frowned, thinking about what she and Dorry had discovered in those files. "As long as nobody screws it up."

The sun, which had been sneaking in and out of clouds, suddenly popped out, drawing Jill's attention once more to Ben Jacob's hair. Shiny jet waves, thicker and springier than she'd imagined. No gray. No receding hairline requiring expensive specialists and prescription snake oil.

He started to say something, but suddenly a low grumble

shook the air. In the space of a heartbeat, Ben's body morphed from a relaxed state to ready-for-action.

"Wow," she mouthed softly.

"Well, well, well, if it isn't the woman of the hour," a rancorous voice said. "I just got off the phone with your boss, honey, and you're in big trouble."

Jill grimaced. She knew that voice all too well from the endless Board of Supervisors meetings.

"Mayor Francis," she said, plastering a fake smile on her face. "Kinda early for you, isn't it?" *The bars don't open for another hour.*

"It's never too early to order up a good tar and feathering."

His hubris made Jill's saliva lodge against her windpipe.

"Whatdaya think, Jacobs?" Bud said, laying a pudgy hand on Ben's shoulder. "Size ten, maybe?"

"I beg your pardon," Jill said, swinging around so her briefcase bumped him. For some reason, his hand touching Ben struck her as obscene. "If you're talking about me, I wear a size eight."

Bud repositioned himself across from Ben, careful not to get too close to Czar, who hadn't taken his eyes off the man since the first growl. "I think two buckets of tar ought to be enough, don't you agree?"

His cackle held a degree of satisfaction that made Jill's stomach release a blast of acid.

Despite the cowboy boots, Ben seemed poised on the balls of his feet—as if still on guard. He didn't reply to the mayor's taunt.

"Since you haven't drawn your weapon on her, I have to assume you haven't read the paper." Bud looked at him, waiting for an answer.

"No, sir. I ordered the paper, but my delivery hasn't started."

Jill noticed that he lowered his hand to Czar's harness, as if to reassure the dog that the mayor wasn't a threat. She wished he could reassure *her,* but she knew Bud Francis too well.

"I'll give Everett Davenport a call. He's a friend of mine." *Name-dropper.* "He owns the newspaper that she works for. Or, perhaps I should say *used* to work for. After this fiasco, he owes you big time. Thanks to our illustrious little journalist here, you and your dog are now a big joke."

Jill's confusion was matched only by her anger. "What are you talking about, Bud? My story isn't due out until tomorrow. I have the Saturday Lifestyle page."

"Your story, or, rather, your *screw job,* is in today's paper. Here, see for yourself." He snapped a folded newspaper at her—gut level.

Jill caught the paper before it connected, but the motion threw off her balance. Ben's rock-solid arm shot out to steady her; one big hand momentarily anchored on her shoulder. Czar's muzzle displayed a nice set of teeth but no growl came from his well-trained lips. She enjoyed the brief sense of safety, even though she had a sinking feeling her relief would be short-lived.

When first assigned this story, Jill had been told to slant the piece with a softer, human-interest edge. That was how she'd written it.

She held the paper so Ben could read it, too. The boffo headline read: Going to the Dogs. A four-column color photo drew the reader's eyes to Czar's mouth attached to a body curled in a fetal ball.

"Damn." Jill hated to swear in public—Mattie's Rule Number Six—but it slipped out. She scanned the cutline, spotting the word *attack,* which she'd specifically requested *not* be used.

From the corner of her eye, Jill caught the mayor's satisfied look; she was too dismayed to look at Ben. She flipped to page three where the story continued. On the surface were a lot of familiar words—even a phrase or two that could have been crafted by her hand, but the rest was a miasmic mix of run-on sentences and nonsense.

"Someone will die for this," she muttered.

"With any luck it'll be the writer." The mayor snickered.

She sent him a look any moron could interpret. "That lets me out."

"It's got your name on it."

Jill would have paid the Word God any price for a snappy comeback, but all of her gods seemed to have deserted her. And the bald truth of Bud's words undercut her self-confidence. Jill's writing was her Achilles' heel. She loved to write and aspired to do more: a novel, screenplays, short stories, but was she good enough? She doubted it.

Bud was right on one count. To the world—at least the town of Bullion—this was her story, butchered and flawed though it was. Everyone, including Ben Jacobs, would believe she'd written this drivel, and there was no way to take back the words.

Her fury, edged with inexplicable dismay, made her crumple the newspaper into a ball, which she tossed in the general direction of the mayor. She turned to Ben. How could she explain—make him see the hidden agendas and political eddies that churned within a newsroom?

Uh-oh. The cop face. Stony and unreachable. She didn't try. Instead she bent low to Czar and whispered, "I'm sorry, my friend. I meant well. Truly I did."

His tongue caught a tear, and she turned away before anyone else could see. Jill Martin didn't cry in public: Mattie's Rule Number Three.

BEN WATCHED JILL dash across the street and pick her way through the dozen or so cars in the parking lot. He knew which one she was headed for—he'd spotted it before he'd parked. If he were honest, he'd admit that a part of him had hoped for a chance encounter in the halls of the Bullion County Courthouse.

For the past two days, for reasons that made no sense and that he chose not to dwell upon, Ben had found himself thinking about the Bullion *Sentinel* reporter who'd captured his attention so thoroughly Wednesday afternoon. He'd put out a few feelers and had gained a wellspring of gossip, including the fact that Jill's ex-husband had left her to marry one of Jill's closest friends.

He'd also learned that she had a reputation for tackling tough stories but was in hot water with her boss for painting an unflattering picture of Bullion's mayor—the man who now seemed utterly delighted that he'd succeeded in making Jill Martin cry.

"I don't know what it is about that woman that pisses me off," Bud said, as if Jill were to blame for that, too. "Maybe her holier-than-thou attitude."

Ben hadn't noticed anything of the kind, but he couldn't very well defend her when her story might have compromised his department and his future.

"Glad I bumped into you, Jacobs. Been meaning to talk to you," Bud said with a friendly grin. "This was even better. Killed two birds with one stone. Well one, for sure. Bang." His chuckle sent a shiver down Ben's back.

Neatly turned out in a Jerry Garcia tie and a tailored suit that couldn't quite disguise his paunch, Bud crossed his arms over his chest and leveled a serious look at Ben. "Let's talk. Follow me. My office is right inside."

He sauntered off, obviously expecting Ben and Czar to follow.

Ben glanced across the parking lot as a little red car shot out into traffic; he hoped she didn't do something foolish. *Impetuous people shouldn't be allowed to own high-powered sports cars.*

He gave a tug on Czar's harness, sensing his partner's reluctance to enter the building. Ben felt the same. They used the pneumatic, wheelchair entrance instead of the revolving door. By the time Ben's eyes had adjusted to the dimness, he could see the small, impatient man waving to him from the end of the corridor.

"Behave yourself," Ben said in a low voice meant for Czar's ears only. "In a way, this guy owns us."

Czar made a whining sound.

Ben shoved his tax bill into his pocket as he paused at the building's directory. The Office of the Assessor was on the second floor. He wondered where Jill's absent friend worked.

When Ben walked into the office, the mayor was pouring amber liquid from a cut-glass decanter into a coffee mug bearing his name. At a closer glance, Ben realized the three letters actually represented the logo of a famous beer company.

"What's your poison, son?"

"Nothing for me, sir. I'm on duty this afternoon." Ben gave the place a quick assessment. Mahogany paneling, green baize accents, shiny brass lamps and muted, seafaring reproductions. Someone had class, but Ben was pretty sure it wasn't Bud Francis. Ben had seen the booze-in-the-mug trick before; alcoholics were great pretenders.

"Just a short one?"

"Not a good idea, sir. Thank you anyway." Czar pressed up against Ben's thigh. Ben buried his fingers in the dog's thick coat.

"This is nice, gives me a chance to formally welcome

you to Bullion, son.'' The word made Ben's stomach turn, especially when accompanied by a chummy pat on the back and the smell of whisky.

"Thank you, sir."

Bud moved to a high-back leather chair behind his desk and sat down, motioning Ben to do the same. Political savvy warred with habits ingrained decades ago. *Run. Split. Leave before things get ugly,* a voice in his head urged. Ben glanced down; a corner of the billing notice stuck out of his pocket.

"Actually, I need to get this matter cleared up before my shift, sir."

Bud's watery gray eyes perked up. "What's that? Some kind of tax bill?" he asked, reaching for the bill that Ben had fished from his pocket.

"A supplemental assessment."

"Lemme see."

Ben gave up the mangled copy, reluctantly.

"Let's just call the assessor and get this cleared up."

Ben wasn't surprised to learn the good ol' boy network was active in Bullion; in fact, he'd have been surprised to find out it wasn't, but that didn't mean he wanted to be dragged into it. Favors never came free.

Ben snatched back the copy before the mayor could reach for the phone. "Thank you, sir, but I need to make every effort to meet the people I'm serving. So, although I appreciate the offer, Czar and I will check it out for ourselves."

He headed for the door; Czar led the way.

"Before you go, son. There's one thing you should know about Bullion," Bud said, his voice serious and full of portent. "We don't go much for those liberal, tree-huggin' environmentalists who think they know what's best for us. Change is comin'—ain't any way around it or you 'n that dog wouldn't be here, but we're gonna be making those changes on our own terms, and we don't need no nosy, do-good reporter buttin' in—even if she does have a nice ass. Plenty of other asses around.''

"I would have to agree with you on that, sir," Ben said, employing every ounce of self-control to keep his lips straight. "If you'll excuse me, I have a lot to do before my shift."

Bud nodded magnanimously. "Just keep in mind what I told you. And you don't have to worry none about your reputation in town. I just said that to get Jill's goat. Nobody gives a hoot what that rag prints. Nobody that matters, anyway."

Ben took care of his tax business as quickly as possible then jogged to his car. He tried to digest the import of the mayor's words as he eased the Blazer into traffic. He had two hours before his shift and a long list of chores—including hauling his trash to the dump, but first he wanted to make sure the fire-red Toyota wasn't at the bottom of some gulch.

"Hey, pal," he said as Czar popped his head into the cab of the vehicle through the connecting window. "Her car's not at the *Sentinel*. Maybe she went home."

Since he had to pass by Jill's house on El Capitan Drive to reach the county dump, Ben didn't feel that his concern was intrusive. But the car wasn't parked in front of the upscale town house where he'd spotted it yesterday while on patrol.

Unsettled but lacking other options, he continued on to the waste disposal site. Ben let Czar roam while he unloaded the last of the detritus from his move. It felt good to finally be settled. He had a good feeling about Bullion—even if he had certain reservations about its mayor.

He whistled for his partner, but Czar didn't respond.

Ben put his hands on his hips and looked around. He expected to see the dog poking into some nasty sort of garbage, but instead saw him standing on a slight rise a hundred feet away. Puzzled, Ben followed.

"Whatcha find, pal? A dead body?" He was only half joking. Czar's nose was something to be reckoned with.

The dog made a whining sound as Ben approached, his focus trained on something in the distance. Ben squinted but couldn't see anything suspicious. To the north, a bowl-shaped plateau sat surrounded by oaks and pines. Beyond that, the terrain turned mountainous with rocky inclines and steep canyons.

Czar made a noise that sounded like a reprimand.

"You're going to make me work for this, aren't you?" Ben muttered, jogging back down the hill to retrieve his field glasses.

He returned a minute later and scanned the horizon. A little red car shining in the midday sun in the middle of an open field that had been pointed out to him as the entrance to the Excelsior mine. The Ex—as Jimmy Fowler, Bullion P.D.'s resident know-it-all, called it—had been one of the richest mines in the entire Sierra Nevada a hundred years earlier.

"Now it's just a nuisance," Jimmy had explained. "Local lovebirds used to park up there at a spot called Lover's Leap, but nowadays it's a hot spot for taggers and dopers."

Maybe she used to go there with her husband, Ben thought, turning away.

Czar swiped his knee with his paw.

Ben looked down. "What? Are we supposed to just drive over and say hello?"

Czar took off as if Ben had just answered his prayers. Grumbling under his breath, Ben followed. After closing the rear hatch behind the dog, Ben climbed into the Blazer.

"You know, you're in bad shape, buddy boy. You're worried about this woman, and I'm not even sure I like her."

Czar popped his head through the window from the rear compartment, pressed his nose against Ben's ear and snorted.

The loud, wet puff of air was Czar's private wake-up call to Ben. Laughing, Ben wiped away the moisture with the heel of his hand. "All right. I'm attracted to her. But it's not the same thing. You use different parts of the anatomy. I'm not going down that road again. Janine was gorgeous, but look how that turned out," he said, reluctantly turning left instead of right.

Instead of examining his reasons for going to the mine, he thought about his former lover, Janine Fitspatrick. Worldly and engaging, Janine had shared his interest in gourmet cooking and murder mysteries. Ben truly had enjoyed their relationship while it lasted. They'd been dating for six months before Ben discovered her drug use.

"Recreational cocaine," she'd called it.

"Against the law," he'd called it.

What had unnerved him most was that she'd fooled him on both a personal and a professional level. He didn't plan to let himself become that blind again, even if his sister despaired of his ever finding a mate.

According to Joely, Ben's personal life was as hopeless as a Woody Allen movie. "What about love?" she'd asked while helping him move.

Ben's estrangement from their parents meant Joely was the only family he had, and he welcomed her visits—and was prepared to put up with her nagging.

"Hey, if the right woman were to walk into my life tomorrow, I'd throw out the welcome mat and make Czar sleep on the floor, but until that happens he sleeps at the foot of my bed,'' Ben had vowed as they'd unpacked his kitchen boxes.

"Why is it I get the feeling your idea of a welcome mat involves a lie detector and an FBI check?'' she'd retorted, tossing him the salad spinner. ''Just promise me you'll give dating a try again. There has to be at least one eligible girl in Bullion.''

As he eased off the gas to round the bend, Ben pictured Jill Martin. Bright, buoyant, intriguing. But the mayor had as good as ordered Ben to stay away from her. Plus, she'd apparently skewered him in her story. He had absolutely no business tracking her down. Except to find out why she'd done it.

"Woof.''

"I know, boy. Red rice rocket at one o'clock. And there's Ms. Martin, too.''

The gravel entrance was deeply rutted, but the Blazer handled it with ease. In an area the size of a football field, the small red car stood out like a cheerleader on the fifty-yard line.

The woman leaning against the car wasn't cheering. ''She doesn't look too happy to see us.''

Czar's low moan verbalized Ben's feelings completely, but he couldn't turn back. He had to speak to her even though he didn't have the slightest idea what to say.

She didn't give him a chance to worry about it. She advanced on the car, shoulders set, eyes flashing. He pushed the power window control.

"If you've tracked me down for an apology, you can go to hell.''

Ben looked at Czar; the dog pulled his head back into the shell, abandoning his partner in his moment of need. "Coward,'' Ben muttered. He turned off the engine and opened the door.

He followed as Jill stalked back to her car—wobbling on the rocky ground in black pumps that emphasized her slim ankles, curvy calves and great knees.

"The way you took off out of the parking lot made me think I might find that tin can of yours crumpled at the bottom of some ravine," he said.

She spun around. "I'm a very good driver."

"Even when you're upset?"

"I'm not…" She didn't bother finishing the lie. Her cheeks reddened with a girlish color that made Ben want to smile. He'd bet a paycheck she hated those blushes. She wouldn't meet his eyes.

"Correct me if I'm wrong, but you and Mayor Francis don't like each other, do you?"

She smiled. Such a simple act, but one that transformed her face from merely attractive to gorgeous. Ben almost flinched.

"Loathe is a good word. Scurrilous is another. Don't get me started. That's what I've been doing for the last twenty minutes—communing with the Word God, composing a thesaurus of adjectives to define the nature of our esteemed leader." She practically spat the word *esteemed.*

Ben asked the question that had been on his mind ever since he'd first interviewed for the job and met the mayor. It wasn't the sort of question one asked in a political workplace like a police department until one knew all the players and which team they were on. "How'd he get elected?"

Jill threw up her hands. "My point exactly. Good ol' boy politics, I guess. If I could explain politics, I'd be writing for the *New Yorker.* All I know is he's got connections that go back to God himself."

Ben studied her as she threw herself into a soliloquy about mountain politics and the abuse of power. She was wearing a power suit and high heels. Her thick cascade of red-gold hair was tangled and windblown. He hadn't thought professional women had long hair anymore.

"You're not one of them, are you?" she asked, eyeing him suspiciously.

"Too early to tell. I don't even know the names of all the players."

Her scoffing sound mimicked Czar when he was impatient. "Well, grab a program, stranger, 'cause things are heating up and you're gonna get caught in the crossfire if you don't watch out."

"Is that so? I thought this was a peaceful little mountain town. No big-city problems."

"Different scale is all," she said. "Instead of drug lords and prostitution, you've got kids getting drunk and driving into the river. Bad things happen, but so do good things."

His sister called him cynical, but Ben preferred the term world-weary. It was one of the reasons he'd chosen Bullion. He'd hoped the smaller town might still possess some fundamental values that had gotten lost with urban sprawl.

"What kind of good things? Give me an example."

"Last spring, I did two stories about the homeless. One was on a single guy, the other was about a mother with three kids. I spent twenty-four hours with each of them. When we ran the stories, the outpouring of support from the community was overwhelming."

"Money? Food?"

"Yes, but more importantly, we'd succeeded in putting a name on the nameless, faceless people we all try so hard not to see. My female subject wound up on the street after she broke her shoulder in a car accident and her boss canned her. She slept in her car and farmed out her kids to relatives, but she never gave up."

Ben's blood quickened at her passionate recitation.

"After the story came out, she had job offers, found an apartment and got her kids back."

Her enthusiasm warmed him. "And the guy?"

A frown skidded across her face like a cloud. "He was...is..."

Ben waited.

"Bobby Goetz is a loser."

The sadness in her tone surprised him. It must be tough to have such a soft heart in her line of work, he thought.

"I wanted to help him, but the truth is he doesn't have much ambition. He's...troubled."

"And you're a Good Samaritan." He didn't mean to sound sarcastic, but he'd dealt with scores of social workers over the years and invariably one or two wound up being raped or brutalized by the very people they were trying to help.

She straightened as if he'd poked her with a sharp stick. "I did what I could to help, but after a while I realized he was using me and the system. I'm not stupid."

"And he's okay with that?" Ben asked, knowing there was more to the story than she was telling him.

"I guess so." Jill backed up a small step, as though his observation invaded her space. Ben recognized the evasive look in her eyes, even though she kept her gaze trained on the ground. *Guilty.*

"He still calls the paper once in a while," she said. "He'd like to see me do a follow-up story."

And... Ben knew from experience sometimes the best way to get answers was to be silent. An instructor once told him: "Nature hates a vacuum, guilty people hate silence."

"Okay," she said huffily. "So he pesters the heck out of me. It's nothing I can't handle." He knew she believed that. The social workers who got beaten up also believed it.

"Anyway, the point is—Bullion is a good place to live, and contrary to the evidence in the paper today, I'm glad that you and Czar are here. I did some research, and police dogs have been shown to reduce crime in some areas by as much as fifty percent. Just the animal's presence—not even the physical threat—can diffuse a situation."

Ben tried to remain unmoved by her praise. She'd expressed the sentiment he preached to any and all listeners, and it felt great to hear the words from other lips, particularly lips as appealing as hers.

"So, tell me what happened with this story." He'd read the article before leaving the courthouse. What puzzled him was the banality of the writing. At moments it read well and seemed to hold true promise, then the flow would disappear, leaving behind a vapid, meaningless sequence of words.

Ben pulled the wrinkled copy from his hip pocket. He read aloud, "In the wrong hands, a police dog is a lawsuit waiting to happen. And Czar is one such police dog."

She threw up her hands and paced. "I don't know what to tell you. I just spent the last half hour trying to find out what happened. Will Ogden, my editor, was at lunch. The managing editor left this morning for San Francisco. All the copy editors work at night and won't answer their phones during the day."

She sighed. "Even if I told you someone butchered my copy—which someone did—you won't understand how crucifying it is to see your byline on a story and know the words aren't yours."

Her anguish came through loud and clear. Ben promised himself he'd visit the library and read some back issues to get an idea of Jill's writing style.

"Don't you keep a copy in your computer or something?" he asked.

She dug a hand beneath the cascade of hair at the base of her skull as if to massage away her tension. "Of course. I went to my office after I left the courthouse. I planned to print out the original and leave it under your door." She pursed her lips and looked toward the towering bull pines ringing the opening. "But it was gone."

Ben believed her. He couldn't say why but he did.

A sudden bark broke the silence between them. Ben felt guilty for leaving his friend unattended for so long. He jogged to the Blazer and opened Czar's door. Normally, Czar would wait for Ben to attach his lead or give him a command, but this time he cleared the door before Ben had it completely open. The impact almost dumped Ben on his keister.

"Czar!"

The dog loped across the barren lot. Even from a distance he could sense Czar's joy at seeing Jill. Ben was puzzled. Czar *tolerated* people. He accepted Joely and the kids, but the only human he displayed any affection for was Ben—which was the way it should be.

To his further surprise, Jill looped her arms around the big dog's neck and hugged him. No fear of shedding hair or dog drool.

None of this made sense. Ben hated things that didn't make sense. He'd had enough of that growing up.

Jill straightened as he approached. Ben did his best to keep his inner turmoil concealed.

"Listen," she said with an almost fatalistic tone. "Land Barons is throwing a black-tie affair at the Ahwahnee Sunday night to woo prospective investors to buy lots in Excelsior Estates." She looked around, her eyes suddenly wistful and a little sad. The sun glinting off her hair made it more copper than gold. "They plan to turn this place into a paying gold mine again. Homes, shops, a golf course."

He didn't have any trouble interpreting her tone. "And this is bad?"

She shrugged. "You have to decide that for yourself. If you come with me to the gala you can mingle with the powers that be—old money, new money, no money. That's me." She forced a laugh. "Bring along a scorecard, line up the players. The mayor and his cronies will be there."

"Is this a date?" he asked, hoping his amusement didn't set off her touchy temperament.

Her cheeks blossomed with color and she focused on smoothing Czar's coat in place. "I have two tickets. I have to go. For the story. But I'll give you the other ticket if you don't want to go with me. I...I'd understand."

Ben hesitated. Not because he had any intention of declining her offer, but because he enjoyed watching the myriad emotions play so eloquently across her face.

She was right about his need to get a handle on the political climate of his new world. And despite the fact he'd been warned otherwise, he wanted to know more about Jill Martin, too.

Czar barked as if impatient to let Jill off the hook.

Ben shot him a quelling look. "Yes. I'll go with you."

CHAPTER THREE

JILL PULLED into the parking lot of the Bullion Sports Center three minutes ahead of schedule. The Time God owed her.

Saturday mornings from ten-thirty to eleven was the Mommy and Me swim class—Jill's chance to fill a maternal void and help Penny give the twins quality time. The eighteen-month-old toddlers sometimes got shortchanged since the arrival six months earlier of their little sister. Lisle, the very demanding demon beauty, was home with her daddy.

Looking around the parking lot, Jill spotted Penny's Jeep Cherokee just arriving. The Baylors had invested in the larger vehicle when they first learned Penny was pregnant; now Penny cursed it as too small for three infant seats, toys and diaper bags.

Jill grabbed her tote and got out of the car, relishing the perfect autumn morning; the air was so crisp and clean it almost hurt to take a deep breath. She inhaled deeply anyway and pushed away the niggling worries—Peter, Clarice, and especially Dorry.

After half a dozen calls, she'd finally gotten someone to answer at Dorry's number at nine o'clock last night. But the slurred voice—one of her brothers most likely—was no help. All he said was, "She can't come to the phone right now. Don't call back."

Jill would have hopped into her car and driven to the

Fishbank house, if its street address had shown up on any of her maps. Unfortunately, once one left the city limits, the maze of country roads was a cartographer's nightmare.

"Hello, my little swimmers," Jill said, opening the rear door on the passenger side.

"Nooo…." Penny screeched. "Don't use the 'S' word."

Jill blinked in confusion. She looked at the twins, who smiled drool-laced grins but didn't offer any explanation. Fraternal, not identical, the boys were as different in personality as in looks. Rambunctious Tristan, a miniature Nordic god, could have passed as Jill's offspring; introspective Trevor favored his mother's warm, Mediterranean coloring.

"That's why we're late. Just as we were leaving, their daddy said,'Have a great time 'S'-ing,' if you get my drift, and they came unglued. Major tantrum. I don't know why. They loved it last time."

Jill tickled Tristan's pudgy tummy, drawing a high-pitched baby giggle that gave her heart a funny twist. "So, what are we doing here?"

"We're going 'S'-ing. We're just not going to call it that," Penny replied as if that went without saying and Jill purposely was being obtuse.

"Well, we can't call it 'S'-ing. That sounds dirty."

Penny, who was busy stuffing baby gear into two bulging, brightly colored diaper bags, gave an elaborate shrug. "How 'bout snorkeling?"

"Snorkeling?"

"They don't know what it means. Next week we can change it to something else. You can pick."

Jill had long ago decided that motherhood involved some serious rearranging of brain cells, but being a good sport, she leaned close to the towhead strapped in the thickly padded gray and maroon car seat and said, "Okay, Tristan B., ready for a little *snorkeling* with Auntie Jill?"

He held out his arms to her.

"Good boy. We'll *snorkel* till we drop." She kept up a running dialogue of nonsense as she unsnapped the chest band and loosened the two shoulder straps.

"You're awfully perky this morning," Penny observed, handing her one of the diaper bags. "Oh my gosh. You saw Peter, didn't you?"

Jill tugged down Tristan's sweatshirt. "As a matter of fact, I did, but not in the way you're implying."

Penny pinned Jill with a suspicious stare. "How then?"

"Two cars passing in the night. Pausing briefly at a stoplight."

"Go on."

Jill made fish lips at Tristan, who giggled and tried to make them back. "Just that. I stopped. He, I mean, *they* stopped. And that's it." *I wish.* "Since when do car agencies rent luxury cars? How pretentious!"

Penny gathered up Trevor and slammed the door shut. "You're hiding something. Tell me the rest."

"Nope. Too humiliating."

They hurried toward the two-story cinder-block building that would have looked like a prison if not for the burgundy and teal stripes running at geometric angles across it.

Penny cuffed Jill lightly. "Even better."

"You're not being very supportive. This is traumatic stuff."

"Bullfarkle. Peter's gone and you're a hundred million times better off without him, even if you won't admit it. Tell me."

Jill glanced around. The parking lot seemed more packed than usual but no one was near. "After work, I ran by the market for some cat food and a frozen pizza."

At Penny's exaggerated gagging sound, Jill said defensively, "It was a Wolfgang Puck gourmet pizza." It probably would have been good if she'd had any appetite left by the time she got home. "Anyway, there I was cruising along, thinking about an obit I'd just written for some thirty-year-old guy who left behind a wife and three kids."

"Local?" Penny interrupted.

"His grandmother lives here. He lived in Reno."

"How'd he die?"

"Cancer."

"What kind?"

"How would I know?"

"You're the obit writer. You should know. I think they should publish cause of death so we know what we're up against."

"Ghoul."

Penny made a *hmmphing* sound; she paused at the entrance, waiting for Jill to catch up. "So, anyway, you're driving along without a life of your own, thinking about death and…"

Jill made a witchy face at Tristan; he smiled back. "So, I'm stopped at a light, and I happen to look over and there's Peter. In the Lexus." She hurried along the corridor that smelled of sweat and chemicals. "But, I'm there in my sports car. And I *could* be on my way to a party. Right?"

"With your cat food and frozen pizza."

Jill stuck her tongue out at Penny's back.

"Then…" Penny prompted.

"The light changed. My foot slipped off the clutch and my car stalled."

Penny let out a howl of laughter. "You're kidding, right? You're just saying that to make my day."

Jill noticed a particularly buff blonde in a two-piece Lycra number looking their way; she felt her cheeks blossom with color. "That's not the worst of it," she confessed in a low voice.

Penny led the way into the changing room and turned to face Jill. "What could be worse?"

"My car wouldn't start right at first, and when it did I shot across the intersection. Naturally, the light had turned red again. And at the cross street, the first car in line was a cop. He pulled me over."

Jill stood Tristan on the aquamarine bench and pitched their bags into an open locker. She could hear Penny trying to control her laughter. "This isn't funny, Pen."

Penny's giggles machine-gunned in a choking sound. "What did the cop say? No, don't tell me. This is too rich to take in all at once."

"You're a scavenger, aren't you? See a person down and bleeding and you look for gore." Jill pouted; Tristan mimicked her.

Jill thought about the humiliating encounter as she changed into her swimsuit. Once Jimmy Fowler—a decent if slightly redneck cop—realized whom he'd stopped, he'd lambasted Jill for defaming his newest comrade in arms. He lectured for a full five minutes about the worthwhile contribution of the canine patrol and the saintly qualities of Ben Jacobs.

Nope, the details of this ticket were going with her to her grave. The only good thing to come of the whole event was Jimmy's inadvertent revelations about Bullion's newest crime fighter—namely, a sister living in Bakersfield and a brother-in-law who was a long-haul trucker. Facts that Jill found interesting, although wasn't sure why.

"We'll meet you there," she said, picking up Tristan and heading for the pool. She shouldered the door open and walked in—momentarily assaulted by the warm moist air, thick with the smell of chlorine.

"Okay, Tristan, let's see that great physique of yours," she teased, standing the little boy atop a white resin patio table. Gooseflesh popped up on his arms and tummy when she stripped off his snugly outfit. "There's my man. My main man." She held up one pudgy little arm and gave him a high five. She kicked off her sandals and draped her cover-up over a chair. The pebbled concrete under her feet was wet and cold.

She tried to suppress a shiver as she hefted Tristan to her left hip and headed for the pool. "Hey, baby, are we going to have fun or what?" she asked him, trying to keep his attention focused on her. "Remember last week how much fun we had, splashing and bobbing and choking?"

Jill stepped into the water without stopping. Normally she liked to work her way in slowly, but the instructor told her fast was the better way to go with babies, so she stepped down, down, down until the water was midway between her waist and chest.

Tristan had a look of surprise on his face. His little fingers dug into her as she bobbed around, getting him wet up to his shoulders. He locked his legs around her waist but didn't seem overly distressed. "At least you're smiling," she told him. "You know how I hate it when you cry."

Jill saw Penny and Trevor come into the pool area. Penny tossed her towel onto the same chair, intent on getting Trevor into the water with as little fuss as possible. Jill saw his chubby body go rigid and his arms wrap in a death grip around his mother's neck.

Tristan tried to wiggle out of her arms to see his mom, so Jill danced sideways, pretending they were waltzing in the water. His bright baby laughter filled the steamy room. Jill felt a clenching sensation deep within her womb, and the tears rushed to her eyes.

"Is everybody ready?" the instructor asked, joining the group in the pool. "It's blow-and-dunk time."

Jill felt herself tense. This was a bit traumatic for both the babies and their mothers. Even Jill, a pseudomom, didn't like this part, but she knew it was important. Keeping eye contact with Tristan, she kissed his nose, then quickly blew in his face while simultaneously dunking them both underwater. Blinking against the chlorine, she kept her eyes open and she could see his look of surprise, but at least his mouth was closed. They bounced back up.

Tristan bunched up his face and prepared himself for a giant scream, but Jill hugged him tight, twirling around, lavishing him with praise. Slowly, his body began to relax. Jill knew she wasn't a natural at this mom business, but she was a fast study and she'd gleaned all the tricks she could from the real moms.

"Let's do it again, Mommies," the instructor called.

Jill shook her head, making her wet ponytail flip back and forth, spraying Tristan. He laughed, and when he wasn't expecting it, she blew in his face and dunked them both again.

He came up sputtering but still smiling. Jill was so engrossed in the child, she didn't notice the man at the viewing window above them.

SHE HAS A CHILD.

Ben wasn't sure why the idea disturbed him. Was it because it seemed so contrary to the image he had of her?

"Your first time here?" a voice said, cutting into Ben's reverie of the scene below him.

He glanced to his left to find a petite blonde in a two-piece fuchsia aerobics outfit that showed off her anodized purple belly ring. Her crown of frothy curls was clamped into a topknot by a plastic clip. A faint gleam of sweat beaded her forehead and above her strawberry-red lips.

"Yes. Just checking it out," Ben said sociably. That's what his sister had suggested—check out the local health clubs for possible babes.

"I'm Amee. Two *e*'s." She held out a slim hand adorned with sculpted nails the same color as her lipstick. On the third finger, Ben spotted a tiny gold hoop dangling from the glossy nail. No other rings on any fingers.

"Ben Jacobs." He shook her hand, letting go before she did.

"Oh. I thought you looked familiar. You're the new policeman, right? The one with the dog."

"Yes."

"I read about you in the paper."

Ben was curious about her reaction to the story. So far, the piece had earned him a mild roasting by his peers, but nothing adverse from the public that he could see. "Did you like it?"

"Well, I just saw the picture when I was getting my nails done. I don't have time to read much. Your dog sure looks scary."

"He's a pussycat, except with the bad guys."

She smiled sweetly. She probably was sweet. A sweet kid, who didn't interest him in the least. Against his will, he looked over his shoulder at the pool.

"Do you swim?" Amee asked.

"Laps." Ben was disappointed to see the pool empty.

"We have a great lap pool here. Come on, let me show around." She took his hand before Ben could protest and started dragging him toward a door at the opposite end of the room.

"I really don't think a health club is my kind of—" She didn't let him finish.

"You can't make up your mind before you've given the place a chance. That wouldn't be fair. And policemen are supposed to be fair, right?"

She was right; police officers were supposed to be fair. He'd give the place a chance; he'd even give Amee—two *e*'s—a chance, though part of him was on the lookout for a spunky redhead in a black swimsuit.

THE WEIGHT OF HER PONYTAIL, more wet than dry, made Jill roll her neck to relieve the pressure. Tristan used the opportunity to grab a handful of hair and tug.

"Yikes boy, that hurts. Want me to pull your hair?"

Penny bumped her forward, herding Jill toward the car. "Children. Children. Let's get going before my boobs explode. Lisle must be screaming, and at some maternal level I can sense it. Her daddy gets so upset when his little angel cries."

In many ways Jill envied Penny's life and craved a child of her own, but some days she was certain she didn't have the patience or attention span it took to raise a child. She loved her Saturday mornings with Penny and the boys but was usually relieved, albeit guiltily, to head home alone.

Jill had planned on having kids, two, in fact; she knew what it meant to be an only child. But Peter never gave her that option. One day, when she brought up the subject, he told her to count him out.

"This is a joint undertaking," Jill had cajoled. "I can't do it alone, but I really do want kids, Peter. Not right this minute but eventually."

Like a child caught lying, Peter hated it when his elaborate fabrications collapsed around him and usually tried to make it someone else's fault. "Well, you will have to do it alone, if it's so damn important, because I had a vasectomy when I was in college."

Jill couldn't have been more stunned. Hurt, shock, anger were only a few of the emotions surging through her, but he never gave her time to assimilate them. He'd taken her hands in his and said, "I know I should have confessed this before we were married but I was afraid of losing you, Jilly. I had the operation right after Diane gave birth to Dougie. I couldn't stand it that he was retarded."

"Down's syndrome isn't hereditary, Peter," Jill had replied.

"It could be. She's my sister, we share the same genes. My mother's youngest brother was slow, too. What if it runs in families? I couldn't live with that, Jill," he'd pleaded. "You know me, I couldn't stand it if our child was less than perfect."

Jill understood. Peter wanted everything perfect—car, home, work and wife. He had a lot of good qualities, but tolerance for anything that interfered with the order of his life wasn't one of them.

"So, what are you doing the rest of this fine autumn day?" Penny asked, taking Tristan from Jill's arms once Travis was strapped in.

"Oh, not much. Trim my roses, e-mail my dad, maybe take a run out to Vista Road to see if I can find Dorry Fishbank's place."

Penny snapped the harness of Tristan's car seat then spun around. "What did you say?"

"Roses...e-mail...Dorry."

"Are you nuts?" Penny exploded. "You can't go up there."

Jill took a step backward. "Why?"

"Because it's dangerous. Don't you read that rag you work for? The Fishbank brothers are drug dealers. They get busted once or twice a year for growing and selling marijuana."

"So? I don't want to see them."

"Dorry lives with them, Jill. Their parents are lazy ne'er-do-wells." Jill smiled at the old-fashioned word. "Pay attention. I'm serious. Remember what happened last month with those park-service workers? They stumbled across some pot growers' booby traps set up on National Forest land. Richard Morse lost three fingers on his right hand."

Jill grimaced.

"They don't like trespassers," Penny continued. "They hurt people who get in their way. You can't go there."

Jill hated to be told she couldn't do something. "I'm not interested in their little agronomy project. I just want to talk to Dorry."

"Why?"

"I can't tell you."

Penny grabbed Jill about the shoulders. "What are you up to?"

"Nothing. Let go."

"No. You're not going. Even if I have to call the police."

Jill's mouth dropped open. "You wouldn't."

"Yes, I would. I'll call and ask for that new cop. The one you did the story on. I bet he'd be happy to arrest you."

"For what?" Jill cried.

"That was my question."

The masculine voice, low and faintly amused, crashed between them like a bucket of ice water. Jill jumped back, and Penny ducked behind her. Jill saw the too-familiar face of Ben Jacobs and groaned. Penny made a gleeful sound that Jill could happily have shot her for, and shoved her friend aside.

"You're him."

Ben put out his hand. "Ben Jacobs."

"Penny Baylor," Penny said, squeezing his hand in a

robust greeting. "Who said you can't find a cop when you need one?" She flashed Jill a smug look. "Officer, this woman is a danger to herself and probably others and you can't let her do what she's planning to do."

"Armed robbery?" he asked, giving Jill an unrelenting stare that made her all too conscious of her lack of makeup and stringy hair.

"Just plain trouble."

He nodded, as if he understood completely.

"Hey," Jill complained, "that's not fair. I was just going to visit a friend."

His eyes narrowed. "The one who works at the courthouse?"

Penny squinted at Jill, too. "Jill, what have you done?"

"Nothing," Jill cried. How had this gotten so blown out of proportion? "I talked to Dorry on Wednesday, and she didn't show up for work on Friday, that doesn't make it my fault. I just want to make sure she's okay."

Neither looked convinced, but Penny relented first. "I believe you, but you still can't go anywhere near the Fishbank place alone. They are weird, unpleasant people at the very least. Dorry's the only normal one. Those brothers of hers…" She shuddered extravagantly, then looked at Ben. "You'll have to go with her."

Jill started to protest, but Penny held up her hand. "It's your duty. To serve and protect, right? Well, she needs protection. Believe me." She suddenly clamped both hands to her chest and let out a yip. "Time to go. Have lunch will travel."

Penny dashed to the driver's door and jumped into the Jeep. As she was pulling out, Ben said, "Doesn't she have your child?" pointing to the towhead waving goodbye from his car seat.

"I wish that were my child," Jill said softly, then bit her

tongue. Mattie's Rule Number Eight: If you're going to waste your time wishing, wish for rain—at least somebody will benefit from it. "Nope. I just borrow him occasionally."

"THIS IS NOT MY FAULT," Jill complained for the tenth time.

"I didn't say it was," Ben replied, trying to keep a lid on his temper. Something about this woman could push his buttons faster than anyone he ever met.

"You're thinking it. Isn't he, Czar?"

Czar barked.

Ben stifled a groan. In the hour and twenty-five minutes they'd spent on this wild-goose chase, Jill Martin had carried on a running dialogue with his partner, his dog. And occasionally it seemed as though Czar was answering her.

"All I asked was whether or not Juniper was a through road."

"How would I know?" she replied equably. "I've never been on this road in my life."

"I thought you said this woman was your friend."

Her cheeks bloomed. Without makeup, Jill Martin looked sixteen. A dangerous age for a man his age. "I used that word in the generic sense. Dorry and I went to school together, but she was a couple of years ahead of me. We didn't *hang out* together. Plus, her parents got busted for dope and her older brother beat up a teacher. Something like that can really screw up your social life in high school—you know how kids are."

You mean like being the center of gossip when your dad gets drunk and wraps the family car around a tree?

"What I don't get is why you're so worried about her."

"Maybe *worried* is the wrong word. I'm concerned because I couldn't get a satisfactory explanation from her brother last night about why Dorry missed work yesterday. It's not like her."

"People miss work all the time, that's why there's sick leave."

"Not Dorry. She's got a perfect attendance record. And her supervisor said she didn't call in sick. Then when I called during the day, no one answered."

"So she played hooky." They'd been over this ground half a dozen times, but Ben sensed she was hiding something, and he knew from experience that the best way to get information from a suspect was to keep him talking. "And regardless of *her* reason, it's her problem, Jill. How does Dorry's job attendance affect you? Are you working on a story?"

Her mouth took on a mulish set. "I'd rather not say."

"Maybe you'd rather walk back to town," he muttered.

"What was that? What he'd say, Czar?"

Ben shot Czar a warning look. Czar pulled his head back into the rear compartment.

"Why don't you call on your radio again?" she suggested.

"No."

"Why not?"

His hands tightened on the wheel. "Because."

She snorted. "Oh, right, it's a guy thing. Peter—my ex—would never ask for directions, either."

"I'm not calling in again because this is not official business. Do you want me to make it official business?"

Her mouth snapped closed.

"Tell me more about the Fishbanks. Why was Penny so worried about your being out here alone?"

Jill shrugged. "The drug thing, I guess."

"What drug thing?"

"Dorry's brothers reputedly have a pot patch somewhere

up in these hills. They get busted every few months, but usually just one at a time—there are three of them—so the other two keep things going. Must be frustrating as heck for the cops.''

Amos had briefed Ben about the area's problem with large-scale marijuana cultivation; some of these ''businessmen'' invested big bucks in camouflage, irrigation systems and perimeter protection.

The Blazer's right front tire dropped into a pothole the size of a wine barrel. Ben cursed as the steering wheel bucked beneath his hands.

''Thanks for doing this,'' Jill said softly. ''My car wouldn't have lasted a mile over these roads.''

''So, it stays nice and clean while mine gets coated in dust,'' he groused. She was hard enough to take when she was acting prickly and defensive, he wasn't ready for sweet and appreciative. ''Is it always so dusty around here?'

''Heck no, in January it'll be pure mud.''

''I saw a swing set in the yard back there. How do kids get to town for school?''

''There are bus stops on the main road. Or they stay with friends. Some rent rooms from town people.'' She sat up straighter. ''That reminds me. I think Dorry rented a room from Penny's mom one year.''

''Maybe Penny's mother could tell us how to find this place.''

Jill shook her head sadly. ''She died when Penny was in college. Penny dropped out of school to come back home and finish raising her younger sister. That's when she met her husband. He's a naturalist in Yosemite. I think he specializes in native plants.''

''You don't approve of him.''

Her expressive eyes blinked wide. ''Why do you say

that? He's not my type, but he's great with the kids and loves Penny to pieces.''

''What *is* your type?''

Her rueful grin seemed a guise; Ben glimpsed pain and hurt in her eyes. ''Well, if you go by my track record, somebody who thinks he's God's gift to women and has to prove it with every female he meets.''

''How long were you married?''

''Six years. Two good, two iffy, two hell.''

''Why'd you marry him?''

She shook her head in a lighthearted manner that made her ponytail bounce. Ben didn't expect her answer to be honest. ''Good question. One I should be hearing from my mother any day now. She never liked him. Mattie's Rule Number Seven—Never marry a pretty man, he'll spend all his time in front of a mirror.''

She chuckled, but it didn't hold any of her usual warmth. ''I hate it when my mother's right. Penny says I make life a lot harder than it needs to be by trying to prove my mother wrong.''

Ben reflected on something that Joely had said to him during her usual Saturday-morning call. ''Dad's old, Ben. Old and sick. How long do you intend to go on proving to the world that you're nothing like him?''

As if pinpointing the source of his inner disquiet, Jill asked, ''So, tell me about your family. Your sister's a teacher and your brother-in-law drives truck. Are your parents still alive?''

''How do you know that? It wasn't on my bio.''

''I'm a nosy reporter-type person, remember? I ask questions.''

Ben had almost forgotten. ''My family life is private.''

''You asked me about mine.''

''Yes, and all you said is your father's a retired miner

and your mother's a travel agent. They're separated and neither of them lives around here."

She suddenly grinned, and something tight inside him loosened up.

"Boy," she said, lightly poking his shoulder with her fingertip, "we'd drown like rats in the dating pool, wouldn't we? No wonder Penny despairs of my love life." She blushed, apparently realizing her gaffe. "I mean—"

She threw up her hands. "Oh, heck, I may as well admit it. All you have to do is ask somebody and they'll tell you Jill Martin hasn't been on a date since the Fourth of July dance."

"Why not? Are you still hung up on your ex?"

She shook her head emphatically. "Hardly. Our divorce was final six months ago, but our marriage was over long before that. We didn't end things on the best of terms. It's hard to be civil when you find out your hubby's shagging your best friend."

"Penny?"

Jill hooted. "Lord no. Penny and I picked up the pieces of our friendship after Peter moved out. Those two openly hated each other. I meant Clarice. We used to work together at the paper."

Her expression was sad, as if she still felt her friend's betrayal. Ben fought down the urge to reach out and comfort her.

"Clarice is…" She paused as if groping for the right word. "Electric. A perfect size three. White-blond hair, flawless skin, little tiny geisha feet." She looked despairingly at her dust-coated running shoes.

"She comes across as genteel, but believe me, she's a ruthless businesswoman. She was director of Human Resources at the paper when I was hired. After she married Peter, she went to work for Land Barons. You'll meet them tomorrow night." Her smile wavered. "You're still going with me, aren't you?"

He nodded, glancing at his watch. "That reminds me. I have an appointment this afternoon to pick up a tux."

She made a face. "You really didn't have to do that."

"I needed to pick up a few other things in Merced anyway. Maybe we should postpone this hunt. I'll check with Jimmy Fowler tonight. He knows every road, rock and tree in this county. I'll ask him to draw me a map."

When she didn't answer, he stared at her until she made eye contact. Her eyes were a funny shade of celery today, almost the color of her faded L.L. Bean sweatshirt. "You won't try this on your own, right?"

She looked as though she'd like to argue but slumped back sulkily. "I'd have to rent a four-wheel drive to make it up this road. Besides," she said with a pointed glance at the digital clock on the console. "I'm already behind schedule, and it never pays to taunt the Time God."

With arms linked huffily, her bosom was framed for view. Even her bulky sweatshirt couldn't hide the fact she was braless. Ben felt a stirring in his anatomy that hadn't even flickered when Amee had bounced into sight.

"Don't even think about it," he said sternly. He honestly couldn't say he expected either Jill or his libido to listen.

Czar poked his head back inside the cab. Out of the corner of his eye, Ben saw Jill nuzzle her face against Czar's neck. He didn't understand the bond that had developed between the two, but he couldn't fault Czar's taste in women.

JILL WAVED her electronic security card across the brown box on the wall of the entry portal. When the tiny red light flashed to green, she pushed open the *Sentinel*'s heavy security door. She generally stopped by the office after swim class to pick up a paper and check on Monday's obits. Thanks to a wild ride through the back roads of Bullion with an uptight, nosy cop whose physical presence made her body react in ways she hadn't thought possible, she was two hours behind schedule. The Time God would punish her for this, even on a weekend.

She paused inside the threshold to savor the quiet. While the newsroom was separate from Advertising in spirit and ego, the two departments shared a common, acoustically challenged corridor that on weekdays was constantly abuzz with ringing phones and voices.

Jill walked to her desk. Since the *Sentinel* didn't publish on Sunday, the Saturday edition carried the comics, a vital component of her Sunday-morning ritual—curling up on the couch with fresh-ground coffee, bagels and cream cheese, the paper and CNN.

"Hello, Jill," a deep voice said, catching her unaware. She jumped skittishly, bumping into the sharp edge of a desk.

"Will," she exclaimed, rubbing the tingling spot on her thigh through her sweatpants. "I didn't see your Beamer in the parking lot. I thought you were headed to San Jose."

"My car's in the shop. I have a rental."

Her heart rate was just about back to normal when he said, "I had to come in to straighten out a mistake."

His tone filled her with dread. "What kind of mistake?"

"Two of the photos in today's obits got switched."

"Oh no," Jill groaned, sinking into her chair. The wobbly chair made her neck jerk painfully to one side.

Chairs were an indication of one's status at the paper. The lower down in the hierarchy, the worse the chair.

"Who? Not the thirty-year-old guy, I hope. His poor grandmother..." Mistakes didn't happen often, but sometimes the typesetters were in a hurry. Like last week, they'd left out two obits completely.

"Margaret Kendell and Otis Johnson."

Jill gaped. "What? That's impossible. There's no way I could have mixed up a man's photo with a woman's obit."

Jill sprang to her feet and stalked across the desk-strewn space to Will's desk. She whipped open the A-section and studied the page before her. Switched.

She threw the paper to the floor and looked at Will. "I double-checked everything before I left last night. Someone had to have changed them after they were on the page."

Will rocked back in his fancy chair. "Who would do that, Jill?"

His question made her feel stupid. The same way she'd felt on the other recent occasions when she'd complained that her stories were being cut midsentence, that photos and cutlines were being switched and that articles were mysteriously disappearing from her queue. "I don't know," she said. "You tell me. Maybe the same person who butchered my canine-cop story."

Leaning to one side, he reached into his open file drawer and withdrew a Chinese lacquered humidor, which contained his stash of cellophane-wrapped toothpicks. "As I already explained, an unfortunate miscommunication resulted in your story getting edited twice. The new hire—I can't remember his name—may have been a bit overzealous. I'll talk to him next week."

"But why me? Why *that* story? I still think somebody in this place is out to get me." Jill raised her voice, wanting to vent her anger on any convenient receptacle. The lackadaisical toothpick wiggling in the corner of his mouth made a prime target.

"Aren't you being a tad melodramatic? This is a newspaper not a soap opera. I suppose it's possible you've made an enemy in the copy-edit team, but there's nothing I can do about that. I can't be here round the clock. Give it time. I'm sure it'll blow over."

"But what about my missing copy, Will? Did you ever find my original? It went missing from my queue. Doesn't that mean someone has my code and is intentionally sabotaging my work?"

He rocked back, slowly shaking his head. Jill had the urge to use her foot to help him complete the arc. "You truly tend toward the theatrical, Jill. It's more likely that someone was using your computer and forgot to sign out. Your story might have gotten stored in their files then accidentally erased. Get over it, Jill." He sighed. "You worry too much. The *Sentinel*'s just a lousy rag with fifteen-grand circulation. We're not talking Pulitzer potential here."

Jill had never understood his lack of professional pride, but she knew why he'd been hired. His editorials carried the message the owner wanted this town to hear, loud and clear. "I care about my job, Will. And it hurts to know that I've added to the burden of those two grieving families."

He shrugged. His toothpick made the same motion. "Look on the bright side. At least it wasn't one of the paid obits."

Jill bit down on her frustration. She'd already learned the hard way how fruitless it was to alienate the editor. "I'll call the families, but first I have to make sure the corrections are on the copy desk for tomorrow night," Jill said, marching to her desk. "I won't be in town, so I can't come by and check on it."

Will sat up, rolling his shoulders like a cat stretching in the sun. "Ah, yes, the Excelsior thing. Still planning to represent the paper?"

"Why not? Free food and drinks. Peter always stocks

the best booze. Gotta be some perks for working in a place like this.''

His laugh was friendly, but for some reason Jill wasn't anxious to share the fact that she was taking Ben Jacobs as her date. She hurried to her desk before Will could say anything else.

It took two agonizing phone conversations and two telefloral arrangements charged to her Visa before Jill was ready to leave for home. She didn't see any sign of Will as she tugged the heavy door closed behind her.

Drained and saddened, Jill trudged to her car. As she neared it, she heard her name being called.

"Damn," she cursed under her breath, hastily unlocking her door.

She reached for the handle, but before she could open it, Bobby Goetz materialized at her side.

"Hey, Jill, didn't you hear me?"

"Hello, Bobby," she said. "I'm in a bit of a rush."

"I been callin' for days. Don't they ever give you your messages?" His tone reminded Jill of a little boy who didn't understand why he couldn't have his own way all the time.

He was dressed in the only clothes she'd ever known him to wear: baggy denims, gray T-shirt and unkempt army coat with the name patch ripped away. When she'd first met him, she'd felt sympathy for him. Now she could barely stifle her impatience.

"I told you we'd get a hold of you when we needed you again, Bobby." Her first story had garnered him so many freebies, he'd obviously decided fame was a pretty easy meal ticket and Jill was his host.

He'd been so insistent in his demands and constant calls, the receptionist had dubbed him Jill's "stalker."

"But I thought of a new angle," Bobby insisted, a plaintive tone adding a certain thickness to his slight southern drawl. "That's what you call it, don't you? I figure you could do a follow-up. Show people how I'm doin' four months down the road."

And they thought you were dumb, she silently acknowledged.

"That's the editor's decision, Bobby. Call Will Ogden on Monday," she said, relishing the image.

She started to open the car door, but Bobby leaned his backside against it, pushing it shut. "He's even harder to reach than you."

Although Bobby was taller than Jill by several inches, with broad, albeit bony, shoulders and a certain whipcord look that implied he could hold his own in a knife fight, she'd never felt intimidated by him, even when they were trekking through the deserted streets of Bullion at midnight. Jamal had tagged along for photographs, but Jill was never worried about her safety. Bobby was too lazy to be more than a nuisance.

She tried pulling on the door again. "If anything comes up, I'll call."

His hand clamped down on her forearm, not painfully, but firmly enough to startle her. "Bobby—"

He stepped closer. Too close. She could smell ripe body odor and stale cigarettes. "It ain't fair, Jill. You can't just use 'n then drop me."

"Bobby, there's not much I can do. It's your life and—"

He interrupted her with an expletive. "That is so much bullshit. Didn't you learn nothin' from being on the street? People say we're there because we want to be, but that's bullshit."

Jill yanked her arm back. His grip tightened. She wasn't frightened, but she was getting angry. "Listen, Bobby, I gave you a break. That does not make me responsible for you for the rest of your life.''

He stepped closer; Jill held her ground.

''You don't get it, do you?'' he snarled menacingly.

''No, *you* don't get it,'' an angry voice said from behind Jill. She turned to see Will Ogden, standing arms akimbo less than a foot from them. She hadn't heard him approach.

''There isn't going to be another story, Goetz, so you'll just have to find some other way to use the system.'' Will's cultured sneer could have turned milk into yogurt. ''Now let her go and get the hell out of here.''

Jill blinked in astonishment at the snarling threat in Will's tone.

Bobby's grip relaxed; Jill snatched her arm away.

Bobby backed up, his hands raised defensively. ''I don't want no trouble, man. I was just talkin' to Jill. It's a free country, ain't it?''

''Maybe to vagrants like you who are only looking for the next handout, but not for those of us who work for a living. Now get the hell out of here. You've pestered her enough, you scumbag.''

Jill cringed. She could never bring herself to hurt a person's feelings, even if they deserved it. ''He's not so bad, really,'' she said, watching the young man shuffle away. ''Just a lost soul looking for help.''

''He's a hybrid—combination user and loser,'' Will said shortly. ''And he looked like he meant business with you. Whoever called him your *stalker* wasn't kidding.''

Jill shivered despite the warmth soaking into her shoulders. She'd never liked that word and didn't think it applied to Bobby, but she wasn't going to argue with Will after he'd come to her rescue.

''Th-thanks for your help,'' she said with a slight stutter.

''Not a problem. I was just pulling out when I saw him

standing over there in the bushes. I decided to wait and see what he had in mind. I think you should report this to the police, Jill.''

Jill shook off her disquiet. All she wanted was to get home. "I'll think about it. Might make good copy."

She slid into the leather seat. She'd meant the last as a joke, but something in Will's expression made her wonder if he'd taken her seriously. She let it go. "Thanks, again. See you Monday."

Will was still standing in the parking lot as she drove out. She suppressed a shudder. Stalkers, gremlins at work, an ex-husband to face... How could life get any crazier? Even as the question crossed her mind, Jill pushed it away. The God of Mischief and Mayhem was always looking for an opportunity to show off.

CHAPTER FOUR

JILL SHIFTED carefully in her desk chair so as not to disturb Frank, who was sleeping peacefully in her lap. She closed her eyes and listened to the mechanical hum of her computer copying her files to a disk. She had to get ready for her big *date,* but even the thought of seeing Ben Jacobs again couldn't override her apprehension at the thought of being in the same room with Peter and Clarice.

Peter's call an hour earlier had unnerved her. The conversation had been short and to the point: he would stop by Monday to collect the last few boxes of his personal belongings.

"You didn't forget about the pictures, did you?" he'd asked.

Jill had cringed. "Nope."

As stipulated by their divorce, Peter was entitled to half the photographs taken during their marriage. Jill and Penny, armed with a liter of merlot, had carefully cut each photo in half and tossed them in a box.

Jill wasn't dreading that meeting as much as she was the one tonight. Monday she'd be on her own turf—the woman wronged who was courageously putting her life back together. Tonight she'd be in Peter's ballpark where he'd have home-field advantage.

Her computer made a soft beeping sound. She pushed the release button and removed the small gray square of plastic. Eyeing the bookcase at her left, she studied the titles a moment before selecting one. With a faint smile, she stuck the diskette between two pages, about midbook, and shoved the novel back in place.

She stared at the title a minute longer: *Gone With the Wind*. *A perfect choice to describe what will happen to my career if this research pans out,* she thought as she turned off the computer.

A gravelly "meow" reverberated across the tops of her cat-warmed thighs. "Frank," she said, picking up the glossy-coated black cat. "Is it chow time, kiddo? I'd better feed you before I get ready for my date."

The idea of walking into the gala on Ben's arm left her a little giddy. Too bad she couldn't get involved with him on a personal level. Everyone knew cops and reporters didn't mix.

"Did I tell you about my choice of escort?" she asked, scratching behind Frank's left ear. "Almost as hunky as his dog."

Frank leaped from her arms and stalked off—tail stiff.

As Jill followed the cat downstairs, she thought about the reasons she and Ben shouldn't develop any kind of relationship.

One, she needed proof that Dorry was just avoiding her—not hiding out because of some threat. Two, she had to figure out if somebody at the *Sentinel* was purposely sabotaging her work, or—as Will suggested—if her imagination was blowing things out of proportion. Third was the Excelsior investigation itself. She planned to get to the bottom of that even if she had to dig her own soil samples. No, it probably wasn't a good idea to seduce the guy they'd send to arrest her for trespassing.

BEN SCOWLED at his reflection in the bathroom mirror as he fiddled with the tiny, pearl-shaped button at the base of his throat. *How did I let her talk me into this?*

The clerk at the tuxedo shop had been about twenty-five, as perky and shapely as a Dallas Cowboy cheerleader and very good at her job. By the time Ben had left, he'd spent just under a hundred bucks.

A noise, he could have sworn it was a chuckle, made him glance down. "What are you looking at?"

Czar eyed him speculatively from the doorway of the bathroom, his front paws framed by the squares of white tile. His haunches rested on the gleaming hardwood floor that Ben had painstakingly refinished right after moving into the house. He'd been overjoyed to discover oak flooring beneath the wall-to-wall olive-green carpet. As Joely had predicted, Czar's nails left scratches, but three Oriental carpet runners helped, and Ben still smiled every time he walked across his floor.

"You can stop begging. I already told you you can't go. She insisted on driving."

The topic of whose car to take had been a matter of hot debate when Jill called that morning to reconfirm their date. For a woman who exudes self-confidence, she sure is insecure, he thought. It was that contradiction that had made him cave on the issue of who would drive.

Czar's bark startled Ben, causing his fingers to undo the tricky button he'd just barely gotten closed. Tractionless on the wood, Czar's nails sounded like hail on a metal roof as he raced off, apparently responding to the sound of a car pulling into the driveway.

Ben glanced at his watch. "At least that Time God of hers keeps her punctual."

He leaned closer to the mirror, twisting the fabric of his shirt until he was sure it would rip. He hated to think how much that would cost.

"Damn," he said when the doorbell chimed.

Ben left the button undone and hurried down the hall; he unlocked the dead bolt and turned the knob, bracing himself for the worst. He hoped—almost prayed—that she wasn't as beautiful as he feared she'd be.

There was no screen door to dilute her effect. Long slanted rays of sunlight shimmered on her floor-length gown of amber satin. Simply designed, the dress escaped being classified as a sultry nightgown thanks to two rhinestone straps that twinkled through the strands of golden waves cascading around her shoulders.

Gorgeous. Worse than he'd imagined. Ben was grateful he hadn't been able to get his collar buttoned because he never would have been able to swallow the lump in his throat.

"Hello," she said, smiling up at him. She must have been wearing flat slippers because she seemed smaller, more delicate than he remembered. She had her hands tucked behind her. The ingenuous pose called attention to the shape of her breasts pressed against the fabric of the dress.

She stared back as if seeing him for the first time. Suddenly she blinked and whipped her hands around, holding something out to him.

"For you. For going with me. I truly appreciate it," she said, offering him a boutonniere in a plastic box.

Her words were spoken softly, almost apologetically, as if she regretted putting him through this torture. Did she know he was feeling tormented by her beauty? Did it show on his face?

Ben looked at the sprig of baby tears—waxy white blossoms that appeared artificially perfect against a too-green leaf.

Elegant. Classy.

"I think so, too," she said. "Much nicer than roses or God forbid, carnations. That's what girls always gave guys on prom night, remember?"

Ben realized he must have spoken the words out loud. He took an involuntary step backward. Focus, he ordered himself. His training had never failed him in the past. It had carried him safely through all sorts of life-threatening jams. He was a master at focus.

But for some reason, his gaze kept getting sidetracked by creamy shoulders dusted with freckles from summers past. Smooth skin that invited touch. As he watched, a cool gust made the hair follicles on her arms prickle.

"May I come in? Or are you ready to go? It's a little chilly in this dress." Her tone was wry. "I thought about black velvet, but Mattie's Rule Twenty-one is never wear white before Easter or velvet before Thanksgiving."

"How many rules are there?" he asked, stepping aside.

"I've always been afraid to ask."

Her nonchalance helped him wrangle his emotions under control while she petted Czar. "I'll be ready in a sec. One last button."

He'd taken two steps toward the hall when she said, "You look very dashing. Like a movie star getting ready to accept his Oscar."

Her tone more than made up for the cost of the tux. "Thanks. So do you." He was terrible with compliments— both the giving and the receiving. He hurried away.

When he returned a minute later, Jill was standing in the door of his living room, Czar at her side. Her fingers, thin and delicate-looking, tipped with a pearlized gloss, ruffed Czar's thick fur. He arched his neck to give her a better field; Ben would have done the same thing.

"Be careful. He sheds."

She pivoted, whisking hairs from her fingertips. "So

does my cat, Frank. It's just something you live with if you like animals.''

He was about to reach for the boutonniere, which she'd set on the table near the door, when she cleared her throat. Ben waited, knowing something was coming, and by the look on her forehead it wasn't good.

''I told you about the purpose of tonight's gala,'' she said.

He nodded. ''The Excelsior Estates development. I asked around, and I get the impression the community is about fifty-fifty, for and against.''

She nodded. ''You won't hear anything but acclamation tonight.''

Ben was fascinated by the play of emotions he read in her expressive face. ''Do you expect your presence to be a problem?''

A stain of red colored her cheeks. ''Of course not. I'm small time, not worthy of notice. It's just that…''

He bit back a smile; she had that little-girl look again. She took a deep breath, drawing his gaze to the swell of shimmering satin. His hand cupped reflexively.

''I think I may have invited you for the wrong reasons, and Penny says I owe you an apology.''

''I don't understand.''

''Well, you would if you were a woman whose ex-husband and his gorgeous new wife were hosting a party and you had the choice of showing up alone or bringing along someone who looks like…you.'' Her hand waved up and down, followed by her gaze, Ben wasn't sure whether to preen or be pissed.

Before he could make up his mind, she turned sideways, displaying a provocative dip of folded satin from shoulder to midback. Her smooth pale skin practically begged to be caressed. He took a step closer.

"I know that sounds awful. Penny called it reverse sexism." She looked at him. "It's shallow and petty and I'm a terrible person for even thinking it, but just look at you in that tux." Her hand reached out and skimmed the surface of his jacket sleeve, much the way she petted Czar. "I knew you'd be gorgeous, and I just couldn't resist the thought of showing up with you on my arm."

She clapped her hand over her mouth. Lifting up the hand, she mumbled, "I had no idea how ludicrous that would sound until I said it out loud. If you'd have said that to me, I'd have decked you."

She cringed a little, keeping an eye on Ben, who couldn't quite decide how he felt about being a sex object.

"I'm a sexist pig. I'm sorry."

Ben fought to keep from smiling. One part of him, a kid he almost didn't recognize, decided to have fun with the situation. He dropped his chin and shook his head woefully. "I feel so used."

She flew to his aid, patting his arm. "Don't say that. I mean, it's not as if I don't find you attractive. I do. Obviously, I do."

"But you're just attracted to my body." Ben could barely say the words without laughing. They came out strangled, as if he might cry.

"Well…yes, but I'm sure you have a very nice mind, too. We really haven't had much of a chance to talk…" Her words trailed off and she looked at him suspiciously. "You're laughing, aren't you? I'm baring my soul here and you're laughing."

Ben let go of his mirth—at ease for the first time in days. Maybe months. "I apologize. I couldn't resist. You were so earnest."

She looked both stunned and sheepish. "I get that way.

Mattie—my mother—says I can't see the forest past my knees.''

Catching Ben's look of confusion, she added, ''I think she means I'm so busy worrying about my own problems I trample over everyone else's.''

Her gaze met his. The last rays of sun slipping through the patio doors made her eyes a rich blend of golds and browns. An image of her lying naked in a pile of autumn leaves took his breath away.

''How about we put all this behind us and go on our date?'' She picked up the plastic flower box—a peace offering.

''I think I can handle it.''

AS THEY PASSED through the rock-and-timber entrance to the Ahwahnee Hotel's great hall, Jill swallowed the lump in her throat. Ben moved with all the assurance and grace of a man in control of his life, and she couldn't help wanting to stay close to him—hoping that some of his confidence might rub off on her.

''The steward said the reception is being held in the Mural Room,'' Ben said, guiding her toward the right with a light touch at the base of her spine. An hour in the intimate shell of her sports car had intensified—to the point of overkill—the attraction she felt for him. Even their tongue-in-cheek debate over the merits of Ricky Martin's music only added to his charisma.

She slowed her pace, content to enjoy the moment. The touch. His amazing good looks.

As if sensing her stare, Ben glanced sideways. His dark eyes were inscrutable but not intimidating. He looked…interested. ''It's getting late. Won't your Time God be mad?''

His gentle teasing was kind, not mean-spirited as Peter's

had been at the end. Before she could answer him, a voice said, "Hello, Jill. What a pleasure to see a familiar face."

Jill pivoted. Her heart slowly went back to its normal cadence when she realized the person addressing her was Mona Francis, the mayor's wife.

"Hi, Mona," Jill said, giving her a friendly hug. "My, you look lovely tonight. Have you lost weight?"

A diminutive woman of Italian descent, Mona embraced life—and pasta—with gusto. Her wide, pleasant grin made her still-beautiful skin light up. "Not an ounce, you flatterer, but I appreciate the lie. Wouldn't it be nice if I could give you a few extra pounds? She's too thin, don't you think?"

Mona looked at Ben expectantly. Jill could read the appreciative gleam in the older woman's eye, much the way an art lover might view a Picasso or Monet. Mona was a politician's wife, but she'd somehow remained untainted by the more sordid aspects of the game.

Jill took Ben off the hook. She swatted Mona's arm lightly. "You're worse than my mother, Mona. Putting my poor date on the spot like that." She took a quick breath then made introductions. Mona's dark brown eyes widened when Jill mentioned Ben's profession. She was a dear lady, but she liked to gossip as well as anyone.

"Bud mentioned your program the other day. Is your dog here?"

Ben shook Mona's hand with solemn formality, then told her, "No, ma'am. There wasn't room in the car. Jill drove."

"Oh, of course. Bud pointed out your car in the parking lot. He's quite a car aficionado—always poking under the hood."

"Speaking of the devil," Jill said, looking over her shoulder, "where is our esteemed mayor?" Jill wasn't looking forward to seeing Bud Francis any more than she was Peter and Clarice.

For the first time Mona looked uncomfortable. "He's taking a little nap in the car. He played an extra round of golf today and needed a quick rest to be at his best." Jill interpreted that to mean he needed to snooze off a little booze. "This is very important to the community," Mona said, "and you know how seriously Bud takes his duties."

Jill had several rather strong opinions about Bud's work ethic, but in deference to his wife, whom Jill really liked, she kept them to herself. "We were just about to go in, Mona. Would you like to join us?"

"Why, thank you, dear. I always hate to walk into a room alone. I'll know a dozen people the minute I get inside, but I just hate that first moment of strangeness, when you think everyone is looking at you." She motioned for Ben to come to her. "Perhaps I could borrow your date for a minute or two, Jill. If I walk in with him, that ought to get the gossipmongers' jaws flapping. What do you say, young man?"

Ben smiled graciously. "My pleasure."

Mona had to reach up to poke her hand through the offered crook in his arm, but she looked as pleased as a girl going to the prom. Jill used the moment to admire her date from behind. His long legs looked absolutely fabulous in the black tux; the material sculpted his broad shoulders then tapered to a snug wrap around his hips. Peter used to complain that tuxedos made all men look alike—obviously he'd never seen Ben Jacobs in a tux.

But he was about to.

"Jill," Ben said, offering her his other arm. "Two beautiful women to escort. How lucky can one guy get?"

Once inside, Mona gave Jill a quick hug then left to join two friends who hailed her. Jill scanned the room—no Peter in sight. She breathed a sigh of relief until she looked up to find Ben studying her.

"Are you sure you want to do this?" he asked.

They were standing near a glass display case honoring the basketry of the Miwok Indians, who'd been very nearly exterminated by the zealous pioneers who settled in this area. She found it ironic that Land Barons would choose such a setting to flaunt its latest acquisition.

"Sure. Why not?" The intensity of his gaze made her blush. "So I'm not a great liar, but I'll be okay. I just have to stay focused on the subject at hand. My personal life is old news, Excelsior Estates is where the action is." She passed him one of the slim, colorful brochures she'd grabbed on the way in. "Here. With your hands full, you didn't have a chance to pick one up."

He tucked it inside his jacket, his eyes never leaving her face. "Being a reporter is important to you, isn't it?" he asked.

"Yes. My job is meaningful, when it's done right." She inwardly cringed recalling the flubbed-up obituary. "But tonight I really have to succeed. I have something to prove."

His questioning look made her explain.

"Peter didn't want me to work. Period. When we were first married, I devoted myself to being a perfect wife and helping him succeed in the company, but there came a point when that wasn't enough. I tried freelance writing for magazines, but it was tough to get established because we moved so often. My financial dependence reinforced Peter's opinion that he was doing me a favor by staying married to me." She raised her chin defiantly. "I have to show him that I can provide for myself. That I'm a whole person, even without him."

Her words came out a little louder than planned, and Jill

glanced around to see if anyone was eavesdropping. Most of the thirty or so people present were gathered around a ten-by-twenty-foot topographic relief map in a glass case. She looked at Ben to suggest they check it out, but when her gaze met his, her mind lost track of all incoming messages.

Dark and intense, his eyes seemed to envelop her. She couldn't remember ever being on the receiving end of such a sexy look; it made her mouth go dry and her knees tremble.

"Only an idiot would think you were less than whole," he said, his voice low and for her ears only. Jill wondered momentarily if he'd meant to say the words aloud, because he suddenly lifted his chin and looked away.

Jill swallowed, not knowing what to say or how to get her brain back on track.

"Jillian," a familiar voice called, breaking her out of her trance. "They let *anybody* into these things, don't they?" The sniping tone was mitigated by a little chuckle. "Did you get your car fixed? It looked like you were having some trouble with it the other night."

Jill turned and took a step back, inadvertently moving into Ben—a very warm, solid fortress. His proximity eased the sudden flutter in her heart, although it was too late to stop the release of acid in her stomach.

"Hello, Peter," Jill said, taking in her ex-husband's new look.

His artfully streaked hair and tanning-salon-perfect skin tone gave him a healthy, all-American look that hinted of crewing on the Potomac. Normally, such *GQ* polish would have worked against a man where Jill was concerned, but Peter's added little-boy-lost quality had been her downfall from the start. It had taken years to figure out what he'd lost—his soul.

Jill saw Peter's eyes narrow speculatively as he studied her date. Ben placed a large warm hand on Jill's bare shoulder. She knew his gesture—whether he'd intended to make a statement or not—did not go unnoticed.

"Peter, I don't believe you've met my date, Ben Jacobs. He's a canine-patrol officer with the Bullion police."

Jill couldn't have asked for a more gratifying look on Peter's face. He recovered in an instant and graciously extended his hand. "Nice to meet you. I'm Peter Martin, Land Barons's associate director of acquisition and development." Peter loved titles. One night after he'd moved in with Clarice, Jill and Penny had brainstormed on possible titles for him. Jill's favorite was: Chief Propagator of Bogus Covenants and Dispenser of Bovine Manure.

"Mr. Martin," Ben said, his breath tickling Jill's ear as he reached around her to shake Peter's hand. The movement had a way of pulling her into the shelter of his body. Jill liked the feeling—more than she cared to admit. There had to be a Mattie rule against this kind of attraction.

"Call me Peter. I'm glad to see Jill's dating again. I was beginning to worry. She fell off a horse once and never rode again. I sure didn't want to see that happen where men were concerned."

Jill's fingers curled around the pen she carried. Sharp— it might pierce that perfidious hide. She plastered a fake smile on her lips and said, "But, Peter, wouldn't I have had to have been with a real man first in order for that to happen?"

Peter gave Ben a look that seemed to say *"Isn't it a shame how some women never get over you?"* then directed a brittle smile toward Jill. "We'll be starting a formal presentation in a few minutes. Time to mingle and drink. There's an open bar, Jacobs," he said, nodding toward a crowded spot across the room. "And, Jill, guess what Clarice was able to find? Château LeReium. Your favorite champagne.''

As if sharing a family secret, he told Ben, "I brought Jill a whole case from France once. Jill loves the bubbly, don't you, pumpkin?''

Jill's stabbing hand started up, but Ben smoothly intervened by blocking her view of Peter's treacherous back. She relaxed her grip on her pen.

But she couldn't stifle a low growl. "You don't know how badly I wish Czar were here. Just a tiny word of German and you could take him out. You'd do that for me, wouldn't you?''

His eyes danced with merriment. "In a heartbeat...*pumpkin.*''

Something sad and bitter left her and Jill laughed. She suddenly realized Peter's little barbs no longer held the poison that enervated her soul. Why? How? Was it because of this man?

Ben's hand squeezed her shoulder supportively. "Are you okay?''

She turned enough to be able to look at him but not lose contact with his hand. "Yes. Believe it or not, I feel great. This is going well, don't you think? My pen is beginning to feel like a pen again—not a weapon.''

"Good,'' he said.

Unfortunately, her stomach chose that instant to complain about its state of emptiness. Ben dropped his hand. "You need to eat. Why don't we divide and conquer? You hit the food table, and I'll get our drinks. What would you like?''

"White wine, I guess. I really am starved. I think I forgot to eat today.''

Ben's right eyebrow rose. "How can you forget to eat?''

She shrugged. "I was mulching my roses and working

on a story—'' *A story that would go nowhere unless Dorry came through.* And then Mattie had called, which had pretty much killed Jill's appetite. ''Anyway, I'll grab a couple of plates and meet you at the map.

''I'm dying to see their artist's concept of Excelsior Estates. I swear they always hire people who live in never-never land.''

BEN WATCHED JILL walk away. She stopped several times to chat with people she knew. To the casual observer, she undoubtedly looked beautiful, charming and at ease. But Ben sensed her calm demeanor was a ruse to hide her vulnerability. He didn't want to care but he did. A part of him wanted to protect her; a part of him wanted her. Period.

Maybe this body came with the tux, he thought as he joined a line behind three men in expensive business suits. *I've got less control than a kid at a prom.*

Of course, he had to acknowledge that the drive had been hell on his libido. The hum of the road. The moonlight. The music. Her scent.

''Excuse me,'' a soft but direct voice said. He turned to find a stunning blonde looking at him. Platinum hair pulled tight to her head. A silver-lamé gown draped with just the right demure about a too-perfect figure. Oddly, the sexy image somehow failed to jibe with the serious look in her eyes.

''Yes?'' His intuition told him this was the new Mrs. Peter Martin.

''We haven't met. I'm Clarice Martin.''

''Ben Jacobs.'' Did goddesses shake hands? He didn't offer and neither did she.

She smiled—at least she moved her lips in what probably passed as a gracious smile in her crowd. Ben noticed it didn't reach her eyes, which were the fairest shade of blue he'd even seen. She glanced around without moving her chin. Unlike Jill, whose hands did part of the talking every time she opened her mouth, Clarice Martin stayed still, as if excess movement might diminish her power.

"I just met your husband. My date is his ex-wife," he said, escalating them to the same playing field.

"Your *date*," she repeated, as if the notion made no sense. She didn't wait for Ben's response. "Jill has strong feelings about me, I fear. But she was never right for Peter. She knows this, but ego often supersedes truth."

Ben was certain Jill wouldn't appreciate this kind of talk. "That really isn't my business, Mrs. Martin," he said, moving forward with the line. He let her draw her own conclusions.

One skillfully penciled eyebrow rose ever so slightly. "A shame."

He ordered a glass of water with a lime twist and the house chardonnay from the bartender. "Why do you say that?"

"Having a man in Jill's life might distract her from her vendetta."

"What *vendetta?*"

"I have a feeling she may try to do something to sabotage this project," Clarice said, her voice displaying real feeling. "You know the media. Any hint of malfeasance can do irreparable damage—even without proof."

Ben silently agreed. He'd been so distracted by Jill's vivacious spirit, he'd almost forgotten her chosen profession.

"There's a saying about a woman spurned," Clarice said with a certain sense of urgency. The look in her pale blue eyes almost made him shiver. She took a step away then stopped, her focus on the beverage the bartender had set in front of him. "You don't drink?"

It wasn't a question, but it seemed to demand an explanation. "I'm a cop. I'm on duty twenty-four seven." That was his standard excuse. It was simpler than explaining what it had been like growing up with an alcoholic father.

She nodded, as if his answer solidified something in her mind. "Please help yourself to the hors d'oeuvres. The head chef of the Ahwahnee is truly gifted. We'll be serving a full-course dinner after the presentation. I do hope you'll stay."

That was a lie. Ben had been dismissed. He couldn't help her so he ceased to exist. *Interesting.* Not particularly pleasant, but interesting.

He picked up his two drinks after stuffing a fiver in the brandy snifter on the end of the bar then went looking for his date. She was right where she said she'd be: surveying the miniature land-development model. She was holding a plate of hors d'oeuvres, a napkin, pen and brochure in one hand and a half-empty champagne flute in the other. A second plate heaped with an artful arrangement of vegetables sat to one side.

He stopped a few feet away to put some perspective on what he was feeling. Beautiful? Yes. But more than that— animated, vividly alive. Watching her puzzle over the map was like observing a child discover the wonders of a tide pool.

She set down her glass, selected a delicacy from the mounded plate and popped a filo pastry puff of some sort into her mouth. She chewed thoughtfully then leaned over to get a better look at something. The décolletage of her dress presented him with a stunning view of her undergarment, a lacy thing that pushed her breasts upward: pale white flesh straining against burnished gold lace. Although totally ungallant, he might have continued to stare if he hadn't caught a glimpse of the mayor eyeing the same landscape.

"Jill." Ben's tone sounded sharp, possessive, even to his own ears.

She straightened, obviously still wrapped up in her thoughts. He wondered if she'd share them with him, or was she actually plotting some secret retribution against her ex-husband?

He held out her wineglass.

She smiled sheepishly, nodding toward her champagne flute. "Peter sent it over." She licked a few crumbs from her fingertips then held out the plate. "Yummy crab puffs. Want the last one?"

He shook his head, sipping his drink. "No thanks."

"I heard you were a health nut," she said with a mischievous grin. "So I stocked up on veggies, too." She produced a second plate heaped with broccoli, tiny carrots, baby corn and jicama spears. "Isn't that a bit incongruous considering your line of work?" she teased.

"Have you bought into that old stereotype of cops who live on doughnuts and coffee?"

"Not at all. I just think it's ironic that you eat so healthy when you have the kind of job that could get you killed."

He shrugged. "There's more danger from burnout and ulcers than from taking a bullet. Diet and exercise help." He accepted the plate of vegetables and sampled a broccoli crown that had been parboiled with a hint of sesame oil. "Good."

Her gaze followed his every move. Her lips parted as though there was something profoundly sexy about a man eating vegetables. The look on her face made him forget to chew. Fortunately, she was distracted by something over his shoulder.

"It's show time," she said, taking a small sip of champagne. She set aside her glass then moved forward to squeeze between him and the display. Her thigh rubbed against his.

Ben's plate wobbled; he set it down with a loud clink. His hastily swallowed gulp of water resonated as if he'd used a megaphone.

At the far end of the glass table Peter Martin raised one hand with the assurance of a man who knows people will stop what they're doing to hear him speak.

"Valued clients, friends. Land Barons is delighted you could join us on the eve of our newest project. Excelsior Estates is particularly near and dear to my heart since Bullion is where I met my beloved wife, Clarice."

He put his hand out to acknowledge the beautiful blonde standing nearby. She didn't nod; she didn't need to.

"Excelsior Estates is a utopia of sorts with options for just about everybody. Behind these gates is a new gold mine, a richness in quality living for both young and old.

"From starter homes for young families to downsized empty-nest homes that are marvels of flexibility and multifunctional use of space, Excelsior has what you want."

The crowd murmured its approval.

As the sales pitch continued, Ben cataloged responses from the people around him—all positive. This audience was chosen well, but a glance to his right told him Jill was less enamored.

"You forgot to mention the views, Pete," Bud Francis called out from a few feet away. "And the airport."

Ben decided the mayor looked none too steady on his feet; his red-rimmed eyes watered under the bright lights.

"And what about the water quality, Peter?" Jill called out.

After a momentary pause, Peter adroitly ignored Jill's comment and addressed the mayor. "You're absolutely right, Bud. I forgot to mention that Excelsior Estates is located on one of the most majestic ridges in the county— a mere six miles from the local airport. Funds have already been allocated by the city council to renovate one runway to make it commuter-jet friendly.''

He looked around, nodding toward some of the men who probably owned their own jets.

''What about the water, Peter?'' Jill repeated.

''What about it, Jill?'' There was a patient, indulgent air to his tone, as if he'd been expecting something like this.

''What about arsenic in the water?''

He seemed to reflect a moment then said, ''We decided to leave it out. A PR thing, you know.''

There was a loud burst of laughter.

Jill's color rose, but she didn't back down. ''Hasn't there been some concern in other mining areas—like Sutter Creek—that the water table might retain elevated levels of arsenic left over from the mining process?''

Peter shook his head like a learned professor patiently indulging a not-too-bright student. ''Sutter Creek is two hundred miles north of here, Jillian. And that area was involved in a totally different kind of mining. Excelsior was a minor gold vein depleted long before the technology that affected those areas was employed.''

Jill stood a little straighter. Ben saw her jaw stiffen. ''There was silver mining here in the early 1900s.''

Peter made a motion of dismissal. ''For a couple of years before the company went belly-up. All they did was make a mess. But we're going to fix that.'' He leaned forward, placing both manicured hands squarely on the display case. He addressed his public, not his ex-wife. ''We're going to make parks where there are piles of sloughed-off rock. We'll give you green grass instead of dust. And bike paths and walking trails where only rattlesnakes now roam.''

"As if rattlers roam," she muttered just loud enough for Ben to catch. He had to bite back a smile. Her points were interesting, but Peter seemed to have answered them.

"Have you tested the water in the existing wells, Peter?" she asked.

Peter's eyes narrowed and he looked about ready to lose his cool, then he laughed, smiling knowingly at those around him. "My ex-wife is of the belief that any growth is bad growth," he told the prospective buyers, as if letting them in on a little family dispute. Then he looked at Jill. There was definitely no affection in his eyes. "This isn't a news conference, Jill. It's a party. But I'll be happy to answer all your questions tomorrow. Just call Clarice and set up an appointment."

Ben was impressed. Peter had outmaneuvered Jill, and Ben could feel her fuming beside him. Then she was gone. He turned around to catch her, but she'd already slipped into the crowd. He started to go after her but found himself face-to-face with Bud Francis.

"What'er you doin' here, Jacobs?" His breath smelled lethal.

"Amos thought it would be a good idea if I met some of Bullion's most prominent citizens," Ben replied. A half truth. Ben had mentioned the gala but had left out the part about his date.

"Did someone say you're with *her?*" The caustic inflection left no doubt how the mayor felt about Jill.

"Yes, sir. I came with Jill Martin."

The man shook his head slowly, "Can't say as I think much of the company you keep." He suddenly lurched forward to finger a green square in the development. "Tha's my lot. Tennis courts across the road from my study. I like watchin' young girls chase balls."

Ben looked toward the door where he thought he caught

a glimpse of copper satin, but Bud tugged on his sleeve impatiently. "This project is going to fund your future dog patrol, you know."

This was news to Ben. "It is?"

Francis nodded. "Tax base. That's where the power is and don't you forget it. Someday people will look back at these years as a boom time and they'll thank me for it." More to himself than Ben, he added, "What the hell was Will Ogden thinkin' to let *her* come here tonight? The paper's got as much to lose if this bombs as anybody."

Bud took another gulp of his drink then said, "A word of advice—don't waste your time on her. Peter says she ain't worth diddly in bed."

Ben felt his temper rising. "Sir, with all due respect, Jill is my date."

Bud gave a wry hoot. "I guess a young stud's gotta let it out someplace." He laid his hand on Ben's sleeve. "Trouble is, we got a pile of money invested in you and can't afford to let something happen to you. So take my advice, son. Dump her like a bag of steaming dog doo. Why don't you ride home with me 'n Mona?"

Fortunately, someone hailed the inebriated politician before Ben could answer. Bud stumbled away. Ben wasn't happy to find out the mayor was a drunken misogynist, but at least their paths wouldn't cross on a regular basis. Bud Francis was Amos's problem.

Ben glanced at the elaborate map. Model children frolicked on a miniature swing set. Too perfect to be real. Ben knew phony when he saw it—he'd lived a whole childhood of it.

He set down his plate on top of the tennis courts then went to find Jill. He needed a dose of reality. Although fantasy might work, too.

CHAPTER FIVE

BEN SPOTTED her standing near an open door leading to the patio. A faint odor of cigarette smoke filtered inside.

"I wondered…"

She put her finger to her lips and nonchalantly leaned back, her ear tilted toward the doorway.

He stepped closer and gave her a questioning look. Her response was so unexpected he almost forgot to think. She reached out and ran the tip of her index finger across the furrow between his eyebrows and down his nose. He often stroked Czar like that; it was their special code of comfort, it said things she couldn't possibly understand.

When she pushed off from the frame, she swayed a moment—as if the movement caught her by surprise. He took her elbow. Her skin felt oddly clammy. "What's going on?"

She shook her head, whether negatively or to clear her head he wasn't sure. "I thought I might overhear some admission of wrongdoing on Peter's part, but he's too clever for that."

"He says you're out to sabotage his project just to get back at him."

She made a scoffing sound. "Of course he'd say that. He doesn't want to admit I might have some evidence suggesting the possibility of tainted water on the property."

"Do you?"

She looked at her toes. "I thought I did, but…"

Ben reached out to draw her chin upward so he could read her eyes; he'd never met a worse liar. "But what?"

"My source disappeared."

"Disappeared? As in Jimmy Hoffa?"

A look of distress enveloped her features. "No. Heavens, no. I think she just decided to make herself scarce because she's afraid of getting involved. People do that, you know. Even friends."

"Dorry Fishb—"

She cut him off by thrusting herself against him and kissing his lips. Although he might have argued that a simple "Shush" would have worked, he couldn't dispute the effectiveness of her method. Suddenly words lost meaning as feelings took over. Her lips were cold, but so very soft and sweet.

The kiss may have started off as a device to stop him from talking, but it quickly escalated to serious exploration. He was about to deepen it—to part her lips with his tongue and taste her, when she suddenly dipped—as if her knees buckled. He lifted his head and locked one arm around her back.

A shiver passed through her body. "Are you okay?" he asked.

Jill's eyes were closed. In the shadowy light, her skin looked too pale, except for an unhealthy slash of pink at the top of her cheekbones.

"A little dizzy," she said softly. Opening her eyes, she looked at him, blinking her long curly lashes to focus. "Do you have that effect on every woman you kiss?"

Ben tried not to smile but he couldn't help himself. "*You* kissed me, remember?"

A blush added to the scarlet glow in her cheeks. "How wanton! Mattie would never approve."

A group of smokers approached the door to reenter the

building, so Ben stepped back. He took Jill's hand and led her to a quiet corner a few feet away. She followed docilely, but he had the distinct impression something wasn't right. "Maybe we should sit down and talk about this," he suggested.

She started to shake her head but suddenly stopped, blinking. With a faint moaning sound, she pulled her hand from his to place it at her temple.

"What's the matter?"

"My head is spinning. Fresh air." She pivoted and rushed through the open door, past two couples standing beside one of the rock columns of the veranda. Ben noticed Jill's ex-husband and wife exchange an interested look.

He ignored them as he hurried to Jill's side. She hadn't gone far. His first inclination was to pull her into his arms, but in the back of his head he heard a voice reminding him that she was a reporter searching for clues that could bring down this development, which the mayor claimed was the key to Ben and Czar's future.

"Are you okay?" he asked, keeping his voice neutral.

Her shoulders rose and fell with a vocal sigh. A vapor cloud escaped in the chilly air. She wrapped her arms around her to disguise a shiver. "My stomach's queasy. Must have been the crab puffs." She glanced back at him. "Or nerves."

Ben was sorry he'd abandoned his water. "Maybe the champagne."

Her chin turned his way as if reading something in his tone. "I only had half a glass. It didn't taste very good. Besides, I decided I was being the worst kind of hypocrite. I can't drink Peter's champagne while trying to put a stop to his project."

Another shiver rocked her. He unbuttoned his jacket, removed it and drew it over her shoulders. When the jacket slipped around her, she seemed to melt backward into his arms. He closed his arms around her. Her chilled flesh was a stimulating contrast to his overly warm body. Her scent was the sexiest perfume he'd ever smelled.

"What kind of cologne are you wearing?" he asked. His tone seemed unnaturally husky. Could she hear the desire in his voice?

She rolled her shoulders as if trying to absorb the warmth from the silk lining of the jacket. "I don't remember. My mother sends me a new bottle every Christmas. No doubt hoping one of these wonder-smells will snag me a man."

Although her words were playful, her tone was flat, drawn. She leaned into him—not suggestively, but for support.

"You need a cup of coffee and something to eat."

She shook her head. "I don't think my stomach…could we leave?"

"Good idea."

She turned around and pressed herself to him in an apologetic manner. "This is terrible. I really did want to introduce you around." He tried to pay attention to what she was saying but was distracted by the feel of her body against his—a perfect fit. "Most of the city council's here…" She stopped, gulping in a breath of air. "I need to lie down."

Ben was at his best when there was a clear course of action. He knew how to make things happen in an expeditious manner; it was one of the reasons he was such a good cop. He could plow through obstacles—be it two gangs ready to hack up each other or an ex-husband ready to cast stones. If Czar had been at his side, the whole thing would have gone that much more smoothly.

This is the last time we take her *car,* Ben told himself.

JILL WASN'T SURE how he did it, but Ben Jacobs seemed to have more control over time than the Time God. Before she could get her thoughts together, he'd collected her things, retrieved the keys and was leading the way to her car, which was parked right beside the exit.

He had to help her crawl into the car. "Damn dress," she muttered, puzzled by the way the words seemed to hang on her tongue as if dipped in peanut butter.

Echoes of the door closing pulsed in her head. "I need aspirin."

While Ben walked around to the driver's side, she groped for the bottle she kept in the glove compartment. Her fingers felt too fat to work properly; the bottle eluded her. She was vaguely aware of Ben filling up the space beside her and watching her.

"Need help?"

Her tongue felt swollen. She nodded.

He located the small white bottle and shook two tablets into his palm. "Two enough?"

He smiled. Sorta. Jill liked it when he smiled. Too bad he didn't smile more often. Maybe she'd tell him that. Someday.

"Need water?"

The yellowish-white pills seemed to glow eerily in the parking-lot light. Her stomach suddenly lurched, and she dropped the pills. "I need to go home," she said, not liking the whiny sound in her voice.

He adjusted the seat and the mirrors, put on his seat belt then turned the key. He took his sweet time exiting the parking lot. Jill's increasing nausea made her snap. "This isn't a little old lady's car. It likes to go fast."

"Well, I don't. Just sit back and relax."

Jill reached down between the seat and the door and

pulled the lever that made her seat recline. Maybe lying flat would help ease her discomfort.

"Which way?" Ben asked. The car crept to a stop. "Are your brakes always this squishy?"

Jill lifted her chin and squinted. "To the…that way." She pointed to the right. "Road goes straight out. Don't get off. Can't get lost."

He turned the steering wheel and stepped on the gas.

"Last stop sign till town. The entrance booth closes at night." Jill was proud to get so much information off in one breath. She felt terrible about not being a better hostess. She knew a lot about Yosemite, but for some reason none of the information was accessible to her at the moment.

She was tempted to open the window for fresh air, but her body was racked with shivers. "Is my head still attached to my neck?"

She saw him glance sideways, his gaze lingering at her neck. "Is it the dash lights or are you green?"

Another serious wave of nausea made her groan. "I'm never going to eat crab again."

Ben stepped on the gas. The car surged forward.

Jill closed her eyes. A bead of sweat formed on Jill's upper lip, and her armpits tingled. She swallowed repeatedly, but the bile kept rising.

She opened her eyes. The moon cast an eerie, disorienting glow. The trees were too tall and the rock fortress walls too far away. "Stop the car," she said. "I'm going to be sick."

He seemed to hesitate. The car didn't slow down in the least.

"I mean it, Ben. You have no idea how hard it is for me to admit that. Mattie's Rule Number…something— never throw up on a first date."

"Your brakes are weak."

She heard his foot pumping the brake pedal, which slapped uselessly against the floorboard. They probably weren't doing more than fifty-five but it felt like a hundred to Jill, whose vision was blurred with tears. Ben grabbed the emergency brake beside Jill's left elbow.

"Nooo," she wailed. "Won't that hurt the car?"

She wrapped her hands around his but couldn't stop him from pulling up on the leather-encased handle. An ugly screeching sound of metal against metal produced a halty braking action.

Jill choked back whatever she'd been about to say. Suddenly she didn't care if he dropped the entire engine in the middle of the road. She needed the car to stop. Now.

Ben worked the hand brake like a pro while easing the car onto the wide gravel shoulder, where on a sunny day there might be a throng of tourists taking in the majesty of El Capitan. At least Jill could be thankful she wasn't going to have to share this moment with a hundred tourists.

As the car inched to a stop, Jill opened the door and leaned out, hoping she might be spared this humiliation by falling beneath the car's still-moving tires.

No such luck. Ben let go of the brake long enough to grab the material of his tux coat, which she was still wearing. The slight rending sound was followed by the noisy purging of her stomach.

As the spasms stopped, the car rolled to a jerky stop. The engine continued to run. Kenny G's expressive saxaphone crooned sweetly.

A hand gently pulled her back inside the car from which she was hanging like a limp rag. Mortified beyond words, she wiped her mouth and nose with the only fabric at her disposal then shuddered when she realized it was the sleeve of Ben's tux.

She was dimly aware of Ben rummaging through her

glove compartment until he found a blue-and-white kerchief she kept on hand for T-top days. He used it to wipe her eyes and whatever awful stuff was plastered to her cheek. She refused to look at him.

"Here's a mint," he said, holding out a little white circle. "Feeling better?"

"A…little," she stuttered, between leftover hiccups. "I might live. Not that that's something I'm proud of."

"Frankly, I'd call that providential vomiting," he said cryptically.

Jill looked at him. "What do you mean?"

"If you hadn't been sick, we might have gotten out of the valley before discovering the brakes were bad."

"My brakes are *not* bad," she snapped defensively.

"They don't work," he reminded her. "And that's not a good thing when you're going down curvy mountain roads in the dark."

A sudden image jumped into her brain: her little red car flying off a mountain curve, plummeting into the icy waters of the Merced River below. "Oh, no," she whispered, a wave of panic cleaving through her.

Ben made a sound of anger, but it must have been directed at himself because he very gently took both of her shaking hands in his. "It wasn't even close," he told her, his voice somber and reassuring. He leaned in and pressed a warm, sweet kiss on her forehead. "The emergency brake worked, and I've been trained in defensive driving."

Jill looked at him, wondering if she should confess her fears. "But I haven't. If I'd have been alone…"

He squeezed her hand. "But you weren't." He seemed to make up his mind about something and reached for the door. "You wait here. Keep the door locked and the engine running. We passed a service station a mile or so back; I'll call a tow truck."

"No," Jill cried, clawing at the sleeve of his fancy white shirt. "I'll go, too. My towing card, my car."

She squeezed between his chest and the steering wheel to reach the lever that opened the trunk. "I keep a change of clothes in my gym bag."

He seemed to shrink back to minimize contact.

I probably smell like eau d' vomit.

Despite the pounding in her head, Jill scrambled out of the car.

"Jill, you're not feeling well," Ben said, getting out. "I'll be right back. If you get scared—"

She stopped rummaging through the black nylon tote bag in the trunk. "My cell phone," she exclaimed. "It's in the side compartment."

Ben appeared a moment later and handed her the slim pink and purple phone. She pressed a button. Even in the moonlight she could see it lacked sufficient signal to make a call.

She handed it back to him.

"The Communication God is on strike?" he asked.

The warm teasing in his tone made her impulsively wrap her arms around him and squeeze. "You're amazing. Not many guys would be this understanding. Thank you."

He went completely still, and Jill realized she'd overstepped her bounds, again. He must think her a terrible tease. First she kissed him, then she hugged him in the moonlight.

Briskly turning back to the trunk, she dug in the bag to produce sloppy sweatpants and an oversize flannel shirt. "Turn your back. This will only take a minute."

He stepped away—apparently to return her useless phone. "Shouldn't you rest? Food poisoning can be a tricky thing."

"What if it wasn't the crab?"

The driver's-side door closed. As she bent over to put on the loose navy pants, she heard the crunch of gravel beneath his shoes. When he spoke, the sound came from in front of her car. "What do you mean?"

"What if my stomach problems and bad brakes are connected?"

He didn't say anything, but Jill sensed his doubt.

"I know it sounds crazy, but it's very real to me now. I'd go crazy sitting here. Can you imagine what I'd be thinking while you were gone?"

"Tell me," he said.

She peeked around the upraised hood of the trunk. "That you were part of the conspiracy, bought off to make sure I didn't find out the truth about the Excelsior project."

"Oh, really," he said with obvious humor.

Jill kicked off her satin slippers one at a time and drove her feet into beat-up running shoes. "Instead of calling for a tow truck, you'd call Peter, who would send his hit men to finish me off and dump my body in an abandoned mine shaft."

She removed Ben's jacket and carefully laid it aside, then unzipped her satin gown and let it fall to the ground. Her fingers were thick and clumsy as she struggled with her heavy flannel shirt.

Despite the stillness of the evening, she completely missed Ben's movement until he suddenly appeared in front of her. "You have some imagination," he said. His voice was low and husky.

He brushed aside her fingers and took over the buttoning. Fatherlike.

She lifted her chin to look at him. Her protest died on her lips. She didn't understand the serious look in his eyes, but she could read the sexual tension behind it. Her lips parted in invitation but immediately pressed closed when her mind cried, *You just threw up and you haven't brushed your teeth.*

Ben finished buttoning then used his knuckle under her chin to keep eye contact. "Do you honestly think I'd let anything happen to you before I have a chance to get to know you better?"

Jill wasn't quite sure how to take that. "Does that mean once you get to know me better I'm on my own?"

He smiled—right before he dipped his head to kiss her.

Jill turned away. "I don't think one mint will do the trick here," she said, embarrassed beyond description.

He ran the back of his cool, smooth hand along her cheek as if tracing her blush. "I think you're afraid something's happening between us and you'd rather not deal with it right now."

His frankness surprised her. Most men played games when it came to feelings. "Well, you gotta admit, my timing isn't the greatest. We have this romantic night, and I puke my guts out."

He lowered his head so their foreheads touched. His hands gently cupped her arms, moving slowly up and down. "I am attracted to you, Jill. Satin or flannel—doesn't seem to make a difference. So a little food poisoning isn't going to turn me off, either."

She looped her arms around his neck. The fine material of his shirt felt liquid beneath her chilly fingertips. One hand tested the solidity of his shoulder muscles; the other toyed with trim, baby-fine hairs at his neckline.

His mouth pressed against hers, but before his tongue could gain entry, she turned her head away and sank against him. Suddenly the tension, her illness, problems with the brakes overwhelmed her. Tears filled her eyes and she pressed her face to his chest. "I'm a mess," she blubbered. "This is crazy."

He soothed her with long, slow strokes against her flannel shirt and murmured soft words of comfort. "You're right. It's crazy to be standing out here freezing to death when we could be home in my hot tub."

Jill looked up. "The Mobrick house has a spa?"

He shook his head. "It's *my* house now, remember. I put one in."

He stepped back, but kept one hand on her arm as if afraid she might collapse. "Are you sure you're up to this?"

Jill looked down at her feet. Nylons with tennis shoes. What would Mattie say? She bent down and used a finger to slip her heel inside the worn shoe. After tossing her dress in her gym bag, she handed Ben his tuxedo jacket then closed the trunk. "Let's go."

"SHOO."

Jill looked at the dog beside her. "Does he mean you or me?"

Czar barked. A solid, throaty *woof* that made her flinch then laugh at her own reaction.

"Both of you," Ben grumbled, nudging her out of his way as he moved from stove to refrigerator. "Peppermint tea will work wonders on that stomach of yours, and even though you're not hungry, I'm starving."

Jill scooted to safety behind the island, Czar at her heels.

He gave his dog a dark look and said nothing. Jill wondered whether he regretted his invitation. Ever since the tow-truck driver had dropped them off at Ben's house, he'd been acting different—uptight. Not that she blamed him. They been squeezed together in the cab of the truck for over an hour.

She looked down at her big toe sticking through a hole

in her nylons. *At least he gave me a brand-new toothbrush and minty toothpaste when we got here.*

Jill moved to a shelf filled with cookbooks. "Do you actually cook this kind of stuff?" she asked, selecting one on Cajun cuisine. "I've become a McDonald's junkie since my divorce."

She caught the obvious sneer that Ben sent Czar. "What? You're not a fan of express cuisine?"

Ben dropped a tea bag in a cup. "Czar and I are a bit more finicky than that, right boy?"

Czar shook his head.

Jill sighed and took out a colorful little book with ice-cream cones dripping with chocolate and colorful sprinkles on the cover. "I used to be a gourmet cook, you know. I studied with a French chef when we were living in Denver. Used to impress the heck out of Peter's clients."

"But now you prefer fast food?"

Rather than reveal her pathetic excuse for a social life—frozen pizza and cat food—Jill flipped open the book. On the inside page was an inscription in red crayon: To Uncle Ben. Love, yur neice, Jenny.

"Your niece and I have something in common, we both love ice cream."

He glanced at her as he popped the cup in the microwave. He pressed a couple of buttons then returned to the refrigerator. When he straightened, his hands were filled with sandwich makings: bread, cheese, mustard, sprouts.

Jill put back the book and walked to the bay window in what was meant to be the dining room. Czar followed. She stroked his long handsome nose, trying to keep the more sordid aspects of the evening out of her mind.

"What time do you have to be at work in the morning?" Ben asked.

Jill turned to look at him. His large, capable hands deftly

slathered bright yellow mustard on dark brown bread. He cut several slices of cheese from a thick brick then arranged some sprouts on top of that.

Jill pictured the contents of her fridge and, for some reason, felt less womanly—and slightly put out. "I usually go in around eight."

The microwave beeped for his attention.

"I'll pick you up at seventy-thirty then," he said, delivering her cup to the island. "Let this steep a few minutes," he advised.

"Not necessary. There's a bike path right behind my house. I can take it straight to work."

He didn't say anything. Instead, he opened a cupboard and took out a plate for his sandwich. "Are you sure I can't fix you something to eat?"

Jill put a hand to her belly. "No, thanks. That little nap in the tow truck helped, but I still feel a bit queasy..." She sighed. "I can't believe you're being so nice about this. Peter would have been utterly repelled. My mother would be rolling over in her grave, if she were dead."

Ben laughed. "That doesn't make sense."

"It would if you knew my mother."

"Tell me about her."

Jill shook her head. "Are you nuts? And ruin a perfectly wonderful evening?" she asked facetiously.

His grin was too intimate, too knowing. Jill dropped to one knee and motioned for Czar to come close. The dog nuzzled the side of her face as if to say he understood completely. In a way, she was a little envious of the beast. It was obvious from observing them that first afternoon that Ben and Czar shared a bond few friends could claim.

You could tell me what's going on in your master's head, couldn't you? she silently asked, holding Czar's head between her hands.

His soulful eyes seemed to say, *Of course.*

"Your tea is ready," Ben said.

Jill gave in to the temptation to study Ben. He hadn't changed clothes, but had kicked off his shoes and opened the top three little pearl buttons of his shirt. The tiny vertical pleats running from shoulder to waist were rumpled, with traces of mascara in spots.

"I'll have your tux cleaned, by the way," Jill said.

"No."

He turned his back to her to reach into an overhead cupboard for a glass. The long clean line of black trousers over a tightly sculpted butt made her mouth fill with moisture. *He'd be gorgeous naked.*

Jill wiped her sweaty palms on the sides of her jersey pants. She couldn't believe such a thing had entered her mind. She reached for the glass of water she'd left on the countertop. It was the first thing Ben had given her when they entered the house, even before he'd taken off his jacket.

Why deny it? She was attracted to this man. Big time. But what to do about it was something else altogether. Even without the external issues facing her, there was the matter of her self-esteem. Peter had done a number on her, and Jill wasn't sure she trusted herself to fall in love.

A sound intruded into her thoughts and she realized Ben was staring at her with an inquiring look on his face. She felt herself blush. *Putting the cart before the horse, aren't I?* "Sorry, a wandering mind."

"Probably from malnutrition. Won't you at least try some yogurt? It would help restore some good flora to your stomach."

The concern in his eyes made her agree to try it.

"Good," he said, returning a second later with a small

carton of peach yogurt. He set it beside her tea then walked around the counter to join her.

The counter separated the kitchen from a rather cavernous room with a vaulted ceiling and a bank of sliding glass doors partially hidden behind tan and white floor-length drapes.

Looking down, she watched Czar sprawl on the floor beside her with a weighty sigh. Jill sympathized. It had been a tough night.

She opened her carton of yogurt and absently stirred the pale peach concoction. "Good thing it's not strawberry," she said without thinking.

"Are you allergic?"

Jill nodded. "Strawberries and anchovies."

"Alone or together?"

The humor in his tone made her grin. "Doesn't matter. They both make me break out in hives."

"Czar loves anchovies."

Jill froze—spoon halfway to her mouth. "I beg your pardon?"

Ben's eyes were twinkling in the indirect light. "Pizza is our mutual splurge. Veggie on my side, meat-lovers on his. With anchovies."

Something too sweet for words blossomed inside her chest. *He buys his dog pizza.*

Apparently not realizing the effect his words had had on her, he sat down in the chair beside her and started to eat his sandwich.

Czar, however, was looking at her as if he knew exactly what she was thinking. A rush of heat filled her cheeks.

"Is the tea still too hot?" Ben asked.

Flustered, Jill shook a big gulp. She winced as it went down. "Nope. Just great. Thanks."

They ate in a companionable silence broken only by

Czar's occasional snore. The yogurt tasted good, but Jill only took a few bites. She didn't think her stomach was ready for too much.

"All done?" he asked.

Jill leaned against the backrest and took a deep breath. "I don't know what happened to me, but I don't want to risk another attack."

"Drink your tea, I added a couple of herbs that will help replace what you lost earlier."

She grimaced. "This whole night has a sort of surreal quality—as though I were standing outside my body watching it happen to someone else."

He chewed thoughtfully, but didn't say anything. Fleetingly, Jill wondered if silence was a police ploy to get people to confess things they had no intention of confessing.

She picked up her mug—a big, yellow, ceramic vessel bearing a Magic Mountain logo. Its warmth soaked into her fingers. "You probably think I overreacted, right? Granted I was borderline hysterical when I thought you were leaving me alone on the road, but what if the mechanic finds out someone tampered with my brakes?"

Ben took another bite of sandwich. When he was done chewing, he washed it down with a swig of tea then said, "That's tomorrow's topic."

Jill shivered. The thought of someone deliberately trying to hurt her was terrifying. "Am I crazy to be worried?" she asked in a soft voice.

"I was there, remember? Something was definitely wrong with your brakes. Tomorrow, we'll find out the cause. There's nothing we can do about it tonight." He put a hand on her arm. "I don't want you to think I'm trivializing your fear, Jill, but I usually advise people who have been through a traumatic experience to focus on what's coming at them, not what they just went through."

"Right," Jill said dryly. "Otherwise they'll miss that jab to the nose."

His lips twitched. Jill wished she was brave enough to kiss him, just lean over and put her lips on his and forget about everything else. But with her emotions riding so close to the surface, it was a bad idea. "You're right. I'll just have to wait until I've talked with the mechanic tomorrow."

Ben cleared his throat. "If you don't mind, I'd like to give him a call myself. I can tell him exactly what it felt like when I pumped the brakes."

"Sure. I'd appreciate that." As she reached for her glass of water, a nerve in her neck became pinched and she flinched.

"Does your neck hurt?"

She rolled her shoulders. "Not as much as my stomach muscles." She rubbed her midsection right at the bottom of her ribs. "I didn't realize vomiting was so physical."

"Well, let's get you into the hot tub," he said. "It might help your aching muscles."

Jill hesitated. She was tempted, but...

"My sister left a suit here. You're about the same size."

Hot, steamy water. Relaxing. Soothing. Ben. Seminaked. She looked at Czar, who wagged his tail and seemed to smile his encouragement.

"What time is it?"

"Nine-thirty."

Early. Too early. Too much time to worry and wonder and stress.

"Okay. Let's do it—go hot-tubbing," she clarified.

His grin made her blush. "Anybody ever tell you you have a way with words?"

His chuckle was big brother–like. He rose and pulled out her chair like a gentleman. The man was nearly perfect, Jill thought. Too bad she couldn't get involved with him, because she sure did like him. A lot.

CHAPTER SIX

JILL GAZED at her reflection in the mirror above the dresser. The bikini—three scraps of bright blue fabric adorned with dainty yellow flowers—was a bit snug, but it would have to do.

For modesty's sake, she tried using her sweatshirt as a cover-up, but it made her legs look like two white clothespins supporting a bag of laundry. After tossing it aside, she tiptoed down the hallway. Ben had promised to leave a towel on his bed. "Go through my room," he'd advised. "I haven't repaired all the decking outside. It's the safest route."

Yeah, right. Safe, she thought dryly as she checked out his bedroom. Masculine, orderly. Pewter walls with textured vertical blinds at both the large window and across one-half of the sliding patio door. A bedspread of Native-American design in gray, burgundy, black and turquoise topped the king-size bed. Oriental runners stretched across sections of beautiful hardwood flooring.

"Nice," she whispered.

After checking to make sure Ben wasn't in view, she dashed across the room to pick up the big burgundy towel at the foot of the bed. Just as she leaned over, something cold touched the back of her thigh. She let out a squeal and vaulted to the bed.

The door to the right opened and Ben appeared, dressed

in black boxer trunks. No shirt. He glanced at her then looked at Czar, who wagged his tail.

Jill instantly realized what had happened.

"Czar," Ben said sharply.

Dancing from foot to foot to keep her balance, Jill was positive every red blood cell in her body had congregated in her face. "Don't scold him. I overreacted. I forgot he was here."

Ben put out his hand to help her down from the bed. "Sorry."

"It...it's okay," she stuttered.

He looked at her—his gaze lingering in a very male way.

"Your sister must be smaller than me," she said, reaching past him for a towel.

"You look amazing," he said, an impish smile flitting about his sensual lips. "But...that's Jenny's suit, not Joely's. I didn't know my niece left one here."

Jill snatched the towel to her chest and wrapped it around her. "Your teenage niece? No wonder it's tight. I'm so embarrassed."

"I know. You blush the prettiest shade of pink." He took a step closer. She could feel his warm breath on her bare neck and shoulders when he said, "Don't tell her I said so, but it looks a lot better on you. If she looked this sexy, her father would never let her out of the house."

Jill's embarrassment disappeared. She couldn't remember the last time anyone had called her sexy. Under Ben's scrutiny, she *felt* sexy.

"Ready?" He took her hand and led her across the patio.

Jill stumbled slightly, bumping into his solid, bare shoulder. The contact seemed to sizzle. He gripped her hand a little tighter. "Have your eyes adjusted?"

She could make out the spa because of the vapors rising

like steam from a witch's cauldron. Private. Cozy. Romantic. What was she thinking?

He let go of her hand and hung the two towels on hooks on the fence, well within reach of the hot tub. "I'll get us some ice water."

As Jill slowly lowered herself into the hot, percolating water, she heard Ben speak to Czar. Instantly, the dog was at her side, respectfully keeping his distance but not taking his eyes off her. Jill decided she liked the idea of being guarded; she felt wonderfully safe.

"Oooh," she sighed, slipping lower until the water topped her shoulders. She'd piled her hair into a pony top-knot using a hair tie she'd found in her purse. She closed her eyes and sank back, letting the warm water caress her aching muscles.

Czar made a sound and she opened her eyes. Ben approached with two tall plastic glasses. Jill's heart fluttered in the oddest way. His broad shoulders tapered to a flat tummy; his muscular legs were covered with a sparse nap that sparkled in the light from the windows.

Her mouth watered as she watched him descend into the tub. When Ben reached the center, he sank beneath the frothy bubbles only to pop up a few seconds later, hair slicked back and dripping wet, like some disciple of Neptune.

The backs of her knees tingled and something hummed inside her.

He plopped into one of the carved-out seats across from her. Breathing space. *Breathe, Jillian.*

"Are you okay?" Ben asked.

Jill squirmed. Did rabid lust fall under the heading *okay?* "Sure. Fine," she said in a squeaky voice.

He reached for one of the plastic glasses and moved

closer to hand it to her. "Drink. Your electrolytes are probably all out of whack."

Something's out of whack for sure, but I don't think water is going to help. Obediently, she closed her eyes and drank. Icy drops slipped past her lips and ran down her throat.

She felt Ben's finger catch a droplet before it reached her clavicle.

When she opened her eyes, his hand was hovering as if caught in a war of wills. She understood completely. With a sigh, she set the glass on the molded plastic ledge and slid closer to him, resting her forearms on his shoulders. Their knees touched. "This is probably nuts," she whispered against the slight stubble on his jaw. "But I'm tired of thinking. I want you to kiss me. Please."

Lips, chilled by the air temperature but warmed by passion, met in a tentative, investigative manner befitting both their natures and careers. For the first couple of seconds. Then, instinct took over.

BEN'S MIND SNAPPED OFF like a flashlight. His arms closed around her wet bare flesh as if he might find a way to crawl inside her skin.

Jill made a little sighing sound that nearly sent the blood surging through the top of his head. Her lips parted and welcomed his tongue to explore the warm, sweet cavity of her mouth. *Tea and toothpaste.*

He shifted slightly so their upper bodies were more closely melded. Ben could feel the outline of the skimpy bikini, the tips of her nipples flattened against his chest. He scooted his hips forward and leaned back, drawing her onto his lap.

She jerked skittishly when her thigh connected with his erection. "Are we going too fast?"

Lifting her chin, Jill pulled in a deep breath. In the light from his bedroom he could see a faint glistening around her lips from his kisses.

Her torso was turned just enough that Ben's hand came in contact with her breast. He tilted his hand palm out and lingered over the tip that strained against the wet fabric. Her responsive arch made him gently squeeze the ripe softness.

"Fast? Slow? To hell with time," she said sotto voce.

A certain wistfulness in her tone made him link his fingers across the middle of her back, letting her use his arms for support. The slash of blue string looped around her neck marred the perfection of her beautiful neck and upper chest. Her breasts peeked in and out of the bubbles; the triangles of fabric teased his imagination.

As if reading his mind, Jill reached behind her back. The scrap of cloth suddenly floated to the surface. Grinning, she ducked down so the water touched her chin. Then the microtop suddenly sailed from the water to land in a puddle beside Czar, who sniffed it with interest.

"Are you shocked?" she asked.

Yes. "A little."

"Me, too," she said, running her hands through the water in front of her. "I swear, I've undergone some kind of personality transplant tonight. I can't explain it, but I feel incredibly liberated."

She stopped moving. Her topknot tilted to one side like the curl atop a melting ice-cream cone. "There I go again— only thinking about me. Completely disregarding your feelings. Maybe you'd rather not be in a hot tub with a half-naked woman."

Ben couldn't keep from laughing. "Yeah, right. My worst nightmare."

She scooted closer, as if testing his interest. "We could

blame my newfound lack of inhibition on surviving a near-death experience, but I don't think that's it. I suddenly feel…renewed. You not only saved my life, Ben, you've made me feel desirable. That's something I haven't felt for a long time. Do you understand?''

''No.''

She looked startled, and a bit hurt.

He pulled her closer and kissed a pulse point in her neck. He could still smell her intoxicating perfume. ''You *are* desirable. Sexy. You're the most beautiful woman I've ever been with, and I can't believe you need *me* to make you feel that way.''

She melted in his arms, framing his face in her hands. ''There's some big-time attraction going on here, isn't there? I've been feeling it all night. In the car…at the party… But it's probably not very smart to act on it, right?''

He agreed but still asked, ''Why?''

She kissed his eyes, the bridge of his nose, his cheek-bones. ''Oh, the usual reasons. We barely know each other, our jobs aren't compatible. I have a cat, you have a dog…''

Ben's brain didn't want to talk; his body demanded action. ''Those sound more like excuses than reasons,'' he argued.

Her knees were demurely folded to one side, her hip resting more on his thigh than pelvis. Ben needed contact of a more intimate nature even if it killed him. He put his hands on her hips and pushed her backward so her body floated in the bubbling jets.

She linked her fingers behind his neck and smiled, like a mermaid tempting her mortal lover. ''I guess there's only one reason that counts,'' she said.

Ben let his fingers spread wide to explore her belly. She

sucked in a breath when his fingers touched her navel. "What?"

"Rule Number One, of course. Never let a first date get beyond second base." The mischief in her eyes made him grin. "Or was it never let a second date get to first base? Do you have a phone around here? I could call Mattie and ask."

Ben snickered as he guided her hips toward him—helping her onto his lap. Two very thin scraps of material were all that separated them.

"No phone. Sorry. But there's a cop on duty if you need help."

Jill's throaty, sexy chuckle made him ache with desire. He shifted his hips to feel her perfect fit against his straining body.

"Wouldn't you call that a conflict of interest?" she asked, wiggling with an obvious need of her own.

"I meant Czar," he croaked.

"We're not a danger to ourselves or others, are we?" she asked, her tongue outlining the rim of his ear. "We're above the age of consent."

When he didn't answer right away, she sighed and said, "I wouldn't blame you if you didn't want to get involved with me. I come with a matched set of emotional baggage, courtesy of my ex-husband and his new wife."

An out. So simple. So generous. At any other time he might have heeded it. Instead, he kissed her then said, "My sister says I have enough pieces to start my own travel company."

She threw back her head and laughed. "Here we are in the middle of this serious discussion and you make a joke. You, who almost never smile." She put one hand on his chest, her thumb moving in sensual little circles above his heart. "I like you, Ben Jacobs. A lot."

Ben couldn't wait any longer. He hugged her fiercely and kissed her with neither finesse nor patience. He wanted her, desired her. Hell, he might even love her. At the moment, all he knew was that he couldn't live without making love to her.

She returned his kisses with an uninhibited yearning that seemed equal to his. He slipped his hand between their bodies. His fingers grazed the elasticized border of her swimsuit then dipped into the nest of curls. She cocked her head to flick her tongue against the roof of his mouth in matching exploration.

Think man, think. You need a condom. You need to hold off long enough to get her inside.

But his mind was focused on a different *inside* all together. He wanted to know Jill from the inside out.

A sudden bark triggered a conditioned response. Ben jumped to his feet, pushing Jill behind him.

The scrambling sound of Czar's toenails against the deck rattled like incoming machine-gun fire. Ben crouched, one hand on Jill's bare shoulder. "Get down," he whispered.

Czar lit out of the protected gazebo and charged across the yard. Ben stared into the blackness to see who or what he was up against. Slowly, like single frames on a video—complete with sound effects—the picture came together: the misty haze from the spa, the twinkling stars above the roof, his partner—his dog—barking like a fool at the neighbor's cat, which had bolted up the plum tree.

"Goddammit, Czar," Ben snarled, sinking into the frothy water.

His fingers tingled from excess adrenaline. His heart was nearly back to normal when he looked at Jill who was sitting across from him—knees to her chest—a look of mirth on her face.

"This isn't funny," he said, trying not to laugh.

"Not if you're the cat," she said, breaking into chortles of pure delight. She could barely catch her breath for the laughter.

She used a knuckle to wipe the tears from her eyes then took a deep breath. "Mattie says there's no such thing as coincidence. I have to assume that interruption came for a reason."

I was afraid you might think that.

"Dammit, Czar, shut up," Ben yelled.

Czar continued barking.

"Czar, honey, leave the cat alone. Cats are friends, too," Jill called—the humor in her tone making the order less than forceful.

To Ben's surprise, Czar stopped barking and trotted back to the spa. He went straight to Jill's side. "Good boy." She patted his head in return for a sloppy kiss on the cheek.

"I like cats," she said, "but if I had to choose, I'd rather be a dog."

Ben's tone was disgruntled when he asked, "Why? Cats get away with murder."

"But dogs get more respect."

She moved to Ben's side, snuggling comfortably against him. She rested her head on his shoulder. He caught a scent of her shampoo above the smell of chlorine and wondered what it would be like to wake up each morning with that smell on the pillow beside his.

"As much as I hate to say this, I think we'd better get out of here before we do something we'll both regret in the morning."

Reasonable words. Smart, even. *Then why do they hurt so much?*

Ben rose, reached behind him and snagged her towel. He held it open for her, then helped her step out of the spa.

"Thanks," she said. She stopped to pick up the bikini top.

Czar followed her—not even glancing Ben's way. Muttering under his breath, Ben grabbed his own towel and hurried after them.

"Do you want to shower?" he asked—trying for normal. No use sounding as desperately bereft as he felt. "There's shampoo and stuff in the spare bath."

She waited just inside the door, keeping to the rug so no drips would mar his floor. "No, thank you," she said with a sigh. "I feel just right."

Just right?

As if hearing his unspoken sarcasm, she winked. "Well, not *just* right, but I feel good. Whole. Better than I have in a long, long time."

Ben relaxed. He understood. There would be other times.

"I'll get dressed and take you home."

She started to leave but stopped. She looked back a moment then held open her arms to him. Slim, feminine and welcoming arms. It wasn't in his power to resist. They hugged in a way that was both healing and full of promise. Not sexy or lustful, but hopeful and tender. When she let him go, Ben felt *just right,* too.

"NICE PLACE," Ben said, pulling into the driveway of her two-story townhouse.

Jill looked at the hulking monstrosity illuminated by the silvery moonlight. Why wasn't her front light glowing? She always left it on when she planned to be out late.

Or had she forgotten? She'd had a lot on her mind when she'd left the house that afternoon.

"It lacks soul, don't you think? I want to sell it and find something smaller as soon as the market turns around."

Ben had retreated into his quiet, serious shell ever since

their hot-tub incident. Jill was still shocked at her uninhibited response to Ben's lovemaking. Where was the repressed, sexually dormant ice cube Peter had accused her of being?

"Wouldn't that happen sooner if the new development went in? More growth, more opportunities?" he asked.

Jill released her lap belt and shifted to look at him. "In order for Bullion to experience new growth—real, solid, positive growth, you need to have some small, clean industries come in," she said, trying not to sound preachy. "Something that will put money in the pockets of those who live here, not in the pockets of people who live in Florida or New York or wherever the Land Barons's execs live."

"Won't the county benefit from increased property taxes?"

"Eventually, but the initial profit goes to people with no loyalty to the land, no sense of community." She reached out to pet Czar's nose. His body was behind the partition but his head filled the space between her and Ben. "The people who live in this area chose it for a reason—quality of life. Why did you move here?"

"My job."

"Wrong answer. I did my research. You're very marketable. You could have gotten a job in half a dozen cities. Heck, make that half a dozen states. But you chose dinky little Bullion. With its rednecks and old hippies. Why?"

Ben took his time answering. "I wanted to get away from big-city problems—crime, noise, apathy, bloodletting, decay. I wanted to see the color of the sky more than five or six times a year. And sit in my yard without worrying about drive-by shootings."

She nodded. The warm glow from the dashboard cast soft shadows over his features; the candid look in his eyes made her heart turn over. *I wonder if love at first sight really is possible.* "That's it exactly," she told him. "And very eloquently put, I might add. But that quality of living is bound to change if Excelsior Estates goes in—its very size almost guarantees it."

"I can't help but admire your conviction, but don't the people moving into those new houses deserve a chance at that dream? Won't their money benefit the community with better schools, more parks?"

Jill smiled. It was fun to argue with someone who fought fairly. Respectfully. "The first lots—the showy ones with the killer views and golf-course access—will go to people who can afford to jet in and out at will. Those people may buy a few necessities from the local grocery store but they buy their clothes at Saks Fifth Avenue."

"But the big ticket homes still help the tax base, don't they?"

"That depends on what they cost in the long run," she said, thinking about the cleanup costs in places like the Love Canal.

"You're referring to the water issue."

Jill sighed. How could she make him see this wasn't a personal vendetta? In order to explain in detail, she'd be giving up information she planned to use in her story. But some things were common knowledge. "In Sutter Creek, houses were built on mine tailings. When kids started getting sick, they tested the water and found high levels of arsenic.

"The feds kicked in something like three million dollars for the cleanup, but that's just the tip of the iceberg. The people who built homes were left holding the bag. They'd spent their life savings to build their dream homes only to find they couldn't sell and didn't dare let their children live there. It makes for an infamous scandal that hurts the whole area.''

Ben sat forward, his arms resting on the steering wheel. He seemed to ponder her points carefully before he said, ''So, all you're saying is test the water before they start building. That makes sense.''

''Unless,'' she argued, ''you're an out-of-state developer who has already sunk big bucks into the project, via payoffs and bribes. At that point, you can only redeem your investment by selling lots.

''And if you have a city council that's gone out on a limb to build a jet-friendly runway at the municipal airport, your politicians are going to be more concerned about their jobs than the water.''

Ben turned his chin to face her. In the light from the police radio, his expression looked serious. ''Didn't you say Land Barons is multinational? Would such a high-profile company risk that kind of negative publicity?''

Jill threw up her hands. ''Maybe they don't know about it because the person behind the project failed to tell them.''

His eyes narrowed. ''Your ex-husband.''

She turned her head to look out the window. ''I don't know. I used to trust people. I used to believe everything Peter told me. I used to think Land Barons was a classy operation. But that was before I bought one of their homes.'' She squinted at a spot near the garage door where the cracked stucco was pulling away from the trim. ''All the homes in this subdivision show shortcuts in building and substandard materials. Land Barons is big on image, but image isn't everything.''

Ben said nothing. The silence was broken by Czar who made an unhappy sound in his throat.

Jill patted his nose. ''When this proposal first came before the city council there was talk of a new school—that carrot got a lot of people behind it. The *Sentinel* backed the project big time. Voters passed Measure C—a municipal bond to raise money for civic improvements, including a school. Did you see a school anywhere in the model we saw tonight?''

Ben frowned.

"No, because there wasn't one. Empty promises. I can tell you all you'd ever want to know about those.''

"Why'd you stay with him?''

Jill knew that question didn't come easy. Ben wasn't the kind of man who pried into other people's lives for the fun of it. A small, self-deprecating chuckle rumbled through her hollowly. "I've thought a lot about that and all I can say is Peter undermined my self-confidence to the point where I believed I couldn't make it on my own.''

She sighed, then added, "I know you have your doubts about me, my job. But I'm truly not doing this for revenge, Ben. If the water in that area is safe, then I promise you I'll back off. And I'll wish Peter and Clarice every happiness, and go about my merry way.''

She took his hand, which had fallen to the seat between them, and brought it to her cheek. "Do you think our being together in the spa had something to do with my newfound maturity?''

His fingers uncurled and cupped her jaw. "I probably shouldn't mention this, but Clarice told me she was hoping I was involved with you so you'd be too distracted to give them a hard time about the new development.''

Jill bounced back, but she didn't let go of his hand. "That woman has enough gall to choke a rhino. What did you tell her?''

Ben smiled. "That you were only going out with me for my body.''

It took her a minute to realize he was kidding. This playful side was so disarming she almost jumped into his lap and begged him to take her inside. She looked at the house's black, uninviting windows and seriously considered asking him in—until she remembered the mess she'd left behind. Five changes of clothes thrown every which way.

"You're dangerous," she said. "You make me want things I have no business wanting. Not yet, anyway. Not until we've had time to get to know each other, to fill in the blanks."

His sigh matched hers. "I know just what you mean." He opened his door. "I'll walk you in. You should leave the porch light on."

"I thought I did."

BEN WATCHED as she picked up her satin bag and silky shawl, which was bunched into a pudgy roll. The fancy bag looked incongruous with her sloppy sweats and scuffed tennis shoes. Her hair was pulled back in a limp ponytail. Damp spirals dangled at her neckline. He saw her try to suppress a shiver.

If it were up to him, he'd carry her upstairs, tuck her in bed then crawl in beside her. Maybe if she was there beside him, he'd be able to sleep without dreaming about her.

"Hey, sweetie," she called, kneeling to peer into the rear compartment. "Come tell me goodbye."

Ben was still confounded by Czar's attachment to Jill. He'd barely left her side the whole time she was at the house. He'd even followed her to the bathroom and waited outside the door.

Czar's head poked through the opening.

She looped her arms around his neck and squeezed. "G'night, big guy. You're a good dog, even if you do have bad manners where cats are concerned."

It dawned on Ben that maybe he could trust Czar's judgment where Jill was concerned. Czar hadn't cared for Janine in the least—in fact, he'd shredded a pair of her expensive shoes one night when she'd stayed over. Czar hadn't responded like this to any of his dates. Maybe his partner knew something Ben didn't.

He gave the dog a quick pat on the head then got out, taking the keys with him.

He paused and looked up. Above him, the sky was awash with stars.

"I swear it's colder here than it was in Yosemite," Jill said, joining him, her bundled shawl clutched to her chest.

Despite his heavy Bullion P.D. sweatshirt, Ben shivered. "Maybe it's just the letdown after being in the spa."

Jill chuckled softly. "There's letdown, then there's *letdown*. I don't think the God of Passion and Desire is ever going to forgive me for that one."

"There's a God of Passion and Desire?" he asked, joking.

She nodded. "Oh my, yes. He sits on my mantel. You can't miss him." Her lips pursed mischievously. "I used to hang my keys on him, if you get my drift, but Penny said that was sacrilegious."

Ben hooted, picturing the image all too clearly. He had to admit that despite his unappeased sexual frustration, he couldn't remember the last time he'd laughed this much.

Czar barked, a serious request for attention. Ben felt a fleeting stab of guilt at having ignored his friend all evening. "I'll be right back, boy. We'll stop for a run in the park on the way home," he promised, closing the door.

Czar's bark rattled the windows, but for the first time, Ben didn't give his friend the attention he deserved. Ben's mind was on the beautiful woman beside him. Could he really be falling in love with Jill Martin?

"Quiet," he ordered sternly. In German.

Jill had started walking toward the house—one hand poking in her purse when she suddenly cried, "Damn. I left my keys with the car. What was I thinking?"

Ben groaned and shook his head. "It never crossed my mind either. I'll run you over to the garage—"

"No," she interrupted. "There's a hidden key by the side door."

Ben frowned. Jill's townhouse was the corner unit. Its side yard was fenced and private, but the lone streetlight was half a block away. "Let me get a flashlight."

"Good idea. I don't use that door because the gate sticks. I asked the maintenance guy to fix it about three months ago, but he's an old crony of Peter's. I guess I'm last on his list."

Ben decided he'd have to look into that. Discrimination of any sort rankled him.

When Ben opened the Blazer's door and reached for his large, heavy-duty flashlight that was clipped in place under the dash, Czar made another bid for attention. "Sorry, pal. Just a few minutes more."

As he hurried after Jill, he heard a creaking. The redwood gate was open when he reached it, but propped slightly askew.

Czar's low whine followed him, but the sound failed to register in his brain. Ben flicked on the flashlight as he entered the small patio area at the side of the house. A narrow step led to a painted door. A concrete path continued to the rear of the house.

Two large garbage cans on wheels were pushed up against the fence. He found Jill squatting beside a couple of empty clay pots near the stoop.

Ben flashed the light around; he spotted the hidden key right away—a lone gray rock sitting beside the welcome mat. "You know, that's a dead giveaway," he said. "At least bring in a few other rocks to give the burglar a challenge.''

He could have bitten his tongue when he saw how exhausted Jill looked. The night was catching up with her.

She unlocked the door then turned and motioned him closer. "You're right," she said. "I'll go rock shopping tomorrow, but right now…" She leaned across the distance and placed her lips on his.

His flashlight made a clunking sound when it hit the concrete. He put his arms around her and closed the gap. Ben wanted more, everything he'd come close to having in the hot tub and then some. He wanted her with a force he hadn't dreamed possible. It made him ache all over, from the inside out.

When the pain became unbearable he pulled back, looking to the starlit sky for help.

"I feel it, too," she said softly. At least Ben thought she spoke; maybe he was hearing her thoughts. It frightened him a little, but not enough to let go of her.

When he looked into her eyes, she sighed—a wispy sound that filtered into every corner of his being. She rested her forehead against his. In the far distance was a faint hum of cars on the highway. Her home was only six blocks from the hospital so there was more street traffic than there was near Ben's home. Even closer was a persistent bark, which seemed to set off other dogs in the neighborhood. Dimly, Ben realized it was Czar leading the chorus.

That really isn't like him, one part of his brain said.

Jill levered herself back, disconnecting her body from his and unloosing her arms from around his neck. Ben felt strangely bereft.

"I wasn't expecting this when I asked you out," she said.

Ben liked her honesty. "Me, neither. Can we do it again?"

She looked at him questioningly. He started to laugh; so did she. It was a good release from all the tension, both sexual and unspecified. He rested his free hand against the jamb of the open door.

"I meant go out," he clarified. "Preferably without car problems, food poisoning and barking dogs."

She drew in a deep breath and let it out slowly. "I'd like that."

Czar's barking intruded into his consciousness. "I'd better go before Czar wakes up the whole neighborhood. Maybe he's jealous. I've never seen him take to another person like he's taken to you."

"He's a wonderful animal. Very intelligent, with excellent taste in women," she added, grinning impishly.

Ben bent to retrieve his flashlight. As he fished around in the darkness he heard Jill open the door and flip on a switch; she tried it several times but nothing happened. "The bulb must be burned out."

She turned on the kitchen light and a warm glow seeped into the little patio area. Ben saw the handle of his flashlight beside a flowerpot and picked it up. "Lock up when I leave," he ordered.

She saluted. "Yes, sir."

Spunky. That was what Amos had called her, and Ben had to agree. At the moment, his heart felt full of good feelings; some he could identify, others might take a while.

"G'night," he said, his voice sounding strange to his ears.

He didn't want to leave. Something made him want to stay right there and never let her out of his sight, but his rational mind kicked in. Besides, his dog was barking like a maniac. "See you tomorrow."

He waited until he heard the door close and the lock click in place then he made his way past the sticky door. Maybe tomorrow he'd run by while she was at work and plane off the excess wood at the bottom of the door.

Czar was still barking when Ben reached the car. He unlocked the door and started to slide in when he realized Czar was trying to squeeze his body through the opening between the two sections of the vehicle.

"Czar!" he cried in alarm, releasing the lock on the rear doors. He whipped open the rear driver's-side door. "What in the hell do you think you're doing?"

As soon as the door was open, Czar did a reverse crawl to extricate himself from the opening then bolted past Ben, who stood dumbfounded by his partner's behavior. "What the...?"

A sudden knife blade of fear arced through him. Ben looked to see where Czar had gone, but the dog was already around the corner of the house. Ben charged after him. "Czar."

He'd only taken two steps when he heard the report of a gun. There was an answering whimper.

Ben's fear changed to pain. But through the haze of agony came years of training. He shut off his mind and let instinct take over. He dived for the Blazer and, using the door as a shield, picked up the mike.

"Officer down, 4403 Heather Ridge Court," he cried. "Repeat—officer down."

CHAPTER SEVEN

THE PAIN STOPPED without warning. One second there was nothing but pain; the next there was nothing. Period. Jill opened her eyes, trying to absorb what was happening to her.

She saw action—too much to follow all at once—but heard nothing. It was like watching a television show with the mute button on. People in sloppy green outfits gestured frantically over a prostrate figure on a moving gurney. Three women poked, prodded and attached clear tubes to the still, lifeless form while two men in orange jumpsuits pushed the mobile cart toward a brightly lit cubicle. Jill sensed this was her body on the table, but she didn't feel overly alarmed.

A gangly, earnest-faced man with a mop of curly, orange-red hair and thick glasses rushed through a pair of swinging doors; he gestured with impatient motions for two more nurses to join him.

"Wow," Jill uttered, although no sound reached her ears.

That one word suddenly brought a flood of images as sharp and clear as if she was reliving them. First, that terrifying instant of awareness when she knew someone was in her house. She'd turned to flee but the hooded figure in black had charged—weapon raised. Another gift from her mother—a heavy brass phallic-shaped statue. The God of Fertility.

"Ben," she'd screamed.

The intruder had grabbed her by the hair and yanked backward.

Through the black cloak of panic one word had formed in her mind. *Fall.* A self-defense instructor once told her, "When there's no other defense, use your body as a weapon. Go limp. The dead weight will throw your assailant off balance."

The statue whooshed past her ear, grazing her collarbone. Her shoulder exploded in neon pain—right before the intruder landed a second blow near her temple. The movie screen in her mind went black, and Jill blinked, bringing her attention back to the present.

The redheaded doctor suddenly jumped up on the gurney, straddling her body. He seemed to be shouting at the others. Jill "moved" closer to the action.

Am I dead? Truly dead?

She looked closely at her body. Her skin, always reluctant to tan, was the color of pumice. Her hair was matted with some sort of black gum. Her features, which she often cursed for being too Scandinavian, were slack, as if her soul had taken the air out of her skin when it left. Jill was grateful her eyes were closed; she didn't want to see them empty of life.

White sheets covered her haphazardly. Her arms dangled like broken puppet pieces with tubes for support; no one was manning them. Snippets of her clothing were lying in a heap in the corner. Her exposed skin looked slightly bluish, but Jill didn't feel cold. She didn't feel anything, just a surreal sense of witnessing a life-or-death drama.

"Please, don't die." She addressed the body on the table. "You have to fight. You have a lot to live for...your work, your cat...Ben."

Ben. She pictured his sweet, handsome, loving face. *He*

might be the one. We both felt something...something good, dammit! She silently railed against fate's injustice. *So close, so very close.*

Suddenly a ripple of commotion passed through Jill's awareness—as if a distant door opened and another presence entered the same dimension of consciousness. She looked away from the frantic scene below her and focused on the tumultuous wave of images surging into the periphery of her view.

"Ben," she called out as he charged across Tri-County Hospital's emergency room. He was pushing a second gurney while two paramedics ran to keep up with him. He wore a bulky, much-too-large jacket with a Bullion Police Department emblem on it. Unzipped, she could see his bare chest heaving. The sweatshirt he'd been wearing when he took her home was partially tucked beneath the patient's head like a baby's security blanket; crimson stains, wet and fresh, were smeared like finger paints. The small figure on the gurney lay hidden beneath a mound of gray blankets.

Somehow Jill knew the identity of the victim on the gurney even before one of the paramedics pulled away a blanket. *Czar.* Jill's heart started to crumble into little pieces; a terrible heaviness weighed her down. Where before there was lightness and a sense of peace, now Jill felt a fearsome sense of loss.

"No, please not Czar. Don't let him die. Ben would be heartbroken. You can't let it happen," she begged whatever forces might be listening. "Take me instead. Just don't take Czar."

She moved closer to the gurney, which Ben had pushed into the cubicle adjoining her little theater. She studied Czar, her newfound friend. The majestic animal looked small and pitiful against the starched white sheet. Ben gently worked his sweatshirt out from under the dog and flung it into a corner; he motioned for someone to help him. Jill could tell he was near the breaking point.

The two paramedics hung back, looking helpless and distressed. Suddenly a door on the far side of the room snapped open and a small, Mediterranean-looking man in evening wear barreled through the portal. Jill recognized the socially prominent doctor from his high-profile lifestyle. She didn't trust him to care about a dog. She *moved* closer to Czar's side.

Without knowing how, Jill suddenly could *hear* a powerful din of noise. Ben's voice came through loud and clear. "Doctor, you've got to help my partner."

Jill flinched at the raw agony in his voice. Was she to blame for this? Did Czar get in the way of the person who attacked her? Did he come to her rescue?

"Good God, this is a dog," the doctor exclaimed.

"Czar is a police officer who was wounded in the line of duty. And you damn well better treat him."

Jill could see the doctor didn't appreciate Ben's threat, but something—maybe pride—made him whip a small, lighted penlike apparatus off a nearby tray of sterilized instruments. After making sure his protective gloves were in place, he leaned over Czar and flashed the light into the dog's unresponsive eyes. Next, he carefully examined the wound below Czar's right ear. Matted blood, thick and chunky in spots, was plastered to the black and tan fur.

"Not good," he muttered. "Nurse, cut off this damn collar."

Ben stepped back to give the medical-team room to maneuver, but he never left Czar's side. He glanced toward the adjacent cubicle. "She's gonna make it, isn't she?" Jill heard him ask the doctor.

"The wound isn't deep, but it breached the cranium,"

the doctor said, taking a nasty-looking instrument from the tray.

"I meant the woman over there. Is she okay?"

The doctor didn't look up. "I have no idea. I can only work on one patient at a time."

Jill didn't care for the man's bedside manner. She felt as useless as an empty glass after a party.

Maybe I can reach Czar's spirit and encourage him to fight. Jill inched closer. She tried not to think about the ghostly aspects of her situation. She didn't feel dead. In a way, she felt more alive than she could explain.

"Czar," she called. "Czar, my friend. Don't be afraid. Be strong and brave. Fight. Think about Ben, don't lose sight of Ben. He loves you, boy. He needs you."

Jill reached out her hand to touch the still form of the dog. She didn't like the eerie image of other hands passing through hers as the doctor and nurse performed their duties.

"I don't know a dog's physiology," the doctor said. "I don't know what got damaged. And he's lost a lot of blood. Where's the damn vet?"

"His answering service said he went to Reno," the nurse answered. "They're trying to track him down."

"Stay with us, Czar," Jill coaxed. "You can do it."

The doctor put a stethoscope to Czar's heart. "His heart is strong, but I don't get any reaction in his pupils."

"No." The heart-wrenching cry was enough to stir the dead, or even those on their way to the hereafter because, from the corner of her eye, Jill saw her body twitch as if someone had poked it with a cattle prod.

The flatline on the heart monitor went haywire. The doctor, who was standing to one side looking downcast and defeated, suddenly cried out, "Holy cripes! She's back!"

Jill didn't feel back. She looked at her hand and saw a white light pass through her essence. Her fingertips, which had been pressed against Czar's bloodied fur, began to disappear as if drawn downward.

Jill wasn't afraid, but she did feel a heavy sadness and deep regret. How could fate be so unkind to give her love, then take it away just like that? She looked at Ben who was talking excitedly, but Jill could no longer make out his words.

As the white light consumed her, she felt a friendly entity press up against her. A strong, loving presence that looked like Czar. *Czar? No,* she cried. *We can't both die. No. I refuse to go.* But as her essence continued to sink lower and lower toward the gurney, Czar eased past her in the direction of the other operating table. Right toward her body.

Jill's confusion made the pain in her head all consuming, but she thought she heard a reassuring voice say: *Trust, Jill. This is about healing, not dying.*

The light turned blinding, the roar of pain deafening. When it became too much, her mind switched off, and the world went black. And very still. Jill reached for oblivion, the sweet peace of not knowing and not worrying. It was all she could do.

"WHAT CAN I DO?" a voice asked.

Ben looked up from the waiting-room chair to find Amos Simms standing beside him. Others had asked him the same question over the past four hours. *Has it only been four hours?* It seemed like a week since he walked away from Jill Martin's back door and into a nightmare.

"Tell me you've caught the guy who did this."

Amos's gray head shook from side to side. "We will, though. I guarantee it."

"Have her parents been contacted?" Ben asked.

"Done," Amos said. "A neighbor came running when

the ambulance arrived, and Jimmy took her statement. She had all Miss Martin's emergency numbers.''

Ben rose and walked the eight paces to the far wall—he had the routine down pat. Fatigue muddied his brain but he refused to leave until he found out what was happening to Jill.

"Sounds like Czar's going make it. Shouldn't you be home in bed?" Amos asked.

"Not until I hear about Jill."

Amos raised his eyebrows. "I think you'd better tell me about this."

Ben straightened. Out of habit his hands went to his belt, which would normally be outfitted with his patrol paraphernalia. No belt. Sweatpants. He glanced down at the borrowed Bullion P.D. jacket someone had given him. His sweatshirt had been soaked with Czar's blood. And Jill's blood.

A shiver passed through him. He walked to the chair and sat down.

"I left her at the door, I heard the lock click. When I got back to the unit, Czar was going ballistic." Ben's deepest regret was that he hadn't paid more attention to the signals his partner had given him. "When I opened the car door, he bolted past. I'd just started after him when I heard the shot. Small-caliber pistol." Ben tried not to relive the sickening sound of Czar's whimper. "I called for backup."

His first impulse had been to storm the house, but his training helped him past that momentary burst of panic. He'd advanced swiftly but cautiously. He'd inched around the corner of the fence. About twenty feet away on the lawn a mound lay outlined by the light of a neighbor's porch light that suddenly switched on. Czar.

Ben had raced to his prone comrade. A seeping gash near Czar's right eye appeared to be the only wound, but it looked nasty. Ben had wrapped his sweatshirt around Czar's head, applying pressure to the spot.

He'd scanned the area for any sign of the assailant but saw nothing out of place. In the distance, a car engine had revved to life but no screeching tires bespoke panic.

"Jimmy was first on the scene," Ben told Amos. "I put him in charge of applying pressure to Czar's wound while I checked on Jill." Ben had made it clear he'd hold Jimmy personally responsible if Czar died. Unfair, of course, but Ben had meant it.

After shrugging on Jimmy's too-large jacket, heated from the other man's hefty body and smelling of stale sweat, Ben had dashed to the dark, silent house.

"Jill was on the floor. The assailant had apparently exited via the patio door. It was standing open," he said, his voice oddly disconnected from the horrific memory of seeing the woman he'd just held in his arms lying on the floor in a pool of blood.

He'd tried to detect a pulse in her neck, but his fingers had felt disconnected from his body. He'd been afraid to move her. Terrified, actually. He'd knelt beside her like a useless child on the verge of tears.

"Jill," he'd called over and over. "Hold on, sweetheart. The paramedics are almost here. Stay with me, baby. Don't give up. Please don't die."

"I talked to one of the paramedics," Amos said.

Ben turned away. He knew he'd behaved like a madman, demanding two gurneys. There'd been a heated argument over where to take Czar. Jimmy had quietly relieved Ben of his weapon.

Amos laid a stubby, freckled hand on Ben's shoulder. The look in his eyes was one of compassion. "Jimmy said you were real shook up about both of them. He wasn't surprised about Czar, of course, but he couldn't figure out what you were doing with a newspaper repor—''

Ben interrupted, "We were on a date. She's a reporter— not a felon. I like her and I plan to see her again."

If Amos was shocked by Ben's reply, he didn't let on. He stood quietly a moment, then said, "I like her, too."

Ben almost lost it. He turned away to pick up the cup of cold coffee someone had given him. Its bitter taste seemed apropos.

Amos took out a small notebook and clicked his pen into action. "Jimmy said something about her car. What's that about?"

Ben suddenly felt queasy. What if Jill was right about her brakes? What if someone was out to get her at any cost?

He gave Amos a rundown of their evening's adventures—leaving out the part about the hot tub.

"I'll call the tow shop in the morning," Amos said, returning the notebook to his pocket. "Could be coincidence. Jimmy seems to think she surprised a burglar. I'll send a team out first thing in the morning."

Ben wondered if now was the right time to divulge Jill's theory about water pollution at the new development. He decided to wait until the report on her brakes came in.

"You need to get some rest, son. Your vehicle's out front. Are you up to driving?"

"I'd prefer to wait until I hear something. Jill's still in surgery."

Amos started to argue, but stopped when a pair of swinging doors opened at the far end of the hallway and a man walked out. Ben recognized the red hair and ran down the hall.

"How is she?" Ben asked, forcing himself not to shake the answer out of him.

"Who are...oh, you're the cop she was with." His tone was heavy with exhaustion. "We've done everything we can. Repaired the bleeder, put in a shunt. Now, it's up to her."

She was alive. Ben understood that much. He didn't like the man's resigned tone, but as long as Jill was alive there was hope.

"Then she's going to be okay?" It was half question, half plea.

"Can't say for sure. She's still unconscious."

"When will you know?"

The doctor sighed. "If...*when* she wakes up, we'll have a better idea. Head wounds are tricky. And we're a little worried about the lack of oxygen to the brain. Her heart stopped, you know."

Ben's hands opened and closed in fists; he wanted to hit something. Amos touched his shoulder. "Jill's a fighter. She'll be okay."

The doctor looked as though he wanted to believe that, too. "She's in recovery. I wish I could be more promising, but this has been one of the most confounding cases I've ever worked on."

Ben frowned. Before he could ask, Amos said, "How do you mean?"

The man sighed. "Medicine is anything but an exact science, and *miracle* isn't a word I'm comfortable with, but something...inexplicable happened on that operating table. I was sure we'd lost her. We'd stopped CPR. But then out of the blue, she came back." He shrugged. "Maybe she just has one hell of a will to live."

Ben held the words close to his heart. He wondered, for a second, if their feelings for each other had played a factor in her courageous fight. "Can I see her?"

"She'll be transferred to intensive care as soon as she's

out of recovery. You can check with them about their visitor schedule in the morning.'' The doctor started to move away then looked at Ben. "How'd your dog do?"

Amos answered for him. "Czar's the second miracle of the night.''

"I'm glad to hear it. Maybe when he's back on his feet you'll give him a medal. If he hadn't intervened, Jill would be dead for sure.''

Ben's heart froze. "What?''

The tired doctor shrugged and started to turn away. "I'm not a forensic specialist, but from the angle of the wounds—one on her shoulder, the other on her cranium—I'd say whoever hit her would have kept on hitting if your dog hadn't showed up.''

Ben's knees buckled. He might have embarrassed himself if Amos hadn't grabbed him by the shoulder and swung him around. "There you go. You found out what you needed to know. Now I'm taking you home. And that's an order.''

JILL REGAINED CONSCIOUSNESS in stages. First, she heard little noises in the distance; then, she picked up bigger sounds, louder and more immediate: the low murmur of voices, the clatter of plastic trays banging against the side of a metal cart, the hum of a heating unit.

Gradually she realized she was alive, but her first, clear thought was *water*. She couldn't remember ever being as thirsty. She opened her mouth to ask for a drink.

"Argrulawah.'' The low-pitched gurgling sound brought a rush of panic. A man in black. The statue. The emergency room. Darkness. *What happened? Why can't I see? Why can't I speak? Where am I?*

Answers came to her as images, which she linked together like a child with a connect-the-dots puzzle. Ben. At her door. Czar. Barking a warning. Bright lights. A safe haven.

Her rapidly beating heart started to slow. *I'm in the hospital. I'm alive. That's a start.*

She directed her focus on opening her eyes. What should have been a simple task required every bit of her energy. She could hear herself panting from the exertion.

She was rewarded with a tentative flutter of eyelashes that told her something was impeding her progress. By concentrating, she sensed something wrapped across her face. *Bandages?* Her first impulse was to reach up and brush it off, but neither of her hands worked.

Suddenly swamped by a feeling of claustrophobia, Jill teetered on the verge of panic. Silent cries of frustration echoed in her head. Did anyone know she was alive, trapped in her mute body?

Jill fought for control. She remembered her father telling her once, "Fear breeds panic, panic fuels disaster."

She took a deep breath. Her ribs felt funny. Actually, her whole body felt strange—disconnected, somehow. *Am I paralyzed?*

She tried moving her leg and heard a rustling sound. *Legs work.*

Logic seemed to dictate that if she'd been revived in the emergency room and brought back to life courtesy of modern medicine then there should be a doctor or nurse monitoring her progress. Shouldn't someone be able to tell she'd regained consciousness?

So where are the bells and whistles? Where's my doctor? Is anybody out there?

Suddenly Jill sensed another presence in the room. She couldn't explain the strange sort of spine-tingling sensation that told her someone had entered her room. She knew it even before she heard the soft whooshing sound of fabric brushing against something. That sound was followed by the smell of a harsh disinfectant blended with a scent she remembered well from her Peter days.

Aramis cologne. A man. Maybe my doctor. Maybe he'll give me a drink if I can let him know I'm awake.

She detected another sound. *Breathing?* Jill didn't know how else to explain it—not raspy and obvious, but soft and steady. *Weird.* What was even weirder was the notion she could "hear" a second breather when a new entity entered the room.

Jill felt as though her ears were actually twitching, trying to pick up these sounds. *Wow. This is bizarre.*

"How's your patient doing, Doctor?" a female voice asked.

The second set of smells made Jill's nose twitch: sweat, breath mints and a faint perfume Jill couldn't identify. Jill realized she could distinguish between the two people in the room quite clearly; the way they moved drew a picture for her. The nurse, quick and purposeful, made twice as many movements as the laconic doctor.

"Stable for now, I think, but what do I know?"

His cavalier attitude surprised Jill. The few doctors of her acquaintance never would have admitted not knowing something, especially in front of a nurse. Or, worse, a patient.

Jill considered staying still so she could hear what other shocking revelation doctors and nurses might exchange, but her thirst was too compelling.

She put all her effort into movement, any kind of movement. Several muscles reacted; she wasn't sure which, but something happened.

"Look, Doctor, that leg twitched."

Jill heard his sharp intake of breath. "I'd heard they have

great recuperative powers, but this is really quite remarkable.''

They? As in what? Women? Jill felt two sets of inquisitive fingers touch her head near her right temple. Despite the tenderness in that area and a steady throbbing that seemed to match the beating of her heart, the pain didn't seem too bad. *Thank goodness for drugs.*

''Maybe the wound wasn't as deep as you thought,'' the nurse speculated.

''It's hard to say, but I thought I saw gray matter.''

Gray matter? Jill gulped. *What if it was the part that runs my motor sensors?* Fighting back panic, she tried to signal the medical team. A smile. A wave. Anything.

The smelly duo apparently noticed nothing.

Maybe a simple sound like, ''Okay.''

Jill tried to concentrate on each step of the process. *Focus on the word. Concentrate. Shape the lips and put a little sound behind it.*

A low moaning sound erupted very close by, but it didn't sound like any noise Jill had ever made.

''Oh, you poor dear,'' cooed the nurse. ''Does it hurt? Do you think he's in pain?''

Of course it hurts. Of course I'm in pain. He?

Someone pressed something round against Jill's chest. Although cool, it felt blocked by the blanket. *Hey, Doc, I don't mean to tell you your business, but maybe if you lift up this sheet you'll see I'm a woman.*

The doctor kept up his probing and suddenly Jill was swamped by a strange sense of vertigo. Something was wrong. Horribly wrong. Nothing felt right. *What's going on? What's happening to me? I need a drink of water.*

''Respiration's up. Pulse is racing. Get Jacobs,'' the doctor ordered.

Ben? Ben. Thank God. He would help her. He'd make things safe. *Ben, help me. I need you.*

As Jill's panic increased so did the pressure of a pair of hands against her shoulders; she sensed the man's reticence to touch her. "There, there, now. Just lie still. Stay."

Appalled by her doctor's bedside manner, Jill vowed to turn him in to the proper authorities. The man had little tact and very little compassion. He acted as though she were a mindless vegetable that could move but couldn't think.

Oh, God. A single bright, needlelike shaft of fear shot through her being. *Am I dying? A vegetable? A mute brain without a working body?*

In the distance, there was a loud whoop of joy. Jill recognized the voice, even from that one indistinct sound. Ben. Irrelevantly, she recalled that for some handicapped people when certain senses failed, others took up the slack. That already seemed to be happening where her hearing was concerned. She heard every single footstep that raced toward her room.

"Thank God!" Ben said, very close to Jill's ear. His face seemed to be pressed against the top of her head. His hands roamed freely across her body. *My body? No. Something isn't right.*

"Just take it easy, pal. We're gonna take off that bandage so you can see." He spoke soothingly, his hand stroking her upper shoulder. Again, she was struck by the very odd sensation of not truly being able to feel him. The solid feel of his hand was there, just not the warmth of his skin. Was she wrapped up like a mummy? Was her body burned?

Before she could finish the thought, she felt him run his hand down the length of her side to her hip. She squirmed, a low gurgle of panic came from her throat. His touch, while welcome, was too intimate for the circumstances.

Again, she was engulfed by the feeling that something was wrong, horribly wrong.

She struggled to get up. Panic worked itself into muscles that didn't seem to read her commands but understood her turbulence. Limbs moved; blankets fell and tape pulled her skin and hair. She was oblivious to everything except her own deep frustration and pain.

Her equilibrium was way off the mark, but she did have a sense of having rolled from her side to her belly and lifting herself into a crawling position. She felt as wobbly as an infant.

"Easy, Czar. Relax now, boy. Take it easy." Ben's voice was low and soothing; his hands pressed forcibly against her shoulders.

Czar? *What's your dog got to do with this?*

"Doc, do you think you could take off his bandage without opening the wound. I think not being able to see is freaking him out."

What is this "he" stuff? What is wrong with you people? she cried.

A horrible yowl—like an animal in pain—filled the room.

Another pair of hands touched her. Cool hands, with a finicky touch, although they too were clothed in woolen gloves.

Drugs! That's it. I'm having a drug-induced hallucination. Her panic subsided and she held still while the cool hands snipped bandages until the fuzzy white film gave way to Technicolor. Jill was so grateful not to be blind, her eyes filled with tears.

Blinking, she looked around. She cataloged familiar images: a bed, an overly bright room, hospital gizmos and gadgets, a nurse—all in white, frowning. Ben—towering

above her. Right things but wrong image. Out of whack.
Like a Picasso painting.

She closed her eyes and counted to three. When she
opened them, she saw a white sheet flecked with a collage
of short brown-and-black hairs. And a pair of animal
paws—dark tan with protruding black toenails that needed
trimming.

Since the image made no sense, Jill decided this bad
dream wouldn't end until she went back to sleep and started
over again. She closed her eyes and let her body relax.

"Whoa, no. I don't think so," the doctor said, reaching
under Jill's tummy to support her in the crawling position.
"Rest is good but now that he's awake I think we should
keep him awake for a little bit to observe him."

Enough with the dream, people, Jill snarled.

"Um, help me out here?" His hands shifted to make
room for another pair. "He's heavier than he looks, isn't
he?"

*Hey, buddy, watch it. I'm hurt and you're worrying
about my weight?*

"He's about eighty-five pounds, we keep patrol dogs on
the light side."

Jill's head began to spin as though she'd been turning
cartwheels. Ben's words battered her consciousness, demanding an explanation, but there was no explanation.
Nothing made sense. Not what she saw. Not what she
heard. Not what she felt.

She was perilously close to tears or biting someone, she
wasn't sure which. Both sounded appealing.

Ben spoke again. "I'll take it from here. He's used to
me, we've been partners for nine years."

Partners?

The smaller, cool hands fell away, leaving the big warm
hands to cradle her weight; in a move so swift she wasn't

sure what happened until it was over, Ben sat down on the bed and pulled her body across his lap. His broad, hard thighs were directly beneath her diaphragm. His hands were now stroking her down the length of her back.

He's petting me. The thought took hold, and while part of her mind rebelled at the idea, another part responded. The long, smooth strokes did have a lulling quality.

Wait a minute, her mind argued. *I can't relax. I have to figure out why everybody is treating me like a dog.*

She opened her eyes again. The dark tan paws were still there, stretched out on the bleached-white length of sheet. Without moving her head, she could see a sea of green tile floor meeting beige walls; she could pinpoint the location of the three people in the room in her mind—a novel, somewhat disconcerting, sensation. She appeared, for all intents and purposes, to be stretched across Ben's lap, and she also appeared to be a dog.

Jill opened her mouth and out came a wail reminiscent of foxes and hounds.

"Shh, boy," Ben whispered. "They don't allow dogs in the hospital. They only made an exception for you because you're a police dog. The vet's supposed to be here in about an hour to examine you. As soon as he gives the okay, I'll take you home."

He petted her head and stroked the side of her face that wasn't bandaged. One small, very human part of her mind thrilled at the touch, so gentle and loving, but her mind raced with a multitude of questions. *Is this reincarnation? Did I die and come back as Czar—an aging police dog? Where's the karmic justice in that?*

Jill groaned. The sound was articulated as a gurgling growl.

"I bet you'd like a drink, wouldn't you, boy?" Ben asked.

Yes, Jill's mind shouted. *And quit calling me* boy.

Jill was vaguely aware of the doctor and nurse leaving and Ben discussing something with them. She'd have paid more attention but her entire senses were overwhelmed by the smell of water.

Without getting up, Ben had managed to locate a plastic pitcher and a stainless-steel, semicircle-shaped pan. With one hand, he poured the delicious-smelling water into what Jill knew was a vomit pan.

Her rational mind rebelled, but a primal need overruled. When he placed the narrow container on the mattress in front of her and levered her chest so she could reach it, she was momentarily stymied. Blocking her access to the fluid was a nose—an alien body part with fine brown and black hairs parted down the middle leading to a bumpy black appendage on the end. It was a good quarter mile long and obscured her view of the bowl.

In a flash of insight she realized she was going to have to use her tongue to lap up the water. She hadn't tried that since Girl Scout camp. She'd been a complete failure.

"Come on, boy. Just a little. For me?" Ben's mouth was close to her ear, his tone gentle and persuasive.

Jill lowered her muzzle.

A muzzle, a silent voice shrieked in horror. *I've got a muzzle.* But the more practical side of her smelled water and had to appease a very basic need.

She opened her mouth, as if to take a drink, but misgauged the distance from tongue to dish and lapped air.

"What's the matter, guy? Your depth perception off?" She caught the amusement in his tone. Without knowing how, she produced a low, growling sound in her chest.

He seemed startled. Jill sensed him pulling back slightly. "No sense of humor today, huh?" His spare hand caressed

Jill's neck. "I guess that's understandable. You've been through hell, bud."

If you only knew... Jill concentrated on the dish below her face. She moved closer to it, almost touching the water, then poked out her tongue. It touched the cool water and dragged across the bottom of the steel bowl like an ocean trawler. She focused on pulling as much water as possible back into her mouth.

"Czar!" Ben exclaimed when water squirted sideways out of her mouth and doused his wrist. "Don't tell me you've forgotten how to drink?" Jill heard the worry in his voice, and her first impulse—to bite him—disappeared.

Although frustrated to the point of tears, she dipped her tongue, trying to cup it some—no easy task considering the uncooperative appendage behaved like a sloppy drunk. After several tries, she seemed to get the hang of it, but not before making a total mess of the sheet.

Ignoring a sudden, stabbing pain above her right eye, Jill tilted her head to look up at the man holding her. *I can't drink worth beans, but, boy, can I see.*

In the crisp light pouring into the room from the wide window at the far end of the room, Jill saw details she'd never noticed before. Fledgling lines that would one day frame Ben's full, masculine lips. A small scar—just a skinny white nick, really—that cut a divot in his left eyebrow. A weariness about his eyes as if he hadn't gotten much sleep or was worried about something.

He nearly lost his best friend last night, she thought. A second thought followed right behind. *He* did *lose his best friend. And he got me, instead.*

The notion of her somehow becoming transformed into Czar was still too inconceivable, too ludicrous, too unholy to be true. It couldn't happen. It didn't happen. What she perceived as real simply had to be some kind of hallucination, a dream.

Ben. Look at me. Look in my eyes. Tell me this isn't real. It can't be happening. I want to be me *with you, not your dog. It just isn't fair. I finally meet a man I could fall in love with and what happens? I die and come back as his dog.*

Overwhelmed with unshed tears from a pain that threatened to make her heart explode, Jill willed her mind to reach him, willed him to hear her. Ben suddenly grabbed her face with both hands and held it close to his own. His brown eyes studied her; his lips were pressed in a tight line as he looked for something.

Jill held her breath. *Ben?*

He nuzzled his nose against the funny black blob at the end of Jill's muzzle. "You're going to be okay, aren't you, boy?" His tone was full of concern and love.

A tsunami of grief washed over Jill, carrying her to the blackest hole in the universe. She knew with absolute finality that her life, the one she knew and sometimes liked, was over, and she was stuck inside the body of a middle-aged police dog.

A tear perched on the rim of her eye and fell, getting lost in fur.

Ben's gaze seemed to penetrate to the very reaches of her soul, but Jill knew he couldn't see her; he could only see his friend and partner, a dog named Czar.

BEN KNEW something was wrong—horribly wrong. Czar was not the same dog he'd been the night before.

But before he could begin to figure out exactly what was wrong and how to fix it, a man appeared in the doorway of Czar's room. His half-buttoned lab coat looked as though he'd slept in it. His mop of curly red hair stuck out at bizarre angles. He was studying a chart that he carried in one hand and sipping from a straw stuck in a cardboard carton of chocolate milk that he carried in the other.

When he looked up and saw Ben sitting on the bed, he stuttered, "I...oh, sorry. Wrong room."

Ben recognized him. Jill's doctor. "Wait." Ben let go of Czar's jaw and carefully moved the dog aside. "Dr. Whitehurst, isn't it? I'm Ben Jacobs. We met last night. I was just looking for you when they called to tell me Czar was awake."

For some reason, Czar made a low growling sound. Ben gave him the hand signal to be quiet. "Sorry," he told the wary-looking medic. "He's not himself this morning."

"No problem. Heroes are allowed a few idiosyncrasies." He took a final draw on his straw, then tossed the carton in the round trash can near the door. "If it weren't for your dog, I wouldn't be on my way down the hall to check on Jill."

Czar's head shot up. Ben returned to the bed and put one hand on his dog's shoulder. "How's she doing? The nurse at the desk said, stable, but that doesn't tell me much."

"I wish I could give you a definite prognosis, but all we can do is wait for her body to heal itself. This is the most frustrating part of brain injuries. You just never know what's going on in there."

Czar made an odd, whining sound.

"I talked to your supervisor this morning," the man said. "He told me they think she interrupted a burglary."

Ben could see the man's doubt. "You don't believe that."

"I suppose that makes sense, but like I told you last night, the guy hit her twice. With great force. If you were just trying to get away, wouldn't once be enough to stop a woman Jill's size?"

Ben frowned. Nothing about this case made sense—including this morning's report from the mechanic, which had been ambiguous.

The doctor took a step closer to the bed. Ben felt Czar's interest perk up. "You know what's really strange about this?" he asked.

Ben shook his head.

"Their wounds are almost identical." He put his hand out tentatively. Ben whispered a low command in German.

Czar tilted his head and looked at him as if he didn't have a clue what Ben wanted. "Easy, boy," Ben repeated. "Let Dr. Whitehurst look at you."

Czar didn't move as the man gently probed the bandaged area. "Odd, isn't it? Different methodology—bullet versus statue." He looked at Ben. "Sergeant Simms said she was hit with a statue of some kind."

Ben had visited the crime scene on his way to the hospital. He didn't for a second believe some drug-crazed thief had been looting the house when Jill had walked in. Even without the doctor's opinion, Ben's gut told him this was a hit. Not the most professional he'd ever seen, but definitely intentional.

"They were both lucky," the doctor said, stroking Czar's nose.

To Ben's surprise, Czar suddenly licked the man's hand.

"By the way," Whitehurst said. "The blood you donated came in handy. We had to transfuse her twice."

Ben shrugged, hoping the man wouldn't see how much his words meant to him. "I had to do something. They wouldn't take my blood for Czar."

As if sensing his inner turbulence, Czar leaned against him. Ben absently stroked the soft bushy fur beneath his neck.

Suddenly, the sound of a beeper intruded. Dr. Whitehurst

jumped as if prodded with a stick. "Time for rounds. Jill's in ICU, you know. Visitors are limited to two at a time, close friends and family. Once we remove the shunt I'll transfer her to a regular room." He gave Ben a serious look. "Just out of curiosity. Are you two involved?"

Ben looked at Czar. Last night they'd been involved, very involved. Would they have felt the same way this morning? "Yes," he answered honestly. "We..." He didn't know what to say. *We fell in love? We were poised on the brink of something incredible? We just hadn't gotten around to naming our unborn children?* "Yes."

"Good," Whitehurst said, smiling. "If she knows she has you waiting for her, she might come back to us faster. I'll make sure the nurses know you're to be allowed into her room. Anytime."

Ben felt like a fraud. Just because he'd fallen head over heels in love with Jill didn't mean she felt the same. He'd gotten the impression she cared. He knew she was interested. He wanted to believe their passion was more than a passing attraction, but how could he say for sure when they hadn't even made love?

The doctor was partially out the door when Ben remembered to ask, "Has her family arrived?"

"Her mother got here about an hour ago. Her dad's on his way."

Ben thought he read a note of strain in the man's tone. Beside him, Czar gave a little shudder. "Is something wrong?" he asked.

Dr. Whitehurst sighed. Fatigue made him look older than his years. "According to Mrs. Jensen, *everything* is wrong with this facility—not enough light, too much noise, poor ventilation." He shook his head. "I shouldn't say this. But after meeting her mother, I couldn't help but feel sorry for

Jill. My dad was the same way, and believe me, it's not easy growing up with that kind of perfectionism.''

Czar barked. The tone seemed like an affirmation, and Dr. Whitehurst smiled. ''I'll take that second opinion any day.'' He nodded at Ben. ''See you later.''

Ben glanced at his watch. The nurse at the desk had said the local vet was supposed to examine Czar before they'd release him. For some reason, Ben didn't have the patience to sit around and wait. ''I feel as if Jill's Time God is breathing down my neck,'' he told his partner. ''Screw waiting. You look pretty darn good to me. I say we head home. We can stop at the vet's office on the way, okay?''

Czar's bushy tail made a start-and-stop motion. He turned his head as if to see whether or not his tail was working. Ben couldn't put his finger on what was wrong, but he had to hope Czar's peculiar behavior was due to some residual effect of the drugs they'd given him.

''I brought your leash but forgot a collar,'' he said, returning the useless leather strap to its pocket. ''They had to cut the old one off last night.''

Just that little reminder made Ben queasy. He'd almost lost his best friend in the world. He put one knee on the bed and took Czar's face in his hands. ''That was a crazy stunt you pulled, my friend. You almost got yourself killed, but if it saved Jill's life then I'm going to forgive you. Just don't let it happen again, okay?''

Czar strained against his hands until he was close enough to lick Ben's face. The big scratchy tongue felt good.

''Okay, boy. Let's head out. I'm taking you home, but first I want to see Jill.'' He shoveled his hands under his partner's withers and lifted him into his arms. ''Bet you'd like to see her, too. You're the hero, after all.''

CHAPTER EIGHT

JILL AWOKE with a fierce pain in her head. She groaned silently, reluctant to get up from her nap. Fuzzy dredges of sleep clouded her mind, but not enough to obscure one big fact: someone else was in bed with her. She heard breathing, a little rough going in but even and solid coming out. Her nose twitched as she identified an alien scent: sweat and some woodsy-perfumed deodorant. Male.

She opened her eyes. In the hazy afternoon light seeping from behind vertical blinds, she saw her bed partner—Ben.

And the morning's events came rushing back to her.

The hospital. Czar. Mattie.

Her mother had been incensed that Ben would consider carrying a dog into her sick daughter's hospital room. She'd barred entry like a mother bear defending her cub. Jill had been mortified for Ben's sake, yet touched. *Mattie had seemed really distraught.*

Ben had handled her mother with finesse and great kindness. He'd diffused the situation by leaving, even though Jill had barked her head off in protest. How was she going to get back into her body—if that was cosmically possible—if nobody would let her get close to the inert figure she'd seen lying on that hospital bed?

Hysteria, fear, anger and grief were just a few of the emotions vying for control, but Jill was a master at compartmentalizing her emotions. In the fourth grade, when her mother had been packing for yet another move, Jill had thrown a tantrum about leaving behind her best friend. Mattie had scolded Jill severely. "This isn't a perfect world, Jillian. Don't waste your time crying over things that can't be changed. Focus on what you can control and let the rest go."

What can I control now, Mom? I'm a dog.

Ben suddenly let out a deep sigh. His lips moved as if forming a word or preparing for a kiss. *Does he think about our interlude in the hot tub?* At the top of Jill's list of regrets was not making love with him when she'd had the chance. Not only would she have avoided bumping into the mugger, she'd now have that memory to savor.

Or would that only make this situation worse?

She used her amazingly acute vision to study the man opposite her. Like a little boy, he slept on his side with his pillow scrunched up under his cheek. His dark hair stuck up in little tufts. Gray-hued smudges looked like bruises beneath his eyes. He needed a shave, but the faint stubble gave him a sexy, dangerous look.

Ben suddenly opened his eyes. Immediately alert—none of Jill's usual fuzzy wake-up dementia in sight, he looked at her and frowned. "What are you doing? Why aren't you at the foot of the bed where you're supposed to be?"

He put his index and middle finger at the bridge of her nose and slowly drew them down to the big black tip. "I guess we can make some concessions after what you've been through," he said softly.

Jill adored his voice—so deep and masculine. Comforting. "I got the impression you didn't like the new vet," he said, grinning.

Jill frowned at the memory. Rough hands. Poky things. Thermometers where thermometers didn't belong. *And I thought gynecologists were intrusive. Jeesch.*

Ben playfully batted her ears. "I've heard there's a lady vet in town. Maybe we'll check her out next time."

He sat up and stretched. The covers pooled around his waist, leaving his torso bare. "I'd better get showered. Jimmy's wife said she'd take the tux back for me, but I've got to drop it off at the station. Then I want to run by the auto-repair shop on my way to the hospital."

Jill listened, but her gaze never left his body. What an amazing body it was, too. *Why didn't I pay closer attention to the details when I was a woman?*

Tossing back the covers, he jumped out of bed. *He's naked.* Jill tried to make her eyes look away. Mattie surely had a rule for this: Never stare at a naked man. But another part of her brain said, *You're a dog. Look while you can.*

Jill was beginning to hate that practical voice, but in this case she didn't seem to have much control. Her salivation glands weren't following orders, either.

She'd seen Ben in swim trunks, but she'd been polite and hadn't ogled. And heaven forbid, she wouldn't have dreamed about speculating about his—uh, privates. But there they were. Picture perfect. At ease.

In its flaccid state, Ben's penis hung like a thick pendulum against a nest of dark curls. A searing heat wave surfed across her face and down her body. She felt twitches in places she wouldn't expect dogs to twitch, especially male dogs. Her big tongue lapped at the drool pooling in her floppy gums.

Ben turned slightly and bent over to pick up a pair of white jockey shorts on the floor. Jill lifted her head for a better look. His lean, well-sculpted butt deserved praise, too.

"Amos said the mechanic's report was inconclusive, but I want to talk to the guy myself," he said, starting toward the bathroom.

He paused to open the vertical blinds a few inches. Bright sunlight poured into the room. From the back, his body was equally stunning. His buttocks were a paler shade of tan, not stark white like her flesh. She recalled him mentioning a grandmother who was part Cherokee, which explained his relative lack of body hair.

"According to the report, the bleeder screw was loose, which means brake fluid escaped every time I pressed on the brake. Essentially, I cleared the vacuum, so the brakes wouldn't hold. The lines were intact and there was no sign of tampering, but how did the screw get loose?"

I could tell you my theory if I could talk, but since I can't, I guess you're gonna have to figure it out on your own.

Ben turned. The angle of sunlight glistened through the small triangular thatch on his chest, which funneled downward.

"Do you suppose Jill was right?"

Jill tried to concentrate on his words not his body. *Yes. Of course I was right. Score one for the dog girl.*

"If she was right about the brakes, then she might have been right about a lot of things." His forehead puckered pensively. "Like her confidential source disappearing."

Dorry. I completely forgot about Dorry. What if the person who attacked me got to her first?

Jill barked. Too loud. It made her head throb; unfortunately she hadn't figured out the volume control on her voice yet.

"I know," Ben said, returning to the bed. He kneeled across from Jill and leaned down to pet her head. "Don't worry. We'll get to the bottom of this. I'll do some investigating today while you're recuperating."

She closed her eyes. Ben's state of undress combined with her newly remembered anxiety over Dorry were just about enough to unhinge the very tentative hold Jill had on her sanity.

Fortunately, Ben turned and sprang from the mattress to the bathroom door. ''I'm going to take a shower. Do you want to go outside?''

He lobbed the underwear overhead with a nice shot that wound up hooking the edge of the black plastic clothes basket sitting beside his closet door. Mesmerized by his fluidity and grace, Jill followed his movements—more dance than athleticism—enviously.

He flipped on the light switch in the bathroom. He used the fingers on both hands to massage his scalp then he scratched a spot between his shoulder blades. His muscles bunched like coils of rope. He opened his mouth and made a weird *aughing* sound. Every movement was so masculine—so locker-roomish, Jill felt like a voyeur.

You are a voyeur. No, you're a dog. There's a difference.

He moved farther into the bathroom, and Jill heard the sound of a very solid direct aim hitting the toilet water. Peter would have let his kidneys explode rather than pee in front of her.

A second later, she heard the sound of running water followed by a muffled hum. Something sad bubbled up in her throat to press on her windpipe. Although she'd experienced an initial relief after Peter left—their last few months together had been stormy and unpleasant—she had discovered right away that she missed the small intimacies of married life. Sharing a steamy bathroom mirror. Eating meals—even takeout—with another human being. Snuggling up at the end of a long day to discuss the trials and tribulations of life.

In spite of their current living arrangement, her parents had provided Jill with a very solid model of married life. Once she graduated from college, Jill's parents had gone their separate ways in a baffling move nobody talked about. Now they maintained separate homes in two states. But they'd never formally divorced, and Jill believed they still loved each other.

"They're independent people doing their own things, but just watch," she'd told Penny the other day. "They'll probably wind up in the same rest home together."

Ben's off-key whistling interrupted her line of thought. He stepped from the bathroom with a fluffy, hunter-green towel snugged to his waist. He headed toward her with some obvious purpose.

"Outside, pal. You need to do your business, because I'm leaving you here when I go." He scooped her up by wrapping his arms around her middle, then deposited her gently on the Oriental runner beside the bed.

Her legs were still a little wobbly but her vertigo was gone. With one eye on her, he walked to the door and nudged open the screen. "Come, boy."

Jill took a couple of steps, trying to concentrate on establishing a rhythm. It wasn't as easy as dogs made it look, she thought. By mentally counting out each step to cue each leg, she made it outside.

Ben didn't say anything, but there was a worried look in his eyes as he watched her pace stiffly around the perimeter of the large backyard. Like many homes in this section of Bullion, Ben's was built against a hillside. Scrub brush and spindly pines claimed space in the rocky red soil beyond the fence.

The more she moved, the easier it became. Jill decided what bothered her most about her current condition was her size...or lack of it. Going from five foot seven inches to less than three feet was a bit unnerving, she decided. It made her feel vulnerable; she got dizzy trying to look everywhere at once.

A quick glance at the doorway told her Ben was no longer watching. Good thing. She needed to relieve herself and didn't think she could handle an audience. She selected a sturdy-looking ash. She was a *male* dog, after all. *I can do this. How hard can it be?*

By focusing, she managed to lift her left hind leg. Unfortunately, the momentum screwed up her balance and she staggered drunkenly. She tried again, lining up the tree with her rear haunches. It took concentration, but she finally managed to empty her bladder. Panting from the exertion, she moved to a shady spot under the plum tree and sat down.

The grass beneath her bottom felt soft and cool. She stretched out her front paws and lowered her tummy to the ground. *This is nice.* Suddenly inspired by sensory needs she couldn't identify, she rolled to her back and put her paws in the air, wiggling in an invigorating body massage of sorts.

A loud cracking sound made her stop, return to her belly and look around. By consciously opening her auditory receptors, Jill was suddenly inundated by sound—too many images, too sharp, too close: cars whizzing past, children's voices cackling like geese at a nearby schoolyard, bees pilfering pollen from late-blooming roses.

By concentrating, Jill discovered how to adjust her internal filter. Letting out a sigh, she studied Ben's house in the daylight. One of Bullion's fine older homes, it needed a loving touch, a family to bring it to life.

Something about that idea got to her; it reminded her of all she'd be missing out on as a dog: a husband, kids, work, play, language, friends, movies, hamburgers, wine, chocolate, computers. *How can I do this? How can I live this life when mine was so rich, so full of potential? Why didn't I realize that then? Why did I play games with the Time*

God—thinking I always had tomorrow to live the life I wanted?

Jill knew one thing for sure. If she ever got her body back, there'd be no more waiting, no whining and no what-ifs. She'd embrace life with complete abandon. She'd throw herself at Ben and beg him to love her. She'd be a better friend to Penny and Dorry. She'd be a better daughter.

The sound of a phone produced a sudden unconscious response that took Jill by surprise. Powerful muscles in her hind legs catapulted her past two levels of deck in a single bound, through the open patio door and across the Oriental runner. When she reached the phone, panting, she knocked the receiver off the cradle with her nose.

"Hello. Hello. Jacobs, are you there?" a male voice asked.

She tried to muster a bark but still didn't know how to contact her vocal cords on demand. She felt Ben's gaze and looked up. Black jeans. Zipped partway up. No shirt. The trail of dark curly hair starting at his belly button—an "inny"—disappeared into the fly.

"Aren't you gonna answer it?" He had a cockeyed smile on his lips that made Jill's heart flip-flop. She sincerely hoped dogs couldn't blush.

He lifted one shoulder in feigned exasperation then reached down for the telephone. "Jacobs here." Crisp, polished. Professional.

Jill watched his expression, trying to read the news. Impatiently, he brushed back a lock of wet hair, exposing his wrinkled forehead. "Are you sure?"

The look that followed wasn't very attractive. In fact, it made Jill shiver. She knew she'd never want him mad at her. He listened intently then hung up with a gruff but polite acknowledgment.

He looked at Jill and said, "That was Amos. They caught

the guy who attacked Jill. Someone from the newspaper reported him. They said he'd been stalking Jill for weeks."

Bobby Goetz? No way. He's too lazy to take a swing at me, and he's certainly not smart enough to figure out how to get into my house—even if there was only one hide-a-key to pick from.

Ben seemed to share her doubt. "Something doesn't feel right about this. I'm going to stop at the jail on my way to the hospital. Maybe I'll run by Jill's house, too."

Jill nodded. *Good idea. I need to check on my cat.*

Ben walked to the closet and selected a neatly pressed shirt. White, long sleeves. As he was buttoning it up, he glanced at Jill and said, "You do understand you're staying here, right?"

Over my dead body.

She gulped. That wasn't what she meant to say. Giving a silent apology to the Word God—and any other benevolent soul that might be listening, she did what any good dog did to get her way. She started to whine.

BEN GLANCED at his watch. Amos was due back in the office any minute. He was interrogating the suspect. The suspect that didn't feel like the right suspect to Ben. Just why that was, Ben couldn't say.

Amos walked into the room with his head down, his gaze on the papers in his hand. Czar greeted him with an uncharacteristically friendly woof.

Amos jumped a full foot to the left, bumping into his desk. "What the hell are you doing here? This is your day off, and that dog is supposed to be resting."

Ben understood that the gruffness in his commander's voice stemmed from lack of sleep and stress. Ben was just as edgy. Life was slightly off kilter, and he didn't like it.

Not one bit. He didn't like the changes he sensed in Czar, either.

The dog had actually whined so pathetically Ben had caved and brought him along. "He's…not comfortable being left alone," Ben admitted with reluctance.

Amos dumped his papers on his desk and sat down. "He's not what?"

Czar's tail thumped on the floor. The noise seemed to take him by surprise. A shot of acid hit Ben's empty stomach. He swallowed. "He isn't quite himself yet." *Please let it be from shock,* he silently prayed. *Or drugs. Or post-traumatic stress syndrome.* Anything but what Ben feared—brain damage.

Amos eyed Czar with concern. "Well then take him home and stay with him."

"I can't. I need some information. I'm trying to track down a woman named Dorry Fishbank. Lives in the hills. Family's reputed pot farmers. There may be a link with Jill."

Amos reached for a can of soda sitting in a pool of condensation that had spread to some nearby reports. After a loud gulp, he set down the can and looked at Ben. "Close the door and have a chair."

Ben paced two steps to a wall adorned with framed photographs. The room felt too small. "I'd like to check out this lead right away, sir. I spoke to the mechanic on my way here, and I have to say, I think Jill had reason to be concerned about her safety. When you combine that with what happened last night, I feel I should check out the whereabouts of her source. The woman seems to have disappeared."

"Sit." It was a command.

Czar sat, crisply, his attention on the man behind the desk.

Ben gave Czar a sharp look; he wasn't supposed to do what other people ordered. This small disloyalty was the pin that popped Ben's composure.

He swung around, marched to Amos's desk and pounded one fist in a fairly clear spot. The thud echoed like a gavel. "I need your help. And I need it now. I know you think you've got the perp, but I don't agree."

Amos shot to his feet. He gave Ben a piercing glare, placed both palms flat and leaned across the desk. "Sit down."

Three or four heartbeats passed before Ben found the control he prided himself on. He sank into the proffered chair.

"Thank you." Amos sat, too. He looked at Czar as if expecting the dog to explain Ben's sudden change in behavior. "I'm assuming lack of sleep and worry about your partner's health is to blame for this unpleasant change in your usual rock-steady temperament." A hint of humor shaded his tone, along with kindness. "And maybe a certain amount of guilt over what happened to Jill, but believe me Ben, you couldn't have prevented it."

Ben slumped lower. Guilt. Yes, he felt guilty. He'd let his feelings blind him to what Czar had sensed right off. "I should have been paying attention. I almost got them both killed."

Amos sighed. "I figured that was eating at you. That and the fact you care for her."

Czar dropped his chin to Ben's knee. Ben saw the stapled gash below his ear—red and ugly. *So much to lose. So close to losing it all.*

Ben looked his commanding officer in the eyes. "I apologize. That outburst was deplorable. There's no excuse for dumping my problems in your lap like that."

Amos gave a dry snort. "Don't sweat it. Everybody likes to pound on my desk. Makes 'em feel better."

They sat in silence a moment, then Amos said, "Bad things happen, Ben. Sometimes they happen to people we love. You aren't clairvoyant. You don't possess the highly developed sense of hearing and smell that Czar has. Quit kicking yourself about something outside your control, okay? Now, tell me about this new lead."

Ben knew Amos was right. Hadn't he learned that lesson years ago? He'd done everything in his power to change his father, but nothing had worked. So he'd joined the Navy and moved on with his life. Ben couldn't undo last night's attack but he could follow Jill's hunch.

After briefing Amos on the background information Jill had shared with him, Ben said, "I honestly believe her inquiry isn't a grudge match or flight of fancy on Jill's part. She claimed she and Dorry had unearthed proof of the con- tamination right before Dorry disappeared. The two things might not be related, but what if they are?"

Amos drummed his fingers on the desk. "Did I tell you we found a ski mask and gloves down by the bridge where the indigents hang out?"

"Jimmy told me on the way in. He's pretty happy about the collar. But Jill mentioned this Goetz guy the other day, she called him a loser. She said he'd been bugging her to do a follow-up article, but she didn't sound afraid for her life."

A tight frown encompassed Amos's thin lips. His gray mustache turned down at the corners. "How's she doing?"

Ben shook his head. "I didn't see her this morning. Her mother wasn't thrilled about having a dog in the same room with her daughter."

Both men were silent for a few minutes, then Ben said, "A couple of months ago in Santa Ignacio all five members of the planning board were indicted for taking kickbacks from a developer. That scandal didn't have anything to do with bad water—just broken faith, hollow promises, sewer hookups that weren't up to code, stuff like that. Once the press got hold of it, the whole thing got very messy, and the city was stuck holding the bag. A very costly bag.''

Amos seemed to ponder the information. ''The Excelsior project is supposed to be a biggie, huh?''

Ben pictured the crowd dressed in tuxedos, glittering dresses and jewels. ''Big.'' He thought about the chilly look in Clarice Martin's eyes when she suggested that Jill might upset things with her false accusations. ''A lot of money on the line. The mayor is very gung-ho.''

Amos's mustache twitched. ''I'm not surprised.''

''He doesn't like Jill much, either.''

Amos sighed. ''Bud and Jill have knocked heads over several issues. So, what do you want to do about the Fishbank woman?''

''I just want to talk to her—so I can tell Jill she's okay.'' He reached out to bury his fingers in the thick scruff at Czar's neck. ''I've heard that people in comas can still hear things. And I know this was bothering her. Maybe with one less thing to worry about, she can concentrate on getting well.''

Ben waited while Amos doodled on the corner of his blotter.

''I'll look into it. The emphasis in that sentence was on the word *I*, in case you missed it,'' Amos said sternly. ''*You* are taking a couple of days off. Czar is on medical leave. You need rest, too. Understood?''

Ben felt like a kid being grounded. He couldn't remember his own parents ever exerting their parental authority. *Maybe because they knew it would be a waste of breath.*

A FEW HOURS LATER, with Ben safely occupied on the phone, Jill looked for a path of escape from his backyard. She put her nose to work. Her wonderful, incredible nose. She was getting good at screening out the scents she preferred not to acknowledge.

She sniffed around until she found a path leading to an opening beneath a rotted grape arbor. Keeping low to the ground, she crawled through without a hitch. Once free, she set out toward home. She felt guilty leaving Ben, who was obviously worried about her—Czar, but Jill had to check on Frank, her cat.

After a couple of blocks, Jill figured out how to lope. Czar's well-conditioned body functioned flawlessly as long as she kept her mind out of its business. Unfortunately, the jarring motion gave her a headache, so she had to slow down.

At first, she stuck to the sidewalk like a good pedestrian until a voice inside her head said, *I'm a dog. Dogs go wherever they want.* Lawns, alleys, jaywalking. The novelty of such freedom made her want to bark with happiness.

She was feeling pretty smug as she approached her house—until she realized she didn't have a key—or hands. Fortunately, her broken gate—sealed with a chest-high piece of yellow crime-scene tape—provided access.

She sniffed the perimeter of the slump stone and stucco wall that framed her patio. Most residents had opted for privacy over view and found a way to extend the height of the wall. As soon as Peter moved out, Jill had hired a contractor to build a redwood extension with staggered landings for potted plants.

Jill could smell Frank everywhere. She knew he wouldn't appreciate a strange dog poking around his territory. Cautiously working her way to the patio doors, Jill glanced up just in time to see a black bomb hurtling through space, accompanied by a screech that would have set a vampire's skin crawling.

Frank's claws sank into Jill's skin—needle pricks in a dozen spots at once. Jill cried out in pain and bucked to dislodge the cat that seemed attached like Velcro. Howling and spinning in hopeless circles, Jill was about to bolt for home when she heard the sliding glass door open.

Help me. Somebody. Please. Jill shot into the house, cat still firmly stuck to her back.

A loud epithet was followed by a crash—a bar stool hitting the floor. A man's voice cried, "Whose dog is that? Jill doesn't have a dog."

Peter?

A second voice boomed. "Czar?"

Ben? Jill froze. Frank disappeared. One minute an instrument of torture, the next gone. Frank didn't like men, especially Peter.

Overcome with gratitude, Jill ran to Ben, her delight making her whole body wag, from her tail to her ears.

Ben went down on one knee and clasped her head in his hands. He looked worried and upset. "How'd you get here, boy?"

On foot, of course. What are you doing here? I thought you were still on the phone with Amos.

"You know this dog?" Peter asked.

Ben quickly checked her bandage, her coat. "Czar's my partner. The same person who attacked your ex-wife shot him. He's supposed to be asleep on my bed." *So you snuck out without me? Me. Your poor wounded partner. Hmph.*

Jill turned around and sat down so she could look at Peter. His dove-gray, three-piece suit fit in that certain hand-tailored way. *Who are you trying to impress?*

He glanced at her once then looked away. Peter couldn't be bothered by nuisance things, like animals and kids. Even plants required too much attention. He liked the image plants provided just not the work that went along with them. Same with wives.

"As I was saying," Peter told Ben, apparently picking up the conversation where he'd left off before the ruckus, "Jill was one of the most ordinary people you would ever hope to meet."

Well, thanks a lot, Jill growled.

"I don't mean that in a bad way. On the contrary, she was 'salt of the earth,' 'good people.'" He put his fingers up to frame his words in imaginary quote marks. Jill always hated it when he did that.

"This is such a tragic accident."

Ben, who was still kneeling beside Jill, rose. Obviously working to control his anger, Ben walked to the patio door and closed it before speaking. "This was no accident, Mr. Martin."

Peter looked appropriately abashed. "I didn't mean that like a car wreck or something. I meant more in the nature of a random act of violence."

"We're still investigating." Ben's tone didn't invite a reply, but Peter never let manners stop him.

"But Bud said you've caught the guy. Some doper who pummeled her with one of Mattie's pornographic figurines."

Jill snorted. Peter had never liked the primitive art her mother sent from faraway places.

Ben moved one shoulder a microshrug.

"You think it was premeditated?"

Jill looked at her ex-husband sharply. It was quite a leap from a random act by a whacked-out stranger to a premeditated attack. Was Peter somehow involved? Would he go to such lengths to protect his precious project?

"It wouldn't surprise me that Jill's made enemies," Peter continued. "She can be the most stubborn, single-minded, self-absorbed person you ever met. Especially when she's working on a story. Maybe this had something to do with one of her investigations. Do you happen to know what she was working on?"

A low menacing rumble seemed to come from her throat.

Peter moved closer to Ben who'd paused in front of her Donna Wright watercolor. The piece, *Glacial Falls,* constituted a big hunk of Jill's final award in the divorce settlement. She wondered what Ben thought of her taste in art.

"I really couldn't say," Ben told him. "What's her cat's name?"

Peter made a negligent gesture. "I don't know. She got him after I moved out. I'm allergic to cats." He sniffed for good measure. "I'm starting to get stuffed up even as we speak."

"You can leave anytime."

Peter frowned. "I wish I knew where Jill kept those settlement papers. She told me she'd made a copy for me."

Jill tilted her head. *What papers?*

"Obviously they're not in plain sight and I don't think it would be a good idea to dig through her files or drawers. This is a crime scene."

Peter started to argue. "Sergeant Simms said—"

"Amos asked me to meet you here so you could pick up some papers your ex-wife was supposed to have ready for you. No papers are in sight, so I think it's safe to assume she was attacked before she had a chance to get them out for you." It was obvious to Jill that Ben didn't like Peter.

A low sound—a cross between a purr and growl—emanated from beneath the navy armchair. Jill glanced over, the hair on her back lifting. Frank was a mere three feet away. Jill covered her nose with her paws.

"Is your dog afraid of cats?" Peter asked, looking right at Jill.

"Czar hates cats," Ben said.

With his back to Jill, Ben didn't see Frank inch out from under the chair and approach Jill. Some gleam in the animal's eyes told her Frank recognized her. Frank rubbed up against her with a happy purr.

Oh, Frank, not now. How's this gonna look?

Peter laughed.

Great. Now Peter thinks I'm some kind of wimp.

Ben looked over his shoulder; his frown made her want to curl up in a ball. "He has a head injury," he said stiffly.

Peter snickered. "Jill told me that cat hates everyone but her. I stopped by once to drop off some papers and the damn thing attacked me. I think its name is Frank. That's right. She named him after Sinatra."

His name is Franklin; I named him after Ben. The other *Ben.*

Peter walked over and leaned down to pet Frank.

Don't do it, Peter.

The ensuing hiss, screech and scratch were poetic justice to Jill's way of thinking. When Peter responded automatically by raising his foot to kick Frank, Jill reacted with some wonderful dog's instinct she didn't know she had and clamped her teeth around his ankle.

"Ow," he howled. "Get him off me."

Jill lost her grip but a tooth snagged the fabric of his suit and she heard a satisfying rip.

"This is a four-hundred-dollar suit, Jacobs. Your boss is going to hear about this."

Ben shrugged his magnificent shoulders. White really was his color. "Hey, make a quick move around a highly trained police dog and you could lose a body part. Be thankful it was just your pants."

Frank, who had disappeared during the ruckus, was back at Jill's side, purring contentedly.

"I have a business appointment, and now I'll have to go back to the hotel and change my suit." He turned to leave. "Do you need me to make a statement? My wife and I were at the Ahwahnee when this happened. We have a dozen witnesses, including you."

Ben took a deep breath. "I wasn't under the impression you needed an alibi, Mr. Martin."

Peter looked uncomfortable. "I meant maybe I could help."

Ben frowned. Jill wasn't sure what she expected, but his question surprised her. "What went wrong between you two?"

Peter shrugged. "Jill's family moved around a lot when she was a kid, and I guess she got tired of moving. She wanted to stay put, but I couldn't. I probably never will."

Ben walked to the fireplace and looked at the framed photographs of her family. Her father—looking rumpled but distinguished. Her mother's glamour shot taken last year at Christmas.

"You need a partner to make it in this business," Peter said. "Jill wasn't up to the role. Clarice was born to it."

"Jill wasn't a good hostess?" Ben asked, bending down to look at a wine cooler built into one end of the island. When Peter lived in the house, the unit had been filled with expensive, vintage bottles of wine. Now it was unplugged to save energy.

"She did her part—for a while, but people change," Peter said with a sigh. "Listen, Jill's a good person. I'm sorry for what's happened to her, but time is money and I have to run. You have my number."

He left without saying goodbye. So very Peter.

Jill sensed Ben looking at her. "Come."

Short and sweet. Jill obeyed. She stayed at his heels as he exited the house. So did Frank, although it was obvious he was only going because of Jill—not because of anything the man said.

"No," Ben said, trying to grab Frank. "Cat. Stay."

Frank darted under Jill and batted Ben's hand, claws extended.

"What the hell is going on, Czar?"

Jill looked between her legs. *Frank, you're going to get me in trouble.*

Frank blinked but didn't answer.

Ben braced one hand on the frame of the door. "This is insane."

Come on, Ben. You heard Peter. Things change. Jill turned and trotted to the Blazer—cat at her side.

After a few minutes, Ben joined them. He rubbed a spot above his nose and heaved a weighty sigh before opening the rear door. Jill jumped in; Frank glared at Ben once for good measure then followed.

"A cat," Ben muttered, slamming the door. "I don't believe it."

They drove the six blocks to the hospital in silence; Frank hid behind the gearbox. Ben parked in a spot designated for police then opened the door, clearly intending to leave Jill behind. She barked until he opened the side door.

Concern warred with obvious frustration as he said, "Czar, you can't go. This is a hospital. Jill's mother doesn't like dogs, remember?"

She made little mewling noises that seemed quite effective.

"All right," he groaned, pulling a leash from a rack in the door.

Jill danced excitedly, making it tough for Ben to attach

the lead to the brand-new collar he'd bought at the vet's. "Stop it, Czar. You're driving me nuts. You know that, don't you? And what about that cat?"

Jill hoped Frank wouldn't panic when she left, but he seemed content in the corner.

Ben reached past Jill to close the window between the two compartments. Jill froze as his scent enveloped her. Dang, she liked his smell. "Now, behave yourself," he cautioned. "This is a hospital."

JILL HAD BEEN MOVED to a private room a few hours earlier, the receptionist at the front desk told him, pointing down the hall to the left. Her family was with her, but Ben and Czar were both on her list of visitors.

"Officer Jacobs," a voice hailed as Ben walked down the hall.

Ben glanced to his left. "Dr. Whitehurst."

The man motioned him over. "Good to see you. Czar, you're looking better. Dogs do have amazing recuperative powers, don't they?"

Ben wished he were as certain of that as Dr. Whitehurst seemed. Czar, while physically improving, simply wasn't himself. Ben didn't know how to explain it. Or whom to tell.

"How's Jill?" he asked.

"To be frank, I'm baffled. We've done everything we can, but she isn't responding the way we expected."

That wasn't what Ben wanted to hear. "But it hasn't even been twenty-four hours."

"I know, but we had hoped for some response to stimuli, physical or verbal, by now. We may not know for several weeks if there is permanent brain damage, but the sooner she responds, the better her chances."

"Brain damage? Permanent?" Ben refused to accept what he heard in the doctor's tone.

"While the physical blow may have compromised individual cells or neural pathways, it's the result of the possible oxygen deprivation that has us worried."

He lowered his head and sighed.

Whitehurst looked at Czar, who stared back unblinking. "Even extensive damage to the cerebral cortex won't necessarily impair consciousness," he told them, "but the cortex is aroused by signals from the part of the brain stem called the RAS, the reticular activating system. If the RAS is permanently damaged—if those cells were *suffocated* for want of a better word, the situation would be irreversible."

Ben heard the words; at some level they made sense but not where Jill was concerned. He felt a nudge and looked down. Czar's black nose was pressed against his hand, apparently sensing his master's distress.

"Are you saying it's hopeless?" Ben's grip on Czar's leash tightened. The stiff cord was his line to sanity.

"She scored a three on the Glascow coma scale, which means she's in the deepest coma possible. I want you to prepare yourself for any outcome—even the worst. I've tried talking to Jill's parents, but they're entrenched in denial. I was hoping that you might be able to help them come to grips with this." The doctor looked past Ben's shoulder. "There's Jill's father. He seems like a fine man—very easy to talk to. Maybe he'll be more receptive if the news comes from you."

As Ben turned, he felt a tug on his hand. Czar strained against his collar like an ox pulling a cart. He obviously wanted to go to the tall, lanky stranger.

"Czar, heel," Ben gruffly commanded in German.

The order went unanswered.

Before he could try again, the man turned and looked in

Ben's direction. His gaze fell to Czar, whose tail wagged in greeting.

"Czar?" Ben croaked in confusion. His fingers went numb; the leather leash fell from his grip, and the dog he'd trained from youth and had worked with side by side for nine years suddenly shot across the room to leap about and bark with obvious glee at a complete stranger.

Jill's father didn't seem to know how to react, but after a slight hesitation he dropped to one knee and put his arms around the dog's neck. Czar licked the man's face with obvious joy.

Completely dumbfounded, Ben said, "He's never done that before."

"Maybe Jill's father reminds him of Jill," the doctor said, obviously trying to help. "His scent or something."

Ben swallowed the lump in his throat and slowly trudged across the room. Before he could say anything, Jill's father straightened and threw his arms around Ben's shoulders, hugging him fiercely.

"Thank you from the bottom of my heart," the man said. "Thanks to you—and this brave, wonderful dog—my Jillian is alive. You will be in my will. I promise."

Overwhelmed and speechless, Ben laughed. So did Jill's father. He stepped back and put out his hand. "I'm Nils Jensen. Come. Mathilda will be back any minute. She wants to apologize for her rudeness this morning. She loves Jill more than life itself, and this has been a terrible shock." He leaned down and patted Czar's head. "You, of course, will never be denied access to Jill's room. You two share a common bond."

Ben and Czar exchanged a look. If he didn't know better, Ben would have sworn he saw tears in his partner's eyes.

What the hell is going on? Ben longed to shout. But to whom—the God of Dogs and Cats?

CHAPTER NINE

JILL REGISTERED the room's atypical hospital décor right away: two placid watercolor paintings, country-chic wallpaper and contrasting trim in dusty blue with rose accents. In the far corner, below the wide picture window rested a rosewood cradle with pastel animal-print comforter and bolster. A birthing room.

The God of Irony is smiling on us, Jill thought, following her father into the room.

"Mattie wanted a more homelike setting for Jill," Nils said, heading straight for the bed where her body was lying. No obvious accoutrements of life support were visible.

Jill strained against her leash. She needed to be by her father's side. For some reason, seeing him made her believe everything was going to be all right. If there were a way to get back into her body, her father would figure it out.

She looked around wondering where her mother was.

Nils walked to a cushioned recliner adjacent to the bed and sat down. "I don't want to seem impolite, but I'm working on very little sleep," he said, motioning Ben forward. "Mattie's even worse, which is one of the reasons she made a scene this morning. She told me about it. I hope you understand. She certainly didn't mean to alienate the new man in our daughter's life."

Jill hacked on a swallow that didn't quite make it down her long neck. This had to mean that her father had passed along the news of Jill's divorce to her mother. Jill had let slip the information in one of her emails, but it hadn't occurred to her that her parents actually talked to each other. She glanced at Ben, who looked uncomfortable to say the least.

"Um, sir, I don't want there to be any misunderstanding. I care about your daughter, but we haven't known each other very long. I'm not sure she'd call me that."

Nils hunched forward, folding his hands together. Jill always called it his *thinking* pose. "I didn't mean to put you on the spot, Ben, but Dr. Whitehurst told us you were with Jill when this happened. And when I spoke to Penny on the phone, she mentioned that Jill was very taken with you."

The fink. That's the last time I tell her my deepest thoughts.

Ben cleared his throat then said, "We wanted to get to know each other better. I think the attraction was mutual, but I can't speak for Jill."

I can. I'm crazy about you, Ben Jacobs.

"Czar, quiet," Ben scolded. "I told you no barking."

Nils reached out to touch the still form on the bed. A heavy sigh followed. "As I told my wife, it seems fortuitous that you are a member of Bullion's finest. You can keep us abreast of the investigation into Jill's case. I do hope you're prepared to investigate it properly."

Jill watched Ben, who seemed drawn to the body on the bed. After hearing Dr. Whitehurst's dire predictions, Jill wasn't sure she dared look.

"They…we've arrested a suspect."

"So I heard. Unfortunately, while the young man you have in custody may be a worthless piece of flotsam in the sea of life, he did not attack my daughter."

Ben looked at her father. "I beg your pardon?"

"He didn't do it," Nils repeated.

"You sound pretty convinced of that."

"Because I know Jillian. She had her nose in somebody else's pie and somebody didn't want to share. If you'd care to sit down, I'll explain my analysis of the situation and my theory." He pointed to the overstuffed rocker near the window.

With a brief glance at Jill's body, Ben took the proffered chair. "You're saying you believe this attack was premeditated?"

Her father nodded grimly. "I made a few calls. I spoke to Jamal, the photographer at the paper. He said Jill was working on something on the side. Something she wouldn't talk about.

"I also called the mechanic who worked on her car. His father is an old friend of mine. Although he couldn't prove it, he said he believes someone tampered with her brakes."

Thank you, Daddy.

"The suspect reportedly has been pestering your daughter for weeks," Ben said.

"I'm sure it would make everybody's life easier if this person were convicted of the crime, but I'm afraid little in life is simple. I'm convinced there's more to the story than that."

"Why?"

"Because Jill is a reporter. A damn fine one."

Ben cleared his throat and looked at his hands. "She writes obituary notices."

Jill appreciated his diplomacy, especially since the only thing of hers he'd ever seen was pure garbage.

"Yes. And very well I might add. But, regardless of what that pompous editor of hers says, Jill is more than just an obit writer. She always excelled in whatever she did. As Peter's wife, she gave the best parties, bought the perfect gifts for clients and whatnot, and always managed to look better than her pretty-boy husband.''

Jill lifted her head off the floor to peer at her father. She'd never heard him speak with such passion. She knew he loved her, but up to this moment she hadn't realized how much. Her throat closed and she had to squeeze her eyelids together to keep back the tears.

I took your feelings for granted, didn't I, Dad? I thought because you were so busy, you didn't have time for me. Maybe I'm the one who didn't make time. Maybe that's what the Time God has been trying to teach me.

''Even while she was busy playing Donna Reed for Peter, Jill read and studied. She wrote letters to members of Congress and volunteered at the battered women's shelter. She's the kind of person who doesn't take things at face value, if you get my drift.''

When Ben failed to answer, Nils went on. ''I used to live in these mountains, and I know what happens when you go poking around—sometimes you dig up a nest of rattlesnakes.''

''His prints were on her window,'' Ben said in an official tone.

Jill looked up. *Really? Bobby was at my house? Yuck.*

Nils sighed. ''Jill isn't the type to walk away from something just because it's inconvenient or unpleasant. What if she found out something certain parties didn't want known?''

Great minds think alike, Ben. Although one part of her experienced a moment of satisfaction hearing her theory espoused, another part hoped it was wrong. Better a random act of violence than someone she knew.

Nils studied Ben a moment. ''You look skeptical, but that's because, as you said, you don't know Jill very well.''

Ben rose and walked to the bed. Jill followed, her leash

making a soft hissing sound against the tile. This bed, while still equipped with the workings of a hospital bed, was low enough for her to see over without having to put her front paws on the mattress.

Jill studied her body. Her left side looked almost normal. Someone had washed the blood from her hair and the golden-red cloud lay neatly arranged on the pillow. Her right side wasn't as fortunate. A stark white bandage ran from temple to ear, with purplish bruising extending outward like an oil slick. Her eye sockets looked unusually large, making her face gaunt; her skin seemed a pale shade of magnolia, the same color she'd used to paint her bedroom.

"She looks better," Ben said, a note of hope in his voice.

"Her body is fit, but her spirit is lost," her father said flatly. Jill's heart rose and dropped in the same instant. "I asked a friend of mine—a trauma specialist in Rochester to see her. He's flying in tomorrow.

"I have another friend who's a forensic pathologist. This isn't going to go away if she dies." His tone lacked any bluster. Just solid conviction.

Ben gave Nils a long, thoughtful look. "I thought Jill said you were retired."

Her father smiled. "True, but I was a mining engineer for thirty years. I used to investigate mining accidents and try to prevent them from ever happening the same way twice.

"In a way, my background gives me a unique perspective. I was trained to look at the aftermath and piece together how the accident happened. For once, this might be of some help to my daughter." Jill heard pain and regret in his voice.

Ben rested his bottom on the edge of the mattress near

Jill's hand. "If you don't mind my asking, how did you get into the mining business?"

Nils sat back. "My father and two uncles were killed in a mining accident in Kentucky when I was ten. My mother and two aunts pooled their resources and moved to Minnesota. Mother thought it was flat enough that nobody would do more than scratch the surface with a plow," he said with a soft chuckle. "But when Uncle Sam called, I somehow ended up in a demolition detail. After the war, I went to college on the GI Bill and found I had an affinity for geology and physics."

He pushed up the spectacles that had inched down his nose. "I'm an old scientist who's spent the better part of my life underground. By the time I'm called to a site there's nothing but a gut-wrenching mess of life and limb. I find the answers. I plan to do the same thing here."

Ben didn't answer right away. When he did, he said, "In my job, if one piece of the puzzle doesn't fit, there's a good chance I'm working on the wrong picture."

Nils smiled, as if Ben were a prize pupil who'd just come up with the right answer. "And you can't let it rest until you make all the pieces fit." He nodded his silvery head. "Stubborn. I like that in a person. Let me define stubborn for you. As you may know, we moved around a lot when Jill was a child. One year—I think Jill was in the third grade—we moved three times. She started school in a tiny town in Tennessee where she was chosen to be in the class play. A simple little story about a princess, a frog and a prince. Jill was ecstatic because she was selected to be the princess."

He steepled his long fingers, deep in thought. "Unfortunately, before the play could take place, I was called away to an emergency situation at the Homestake Mine in Lead, South Dakota.

"Jill didn't cry a tear, she just packed up her costume and took it to her new school and convinced her teacher that with a few line changes the play could be adapted to a Christmas motif."

He took off his glasses and wiped them on a wrinkled handkerchief he withdrew from his hip pocket. When he held them up to the light, Jill could see streaks on the glass. He shoved them back on his nose.

"Wouldn't you know it, on Thanksgiving Day I got a call from British Columbia. Ninety-seven miners trapped. I couldn't say no. Mathilda wouldn't hear of staying behind. We packed our bags, drove across the state in a raging blizzard and flew out of Sioux Falls minutes before they closed the airport.

"Conditions in B.C. weren't great. One teacher taught all eight primary grades. Somehow, Jill convinced him to put on her play."

Nils chuckled, lost in the memory. "The frog was a little French boy who couldn't speak English and the prince was the tallest girl in the class, but Jill was the princess. To me, that exemplifies tenacity."

Jill shook her head in amazement. *I don't remember that.*

When she looked at Ben, Jill noticed that he'd unobtrusively taken hold of her lifeless hand and was studying her face.

"Sergeant Simms has given me permission to go to Jill's house," her father said. "As soon as Mattie gets back, I want to take a look at Jill's computer. If I find anything suspicious, I'll let you know."

"Where did you say your wife is?"

Yeah, where is Mom?

"She went to the store to buy some CDs. Not that either of us knows what kind of music Jill likes, but—"

Ben rose abruptly. "I have some in the Blazer. When

we were together the other night, Jill and I discovered we shared the same taste in music. Except for Ricky Martin.''

His gentle teasing—combined with the tender look on his face before he released her hand—made Jill's heart beat double time. He took a step then looked at her. "Czar, stay."

Once she heard the door latch, Jill closed the distance between her and her father. She rested her long muzzle on his knobby knee. He responded with a gentle but firm stroking motion. She sighed, absorbing the solace of her father's touch.

Nils lifted her chin to stare into her eyes. "You're a special animal, aren't you? You have a human look about you, which I guess some might say isn't such a compliment. Did some evil witch put a spell on you, robbing you of the ability to speak?"

Jill barked.

"My, you certainly are well trained." Nils smiled, but Jill could tell his heart wasn't in it. A cloud of worry made him look older than his years. Jill's heart twisted with regret. *There's so much I should have told you. Like how much I love you. And miss not having you in my life.*

Nils levered himself out of the chair and took one long stride to bring himself to the bed. He tenderly brushed a lock of hair from Jill's forehead. "How I wish I'd spent more time with you, dear girl. Where did our time go? Some wicked god—what did you call him? The Time God? Yes, the Time God tricked us into believing we'd always have tomorrow, we got so caught up in our own small dilemmas, we missed out on what was important."

"Have I not told you that for years?" a voice said.

Mom.

Jill dropped to the floor and tried to make herself invisible. She hadn't seen her parents together in almost two years. She'd never really talked to either one about their separation, except to express her concern. Mattie had assured her that both she and Nils were happily pursuing their own "thing," as she put it. Mattie seemed to love her job as travel director at a high-end retirement complex in the desert Southwest. Nils seemed content to putter in his workshop in the Black Hills of South Dakota. Jill had been too wrapped up in her own disintegrating marriage to give her parents' relationship much thought.

"Yes, Mathilda, you did. And you know how much it pains me to say this, but you were right." Nils's tone was wry and self-deprecating—the kind of opening her mother would normally pounce on.

Jill braced for the snide reply.

Instead, Mattie dropped her purse and a plastic shopping bag on the floor and rushed to her husband's side. Nils opened his arms and pulled her close.

Jill's tongue rolled out of her mouth and hit the floor. The unpleasant texture of gritty tile made her shudder.

Mattie turned her head sharply, although she kept her arms locked behind her husband's back. "What's that dog doing here?"

Jill covered her nose with one paw. Her mother hated pets.

"Visiting the woman whose life he saved."

Mattie stepped back. Dressed in navy slacks with an oversize white top adorned with gold embroidered anchors tied together with red satin ribbons, she gave the impression of one ready for any social event. Her white leather deck shoes squeaked against the tile floor as she walked toward Jill.

Oh, no... Jill's heart sped up. She tried to tell herself she was a ferocious police dog, but the quiver that raced beneath her coat was pure terror. *I'm sorry, Mom. I really screwed up this time. I bet you don't even have a rule for this one, do you?*

Mattie lowered herself stiffly to both knees. She slowly reached out. "Thank you," she said, her voice husky with tears. "Thank you for saving my daughter's life."

Her mother's hand was trembling as she tentatively petted Jill's head. *Oh, Mom, I didn't do it. I made things worse. Czar saved my life then I poked my nose in where it didn't belong and look what happened.*

The low groan that filled the air sounded like an animal in pain. Mattie moved back in alarm. "Did I hurt him, Nils?"

Jill's father hunched down beside his wife. "No, dear, Czar's just very attuned to your pain. He can tell how much you're hurting."

Mattie burst into sobs, and Nils helped her to stand. "Come here, love. Come sit with me."

To Jill's immense surprise the two sat together—her mother on her father's lap—in the chair Ben had occupied earlier. Nils tenderly soothed his wife and kissed her forehead. "Be strong, Mattie. Jill needs us to stay focused on the positive."

Jill watched in silent wonder. She couldn't remember her mother ever displaying such vulnerability. Jill knew Mattie loved her, but she wasn't the kind of person who displayed her emotions for all the world to see, or even for the benefit of the other two inhabitants in her small world.

Jill had to look away; the touching scene made her heart feel as though it was being squeezed in a vise.

"How can I be hopeful, Nils, when that doctor referred to her condition as a *vegetative state?*"

Nils wiped away her tears with his handkerchief. "Believe me, dear, miracles happen. I've seen men labeled *dead* get up and walk away from a blast. I hardly think it fair to cast Jill into a potful of vegetables when she's been comatose for barely a day.''

Mattie sniffed. ''What if he was trying to prepare us for the worst?''

''That doesn't mean the worst will happen. Jill's our daughter. She has the blood of two bullheaded people running through her veins. Right?''

Jill watched this byplay with interest. She'd been the recipient of her mother's sharp-tongued criticism often enough to know Mattie didn't have a sense of humor—especially when it came to herself. Mathilda Jensen took life seriously. She'd transferred her experience of moving around the country into a career as a travel consultant. A brilliant strategist and logician, she foresaw potential pitfalls and arranged to avoid them. Unfortunately, this meticulous approach to detail generally made her seem a bit…anal.

To Jill's surprise, her mother smiled. A sweet, girlish grin that made her appear years younger. ''Mother always said I was part mule.''

''And since I'm part ass,'' Nils said with a chuckle, ''we're perfect for each other.''

Jill's eyes opened wide. *Good heavens! They're in love. With each other. When did this happen?*

Her mother nuzzled her father's cheek and sighed. ''I just wish we'd told Jill. About us.''

Nils let out a long breath. ''I know. I've been kicking myself, too. But it seemed so unfair to drop our newfound happiness in her lap when she was going through such a hard time.''

When? How? I need details, people. She crept closer.

Nils let out a rueful sigh. ''Of course, we both know I'd

still be holed up in my workshop feeling sorry for myself if you hadn't sent me that ticket to Bermuda.''

Bermuda?

''Our second honeymoon,'' Mattie whispered.

''Our first. I don't think two nights in Minneapolis count as the real thing.'' He sighed. ''Oh, Mattie, there's so much I'd do over if I could. Work less, spend more time with my family. Why don't we learn these lessons until it's too late?''

Jill spotted the tears in her father's eyes and she ached to put her arms around him. She felt exactly the same, but there was no way for her to tell him.

Mattie dropped her head to his shoulder; they silently wept together. Jill was creeping away on all fours to give them some privacy, when the door opened and Ben walked in. ''I think Jill might like these.''

He stopped abruptly when he realized her mother was present. He stiffened; his demeanor became more polished, more professional.

Mattie jumped to her feet and brushed the tears from her eyes. Nils stood. He, too, wiped his face, but he didn't try to hide it. A second later, he walked over to take the CDs. ''Thank you so much.''

Jill tensed.

After fixing her face, Mattie walked across the room. She extended her hand. ''Hello, again. Although we weren't formally introduced, I'm Mattie Jensen. You're Officer Jacobs, I believe. I've heard a lot about you from the staff and Jill's friends.''

Ben took her hand with great care and nodded. ''Please call me Ben. And this is Czar.''

To Jill's amazement, tears welled up in her mother's eyes again. ''I'm so sorry I was rude to you this morning. I didn't know the circumstances. I—''

Ben put his hand on her shoulder. "Forget about it. We understand. Don't we, Czar?"

Jill barked on cue. Proud to finally have barking down pat.

"At the time, I couldn't imagine why they'd let a dog into a hospital room. Especially intensive care."

"Normally, they wouldn't and I wouldn't have presumed if I didn't know how worried Jill would be about Czar's condition," Ben said.

Nils pushed a button on the CD player. "This dog is welcome here anytime. Anyone can see he's special." All three humans looked at her. Jill squirmed uncomfortably. "There's something very Jill-like in his eyes. They obviously share a special bond."

Oh, Dad, if you can see that, why can't you see me?

Gentle strands of saxophone filled the room.

Jill closed her eyes; she could almost picture herself dancing to the sound of this music with Ben. She imagined his scent. His sweet kiss.

"She likes the music," her father said, lowering himself to the edge of the mattress. He took Jill's hand and gently stroked the unresponsive limb. "Look, Mattie, doesn't she seem more relaxed?"

Jill felt a tug on her collar. "Mr. Jensen, if you need any help at Jill's just give me a call. Here's my card. My home number's there."

Ben took three long steps to the end of the bed and leaned across the distance so Nils wouldn't have to get up.

Nils took the card. "Thank you, Ben. We're going to try to keep someone at her side around the clock. If you're available—"

"Anytime. Just let me know."

Jill's mother and father exchanged a look. "We will."

Jill smiled. Poor Ben might not have recognized the maternal gleam in her mother's eye, but Jill knew what it meant—matchmaking. Too bad Mattie's daughter was a dog.

BY THE TIME Ben stepped out of Jill's room, his head was throbbing. He never got headaches, but this situation probably qualified as sensory overload: too much weirdness, too many feelings, too strong a fear to hold inside any longer. Normally, he'd unload his worries and fears on Czar, but...

Ben looked down at his dog as they followed the sidewalk to the parking lot. Czar's head bobbed as he trotted beside him; his ears were alert, his body looked strong and primed. Except for the small bandage covering the jagged gash that had already scabbed over, there was little to indicate he'd been perilously close to death a mere sixteen hours earlier. But there were changes; this was not the same dog he'd known for nine years.

That fact tore at Ben like a bullet. He wanted to believe it was just a matter of time before everything went back to normal, but that hope felt like an eel in muddy water. Slippery and dangerous.

Maybe things will straighten out in a day or two. Jill will wake up. Czar will be better. I'll find somebody to take that damn cat...

Ben was so intent on his list, he would have collided with the dust-colored Cherokee parked halfway over the curb, if Czar hadn't skidded to a dead stop and refused to budge.

"Ma'am, you can't park here," he started, fully prepared to lecture the driver. Then he recognized the woman sobbing in the driver's seat. Jill's friend. The one from the health club.

The woman suddenly leaped from the car and raced around to where he was standing.

"Officer...Jacobs," she said through her snuffling sobs.

Her eyes and nose were both red and wet. Dressed in faded jeans and an oversize flannel shirt, she looked very human. "Thank God you're here. What providence! Maybe one of Jill's silly gods—the God of Baby-sitting or something— is smiling on me. Will you help me?"

"How?"

She grabbed his hand—the one without a leash—and pressed a black plastic key bob in it. "Keep an eye on things. Just for five minutes. Please. I have to see Jill. I was at my mother-in-law's in Fairfield when Nils called. I just got back into town, and I *have* to see Jill. Do you understand?"

Ben did. Completely.

"Five minutes?"

She nodded but was already racing away. She almost tripped when she turned to call out, "The baby's bottle is in the bag behind the seat."

Ben looked at Czar. "Did she say bottle?"

Czar barked.

Fearing the worst, Ben took a step closer to the sport-utility vehicle and looked inside. Two toddlers—the same pair he'd seen that day at the pool—let out excited squeals and held out their arms. They wiggled and squirmed against their car-seat straps.

Dressed in long-sleeved black sweatshirts emblazoned with some neon-colored television-cartoon heroes, the pair was Macy's-ad perfect, right down to their miniature blue jeans with snaps in the crotch and stubby tennis shoes.

Ben opened the rear passenger door. He felt drawn to the little boy with hazel eyes and reddish-blond hair. "Jill's baby," he said, not meaning to say the words aloud.

"Dah," the child said, looking hopeful.

Something painful pressed against his windpipe. He

stood there frozen until Czar leaped up and started licking the child's startled face.

"Czar," Ben barked, fumbling with the leash.

The little boy let out a cry of pure glee. His brother reached for the dog, jabbering with obvious joy.

Ben had expected them to be scared and screaming, but the pair seemed entranced with the fearsome beast. Almost as if they were welcoming an old friend.

Ben took a deep breath to ease some of the anxiety building in his chest. *This isn't too bad. I can do this.* "Good boy, Czar. Keep them occupied until their mother gets back and everything will be just fi…"

Before the word was out of his mouth, a cry pierced the air. Its decibel level made him put his hands to his ears. Czar whined and dropped to the ground. The children in the car seats looked at each other and started crying, too.

Heart racing, Ben leaned into the car to locate the source of the anguish. He found it in a third car seat.

A white-and-pink bundle. Snowy cap of blond curls. Tiny fists swinging at empty air. Cherub cheeks bright red. Perfect little mouth open so far, Ben could see her tonsils quiver.

Trying not to panic, Ben fumbled with the harness mechanism and picked her up. She was light as a feather pillow and just as soft. He backed out of the vehicle, protecting the baby with his body. Muttering low, inane words, he bounced her in his arms, feeling like a bully.

"It's okay, baby. Your mommy will be right back."

The child continued to wail.

Czar made a snorting sound, and Ben glanced down to see his dog tugging on the strap of a brightly colored diaper bag. "The bottle. Good thinking, boy."

Ben turned around and sat down on the running board. It was a tight squeeze, but he managed. Carefully balancing the baby in one arm, he groped for the plastic bottle. Seconds later, the horrible siren was replaced by a contented sucking sound.

Ben let out a long, deep sigh. "Good Lord, that was brutal."

"But you did it," a voice said.

Ben looked up to see Jill's mother standing in front of him. She smiled and held out her arms. Ben could have gone into them himself for comfort, but he gave her the baby, instead.

She stepped back and gently bounced the child in a soft, soothing motion. "You're very good with children," Mattie said. "Is that innate or do you have a brood?"

"A niece and a nephew. I've never been married."

"Your dog likes those children, doesn't she?"

Ben looked down. Czar had squeezed behind him and was sitting directly in front of the little boys, keeping them entertained with a game of licking fingers.

"He," Ben corrected. "And, yes, Czar has always been very good with children. He adores my sister's kids."

Ben squinted against the bright sunlight. Strangely, here in the bright light, Mattie looked less like a glamorous cruise director and more like a grandmother.

"Have you noticed how much the one twin looks like Jill?"

Mattie nodded. "I commented on it the last time I visited. Jill laughed it off, but I know my daughter, and I know she longs for a baby of her own. Why else would she have stayed with Peter for so long?"

Czar made an odd sound. Ben petted his ear.

"But Peter played her for a fool. He let her believe they'd have a family, but he'd actually had a vasectomy years earlier. Poor Jilly was so upset. She'd put her own career on hold to help Peter in the corporate world, only to have her dearest dream smashed by an egoist.''

Ben felt his gut tense.

''If he'd lie about something like that, makes you wonder what else he'd lie about, doesn't it?''

Before Ben could ask her to elaborate, Mattie said, ''Here comes Penny.''

Penny trudged to the car—her face as fragile as a broken windshield. Ben understood completely. He rose and went to her, letting her muffle her sobs in the fabric of his shirt. He glanced behind him to make sure the twins were okay. His gaze met Czar's. Although it had to be a trick of the sunlight, Ben could have sworn he saw tears in his dog's eyes. *Dogs can't cry.*

Once Penny was in control of her emotions, she stepped back, mopping her face with her hands. ''I can't believe this is happening. I kept expecting Jill to open her eyes and say, 'Just kidding, guys.'''

''Nightmares are so much nicer than real life, you can open your eyes and be done with them,'' Mattie said. The child in her arms appeared to be sound asleep.

Penny turned to Ben. ''Sorry about that. I'm not usually a hysterical wreck. And believe it or not, I'm not in the habit of dumping my kids on a complete stranger.''

Ben shrugged. ''Blame it on the Baby-sitting God.''

Penny tried to smile, but her lips quivered. ''I've got to go home where I can fall apart in private. Thanks, Mattie. I told Nils I'd take the eight-o'clock shift. The kids will be in bed by then.''

Mattie handed her the sleeping child. ''Excellent. Maybe Nils will be able to get some sleep.''

Impulsively, Ben said, ''I could take over at ten.''

Mattie and Penny exchanged a look he couldn't read.

She gave him a smile very much like her daughter's. "That would be excellent."

Ben gave Czar the hand signal to heel. Czar cocked his head curiously. That nasty twinge in Ben's gut returned. He picked up Czar's lead and gently tugged. "I'll see you ladies later, then."

JILL ITCHED. And twitched. She was learning the hard way how unpleasant it was to have hives, with no way to scratch.

Why did I let him talk me into pizza? With anchovies?

Who knew Jill's allergies would migrate with her to a new body? She'd been so eager to please Ben and show him she had an appetite—for anything other than canned dog food—she'd gobbled up every bite. Tiny fish bodies and all.

"What's wrong with you?" Ben asked, his voice hushed as they walked through the corridor of the slumbering hospital. "Do you have fleas?"

No. Jill growled. *But I could use some help here, Mr. Ten Digits.*

Ben seemed oblivious to her distress. A post-dinner call to his sister had left him distant and introspective. Jill wondered how much of that had to do with his father's health. Apparently Ben's father was going to need surgery in the near future, and Joely wanted Ben to put in an appearance.

Ben's, "Not in this lifetime" had seemed pretty adamant.

They paused outside Jill's door. Ben's hand seemed to shake slightly as he laid it on the metal lever.

Well? Jill silently asked.

To her surprise, he dropped her leash and turned away. His deck shoes made a muffled squeak against the tile as he headed down the hall.

Even if Jill weren't a dog, she wouldn't have had any trouble finding him. Ben was standing at the window of the nursery like a kid at a candy store. The dim light from behind the glass showed the depth of his sorrow. *Ben, what's wrong?*

He looked down. "Either way, I'm screwed," he said, his voice a harsh whisper. "If she never wakes up, I've lost the chance of a lifetime. If she opens her eyes tomorrow, I'm just putting off the inevitable." He closed his eyes and sighed. "We both know I'm not marriage material, right? I'll always be my father's son."

Jill ached to hold him, to comfort him. The best she could do was lick his hand. *And I'm my mother's daughter. But, Ben, didn't you see her face today? If she and Dad can rebuild their love after all the bitterness and disappointments they've shared over the years, then anything is possible. Please don't give up.*

Ben dropped to a squat. He scratched Jill's tender, itchy back as if he could divine her hives. She groaned with bliss. "Poor guy. I've been so wrapped up in my own problems, I've ignored you, haven't I? But you still love me. I wish I understood why."

Because you're you, Ben. Because you give more than you know and you care more than anyone I've ever known. And if I could speak, I'd tell you that every day until you believed it.

Jill licked his face. She tasted his salty tears.

Ben took a deep breath. "Come on, boy. Let's go see Jill."

Ten minutes later, Ben and Jill were alone with her body. Penny had given Ben a weepy hug then dashed away. A nurse had checked in on her rounds. After slipping an Andrea Bocelli CD into the player, Ben pulled a chair beside the bed and sat down.

Jill's heart was racing as she wiggled between his knees and the bed. *Maybe I can reach Czar. Maybe if I try hard enough...*

She put her head on the mattress—just inches from where her body's lifeless hand was resting in Ben's palm.

Ben's voice was soft. "Jill, it's Ben. Can you hear me?"

Jill inched closer. She wanted to touch her body but was afraid. *What if I can't get back? What if Czar's spirit has moved on and I'm stuck in this body forever?*

"I'm so incredibly sorry this happened, sweetheart," Ben said, leaning over to rest his chin near her ear.

Without Czar's keen hearing, Jill might not have been able to hear his solemn promise. "Jill, if you can hear me, I want you to know that I love you. I wasn't sure I knew what love is—believe me, I didn't grow up in a house where people used the word. But I know it now. I know, because my life hasn't been the same since I met you, and it'll be an empty shell if you leave me."

Jill leaned in closer. *Oh, Ben...*

"Come back to me, Jill. Please."

Jill closed her eyes and focused on reaching Czar. *Czar, my friend, are you here?*

She didn't hear an answer, only Ben's steady breathing. She pressed closer. Ben's shins provided a rock of support. His left hand rested on her back—a touchstone of comfort. Even if she never got her old body back, Jill knew she'd live out Czar's remaining years in the cradle of Ben's affection.

She wished that was enough, but it wasn't. She was greedy. She wanted it all. She wanted to hold Ben, love him and laugh with him. She couldn't wait to watch him feed *their* child a bottle. She longed to rejoice with her parents in their newly revived happiness. And she needed to tell Penny how much her friendship meant to her.

Filled with needs too great to express, hope too large to contain, Jill closed her eyes and tried again. *Czar, come to me, boy.*

At the corners of her consciousness, a white light appeared. A soothing glow of warmth and compassion. As Jill's heart opened up, so did the portal to another dimension. Essences—spirits—hovered on the perimeter. Some, Jill recognized. Her grandmothers—gone so many years. And then there was Czar.

He greeted her with the joy of a puppy but the dignity of a warrior. They didn't speak. No words could possibly convey the depth of knowledge they'd shared.

They touched, but only for a second—or was it an eternity? Then he was gone.

Distantly, she heard someone call her name.

"Jill? Jill, stay with me, sweetheart. I'm going for help."

No, she longed to cry, don't leave me. But the words wouldn't come. Her throat was too dry and sore. *Ben...*

Her body responded to her panic. Her fingers grasped for something—anything grounded, real. When she felt the tangible grip of Ben's hand—rock-solid warmth pulling her safely back to shore, she held tight. She didn't let go. She'd never let go again.

CHAPTER TEN

"Mom. Dad. Leave."

Jill kept her tone light but serious. After a week of coddling and hovering, she knew she'd go insane if the well-meaning pair didn't follow through with their original plans and rejoin their around-the-world adventure group.

"But, Jillian," Mattie argued after shooing Nils out of the kitchen, "you've only been out of the hospital four days. You're going to need therapy to rebuild the strength in your left side. And I'm worried about your amnesia."

"Temporary amnesia," Jill stressed. "Whitehurst said it was trauma-induced and probably not permanent."

Jill was tired of being treated like an invalid. Each day she showed more improvement. Dr. Whitehurst had taken to calling her SuperJill. *If only he'd quit pestering me about my near-death memories. Those are too weird to share with anyone.*

Her headaches were becoming less frequent and each day she felt stronger. It bothered her that she couldn't remember the events that put her into the hospital, but she hoped her doctor was right and that her memory would return.

"Mom, I love you. You and Dad put your lives on hold for me. You nursed me back to health, but I'm almost a hundred percent now. I refuse to let you miss out on this once-in-a-lifetime trip."

Mattie finished wiping the kitchen counter that Jill had already wiped. Jill bit down on a smile. Her mother was still a perfectionist, but these days Jill didn't take it personally.

"Jill, we came so close to losing you. There's not a trip on this planet worth more than you."

Jill walked across the sunny kitchen. She was glad that all memory of the actual attack had been erased from her mind, so she didn't have any qualms about returning to her home. She snatched the sponge out of her mother's hand. "Mom, it seems crazy that it took a coma to bring us all together, but at least we've learned from our mistakes. We won't let it happen again."

Mattie cupped Jill's jaw with her hand. "You are a treasure. There's so much I wish I'd done differently, but you turned out perfect despite my flaws as a mother."

"Perfect?" Jill scoffed, but inside she blossomed under her mother's praise. "Doesn't that contradict Mattie's Rule Number Eleven—Nobody is perfect—deal with it."

Mattie brushed aside a tear. "Are you sure that isn't Number One?"

They looked at each other and laughed. Then Mattie took a deep breath. "Nils," she called. "Your daughter is kicking us out."

Jill walked into the adjoining family room. Everything appeared back to normal, her unique collection of Gods—ranging from a Mayan jaguar God, Frank's least favorite, to a pair of intricate wood carvings from Bali—were dusted and on their respective shelves of her display case. She moved to the easy chair by the glass door and sat down. Her stamina was returning—she could now climb the stairs to her bedroom with ease. The first few days, Ben had insisted on carrying her. Despite the pleasure it brought her to be in his arms, Jill didn't like feeling helpless and dependent.

Ben. Maybe once her parents were gone, Jill could get

some answers about her relationship with him. He'd been the one holding her hand when she'd opened her eyes. She'd witnessed his joy and fear and something she couldn't name. And he'd been a part of her life every day since that moment. Why? Were they a couple? Shouldn't she remember something that important?

Frustration—a side-effect of amnesia—brought a pulse of pain to her temple.

She glanced up to see her parents conferring in the foyer. By concentrating, she could easily hear their whispered exchange. She didn't understand her improved auditory acuity, but she liked it.

"I think she means it," Mattie said.

Nils sighed. "I told you she was serious. We talked about it last night. She feels badly that we've already missed the first leg of the trip. Run upstairs and finish packing, dear. You are the pro, after all," Nils said. "I want to talk to Ben before we leave."

Jill sank back in the chair and closed her eyes. *I have things to discuss with him, too.* Ever since Ben had said, "When we were in the hot tub," Jill had been racking her brain trying to recall the circumstances of their encounter. Occasionally she'd get hazy images that might or might not be real. Moist clouds swirling around two figures. A passionate kiss that left her a little breathless just thinking about it. A furry weight suddenly landed in her lap. "Frank," she exclaimed with pleasure. The cat had barely let Jill out of his sight since her return from the hospital. Ben had mentioned Frank's odd attachment to Czar— something Jill couldn't begin to explain.

Jill heard her mother walk into the room to get something from the refrigerator.

"Mom, why does everyone seem to assume that Ben and I are an item? Were we dating? Did we…had we…?" She felt herself blush. "I guess you're the wrong person to ask, huh?"

Her mother sat down on the love seat across from her. "I don't have any of the details, but I know Ben's head over heels in love with you."

Jill felt herself blush. "Mom."

Mattie gave Jill one of her patented Mattie-looks. "Jill," she returned in the same singsong tone. "The man was at your side every possible minute. He gave you his blood. He's been dauntlessly helping Nils try to figure out who attacked you and why." She paused. "Are you sure you can't remember anything about what happened that night?"

Jill frowned. She'd heard the story a dozen times. But only a few images—tall, black trees speeding past, a dog barking in the distance, sirens in the cold—stood out in her mind. But nothing made sense.

She'd even lost track of the events of the week preceding the attack. She couldn't recall playing tackling dummy for Czar or going to the Land Barons affair at the Ahwahnee or seeing Peter and Clarice. She smiled inwardly—amnesia wasn't *all* bad.

"Things are slowly coming back," she said. "Too slowly."

Mattie reached out and squeezed Jill's knee. "At least your fine motor skills are returning."

Jill sighed. Her right hand seemed unimpaired, but her left was still struggling. Her fingers felt numb part of the time, and her leg sometimes buckled without warning. She was scheduled to start physical therapy tomorrow.

With any luck she and Czar would both be back to normal soon.

Jill couldn't recall exactly what had happened immediately after she'd opened her eyes, but she'd been told that both Ben and Czar were present. Apparently, she'd cried out and squeezed Ben's hand, not even letting go when the nursing team rushed in. At some point, someone had spotted Czar lying on the floor beneath her bed. He'd suffered some kind of stroke. Once Jill was stablized, Ben had rushed Czar to the veterinarian.

Czar.

Jill couldn't explain the deep connection she felt toward the police dog. She couldn't wait to see him. After spending three days under the watchful eye of the veterinarian, Czar was now recuperating at Ben's. Jill had lobbied to have Czar stay with her, but Ben was afraid there was too much activity here.

Maybe Ben will bring Czar here after my folks leave.

She found it odd that, although she could remember practically nothing of her experience, she could picture, with minute clarity, Czar's soulful eyes.

"I wish I could remember what happened that night," Jill said, her frustration building. "I feel as though I'm letting everyone down. Especially Ben."

Mattie gave her understanding look. "Nobody cares what you can and cannot remember, Jill. We're just relieved that you're alive and well. Seeing you smile is something we feared might never happen."

In the past week, her mother had let her beauty-shop hairdo go. She'd forgone makeup completely. In some ways, she seemed like an entirely different person than the Mattie Jill remembered growing up.

"You know, Jill, this experience has changed me," her mother said as if reading Jill's mind. "I've learned a valuable lesson. I know what's important now. Love and family. And I'm never going to take either one for granted again."

Jill smiled. "I always knew you and Dad loved each

other. I just never understood why you didn't live to-gether.''

Mattie fiddled with the plastic bag in her hands. It was filled with little bottles and jars. "That was all me, Jillian. Nils was totally baffled, and more than a little hurt. He squirreled himself away in that workshop of his and hardly talked to a soul for years.''

She sighed. "I married so young, and women of my day devoted themselves to being a good wife and mother. That was my job. And I was damn good at it.'' She shrugged sheepishly. "The wife part, anyway.'' Before Jill could say anything, Mattie rushed on. "But once you were out of school and on your own, I needed to prove to the world that I was something more than a woman who packed well.''

"Mom, you worked your tail off all those years. I doubt any CEO could have accomplished what you did.''

Mattie sighed. "I alienated the people most important to me.'' She gave Jill a penetrating look. "Which explains why my daughter didn't tell me about her divorce until six months after the fact.''

Jill's heart stuttered. "I was afraid you'd be disappointed in me.''

"Honey, I was relieved for you. I never understood what you saw in Peter. I tried to support your decision, but Nils and I were terribly worried about you. You seemed so un-happy. So lost.''

Jill looked up. A week ago she might have said, "How would you know? I hardly ever saw you.'' But today she let it go.

Mattie's eyes studied Jill's face. "Jill, I know I was hard on you when you were growing up. I didn't want you to turn out like me.''

Jill moved to hug her mother. "What's wrong with the

way you turned out? You created a home for us in every desolate, out-of-the-way place between Canada and Mexico. You're the strongest woman I know."

Mattie's eyes filled with tears. "Oh, sweetheart, you're so forgiving. You're not even mad at Peter and Clarice anymore, are you?"

Jill couldn't explain why, but she felt no antipathy toward either her ex-husband or her ex-friend. "You know, Mom, they have each other, and all I've got to show for six years of marriage is a Land Barons 401-K. Who do you think got the better deal?" She winked.

Mattie rocked back in laughter. "Now, that's my girl."

BEN TOOK a deep breath before pushing the enter key. His computer skills were negligible, but that hadn't stopped Nils Jensen from setting him to work inventorying the files in Jill's PC.

"How's it going?" Jill's father asked before he'd even set foot into the small, bright room that Jill had set up as an office. Since the room was just a few paces away from Jill's bedroom, Ben had taken every opportunity offered to spend time there.

Ben looked up. "Pathetic. A clubfooted snail would be faster."

Nils chuckled. Over the past few days, the two men had established a bond. It wasn't something they discussed, but Ben felt a comfort level with Nils he'd never known with his father. Of course, it helped that Nils was a patient teacher and a good listener.

"My gut says nothing is in here. I'm ready to agree with your theory. Somebody did a very good job of cleaning house. But why go to the bother? Why not just chop the computer into little pieces or introduce a virus into the hard drive or something?"

"If I'm right, whoever did this wanted to find out what Jill knew."

Ben nodded. "Someone other than Bobby Goetz."

"Exactly. When are you interviewing him, by the way?"

Ben frowned. Jill had asked to see Bobby as soon as she learned that he'd been arrested for attacking her. She said she wouldn't believe his guilt until she talked to him face-to-face. Amos seemed in favor of the meeting since none of his other leads had panned out.

"As soon as we can clear it with the D.A. and public defender."

Ben turned back to the monitor. Something wasn't right about this case. Everyone had hoped that Jill would be able to identify her attacker once she came out of the coma, but she remembered nothing—not even the steamy interlude they'd shared in the hot tub.

Ben hadn't known quite how to take that. He'd spent the past week falling in love with a woman who couldn't recall kissing him. The irony would have driven him crazy if he hadn't had so many other worries—including Czar's mysterious setback.

"You know, Nils, even if we prove someone tampered with Jill's computer, we can't connect it to the attack. Jill can't tell us what's missing or when she might have entered whatever isn't here."

Ben's frustration over this case was making him cranky. He was frustrated in other ways, too. Being in Jill's presence while keeping a polite distance was killing him. Even though Jill had no memory of their time together, Ben knew they were connected. And he wished he understood the mysterious bond between Jill and his dog, but he didn't. *Is it because they both nearly died?*

Nils was talking, but Ben had missed most of it. "I'm sorry. What did you say, Nils?"

"I think you need to concentrate on finding Dorry. She may have some valuable information."

Ben sighed. So far he'd gotten nothing but the runaround from Dorry's mother. Something wasn't right in the Fishbank household.

"And someone at the paper may know something that could help us. That Jamal fellow, for example. Shouldn't he be back from vacation soon?"

Ben nodded. He'd interviewed the young photographer on the phone. Jamal had mentioned that Jill had complained about having problems with her files.

"I'm not anxious to tip my hand at the paper. After all, it had to be one of her fellow employees who put us on to the stalker."

Nils nodded. "And if he was trying to cast blame elsewhere, then he…or, she…might actually be guilty."

Ben remembered something Jill had once said. "Nils, is it possible for people on the same system to get into someone's personal files?"

"Absolutely. Integrated systems like the *Sentinel*'s allow an editor or several editors or proofreaders access to the same piece of material." He crossed his arms and leaned against the door. "Jill gave me a tour of the facility the last time I visited. Typically, three or four people have access to her story after she files it."

"Would there be any reason for an editor to go back into a reporter's personal queue and change or eliminate the original copy?"

"None that I can think of. In fact, that sounds rather unprincipled, but I suppose it could happen." He tilted his head. "Did Jill suggest this happened to her?"

Ben tried to recall what Jill had told him about the feature she'd written about him and Czar—the one allegedly sabotaged. "Yes. I think so."

Nils thought for a moment. "It's also possible she logged on as someone else. Then any work she did would take place in that person's queue. Which might explain why she couldn't find it."

"How could that happen?"

"If someone else used your terminal and forgot to log off, you might compose your story in his or her queue by mistake. I'm sure you'd realize your error sooner than later because your pathways and shortcuts would all be different. Why? Is it important?"

"Probably not, but Jill wrote a story on Czar and me. She wasn't happy with the published version and said her original was missing. I thought she was just trying to get off the hook, but now I'm wondering if someone tampered with her work."

Nils's eyebrows shot up. "If Jill said she made a copy, she made a copy. She's very good about backing up her work on disks, which is one of the reasons this search is so frustrating. There should be a nice neat box of backup disks sitting right there." He strode to the desk and rapped his knuckles on the oak surface.

"Have you asked her about them?"

Nils sighed. "She can't remember. Poor dear. She's trying, but I don't want to push too hard."

Both men were silent a minute. "Did you come up here to tell me something?" Ben asked.

"Yes. Mattie and I are leaving. In twenty minutes. We have a flight out of Fresno that will take us to LAX where we catch a plane for Hawaii. We'll join our group as the ship takes off for Tahiti."

Ben rocked forward. "You're leaving? Today? But we haven't solved this case."

Nils put a hand on Ben's shoulder. "I have faith in you, my boy. You and Jill will work everything out."

His cryptic tone seemed to say more than Ben was ready to discuss. "But what about the computer stuff? You're the expert."

Nils walked to a metal filing cabinet and picked up a small plastic box. "I've put everything on a Zip disk. A computer friend is meeting me at the airport between flights. With his help, we'll be able to figure everything out."

Ben slouched down in the chair. "I still don't understand what you expect to find if the stuff's gone."

Nils smiled. "Remember my field of expertise, Ben. By the time I'm called to the scene of a mine explosion, the damage has already been done. Trying to rebuild a decimated computer filing system is like picking through the rubble of a ruined mine, the clues are everywhere, not only in what you see, but in what you don't see—the gaping holes left behind."

Ben shook his head. "Like what?"

"That, my boy, is what I hope to uncover. I'm only guessing at this point, but I'd bet that all the *Sentinel*-related files are missing."

Ben rocked back, thinking. If someone had taken the time to methodically go through Jill's files, he probably hadn't expected Jill back any time soon. Perhaps he'd been counting on her winding up dead or in the hospital as a result of a car accident.

Nils cleared his throat, and drew a thick, white business envelope from his breast pocket. "This arrived in the mail this morning. Jill gave it to me because she said she didn't understand it."

Ben's heart contracted when he saw the Land Barons logo. He scanned the letter while Nils talked.

"Jill and Peter mutually had invested in his company's 401-K retirement plan. The returns were quite phenomenal, and at the time of their divorce, Jill had the option of keeping her share in Land Barons or rolling it over to the *Sentinel*'s plan.''

He paused, as if remembering something. ''Jill felt she should stay with a proven winner, and I agreed as long as she was adequately protected.'' He drew in a breath. ''On a hunch, I called the company's accounting offices last week—and this letter confirms what I was told. Apparently, Peter borrowed against their joint account before the divorce was settled. He lied about it to the judge who wrote their settlement agreement. He's virtually wiped out the entire fund, including Jill's contributions.''

Ben gripped the armrest. ''Is that legal?''

''You can access 401-K contributions through a loan. If you don't pay it back, you owe the government taxes, and I believe there's a penalty for early withdrawal. While it's legal to borrow against the fund when you're married, it's unethical—and perhaps, illegal, as well—to tap into your ex-spouse's contributions. I'm sending this to my attorney.''

''Peter must be in serious financial trouble,'' Mattie said, appearing suddenly at her husband's side. Nils put his arm around her shoulders. She added in a low voice, ''To someone like Peter, money is the equivalent of blood. If he were feeling a little anemic, he might be desperate enough to do something rash.''

All three were silent for a moment, then Nils said, ''Peter has an alibi. Ben and Jill saw him at the Ahwahnee. But what if he hired someone to break into her files while he did something to Jill's brakes?''

Mattie shook her head. ''I can't picture Peter on his hands and knees in a tuxedo fiddling with an automobile's brakes. He might pay someone to do it, but he would never dirty his hands.''

Ben knew she was right. Still, given this revelation about his finances, Peter moved up a notch on Ben's list of suspects.

JILL LEANED her forehead against the door and closed her eyes. By focusing, she could hear her parents' rental car as it backed out of her driveway and sped off down the street. Gone. They were gone. She felt a mixture of relief and fear.

"I supposed I should take off, too," a voice said behind her. "You need to nap."

Nap? "Nap?" Jill spun around, hands on her hips. "That's what my mother just said, too. Look, Ben, I'm thirty-one, not three. I have a life, and I'm tired of sitting on the sidelines of it."

His lips flattened as if trying to keep from smiling. Other frustrations—some she couldn't even name—fueled her temper. "I'm not kidding, Ben. You and my parents have been talking around me like I'm a…a dog, and I don't know what's going on. This is going to stop. Now."

Ben took a slow breath. "Okay."

Her ire dissipated. "Okay?"

He nodded. "I promise not to talk to you like you were a dog."

She heard the humor in his tone. She stepped toward him, fist raised. "I mean it, Ben."

His eyes lit up, but his expression remained serious. "I know."

The impasse lasted three seconds then he leaned down, took her wrist in his hand and kissed her knuckles. "I also know you're not ready for hand-to-hand combat."

A shiver of something delightful, something sexual passed through her. Was there a message in his words beyond the obvious? "How do you know? You're not my doctor."

He glanced up; their gazes met. "I asked your doctor."

Jill gasped. She felt her face heat up. "You didn't."

"Actually, your mother did. I just happened to be eavesdropping."

Jill's mouth dropped open. She knew they weren't talking about fisticuffs any longer. While one part of her was mortified that anyone would discuss such personal things behind her back, another part wanted to know the answer. She needed to know.

She swallowed. "What did he say?"

Ben let go of her hand and moved back a step. Suddenly the foyer seemed overly bright and pretentious. It was her least favorite room in the house. She was tempted to grab his hand and lead him to her bedroom. A much better place for such talk.

"Doctor double-talk."

Jill's gaze narrowed. "You mean like police double-talk? Tell me what he said. This is my body, Ben. I should know these things."

Jill couldn't swear to it, but she thought the color in his cheeks intensified.

"Whitehurst said he wouldn't recommend any physical exertion for a few weeks but, technically, you're in great shape."

Yep, a blush.

She looked at the man across from her. She was drawn to him in a way she didn't quite understand. Something told her they were connected at a level so basic it defied description, but her amnesia had erased any memory of falling in love or playing all those getting-to-know-another-person games. She was forced to trust her instincts.

She cocked her head coquettishly and batted her eyelashes. "So, wanna get naked?"

He almost choked on his obvious shock. "Jill, that isn't funny."

"Who's laughing? That was a test."

His eyes narrowed suspiciously. "What kind of test?"

"To see whether or not you and I have ever been intimate."

His lips repeated the word. "How can you tell from one question? One shock-jock question, I might add."

Jill closed the gap between them. "If you'd pulled me into your arms and said, 'It's about time. I thought your parents would never leave.' I'd say it's a safe bet we've done it."

She was close enough to smell him. The first days home from the hospital, when she spent most of the time sleeping, she'd drawn comfort from Ben's scent. Somehow she always knew when he was in the house.

Ben stood his ground but he kept his arms at his sides. "And by choking as I just did…you've decided what? That we're just friends?"

Jill dropped her chin. Probably. But that didn't mean she wanted it that way. "I guess so," she said softly, staring at her painted toenails. *When did I paint my toenails? Why did I paint my toenails?*

Ben's low chuckle made her want to throw her arms around him and crawl inside his skin. "Oh, Jill," he said, drawing her into his arms. "You have no idea how glad I am to have you back."

She melted against him. *Home. I'm finally home.* She didn't bother to analyze that thought. She was content to revel in his warmth, his comfort.

"I feel as though I should bow down before every single

one of those heathen gods in your family room. I love…having you back.''

Jill heard him stumble over that last, but she paid it no mind. She was too happy. ''You do?''

His lips whispered the word *yes* against her hair.

She looked up. ''So…do you want to get naked?''

His eyes darkened with desire and she thought for a minute he might take her up on the suggestion. He tightened his hold and kissed the corner of her mouth. ''Yes. I've spent a week wanting to do this.'' His mouth covered hers, his lips drawing from her a moan of yearning. Soft yet commanding, Ben's lips knew her secrets, her needs. His mouth pressed for access. His tongue teased and tempted, but she sensed a restraint to his playfulness.

Jill broke it off. ''You're not going to make love to me, are you?''

The cloudy haze of passion cleared in his eyes. ''Not today.''

''Why not?'' Jill blushed, knowing her words sounded as whiny as any seven-year-old's.

''Whitehurst said nothing strenuous.''

''We could take it easy.''

His lips curved upward in a grin. ''I don't think so.''

A shiver of delicious longing passed through her. Maybe it would be worth the wait.

''Besides, I have to go somewhere this afternoon.''

Jill didn't like the sound of that. She'd come to rely on his presence, even though a part of her knew he was only on loan until Czar was released from medical leave.

''Where?''

''Work.''

''Can I come?''

He laughed. ''No.''

''Please. I'll wait in the car. I could take Czar's place. I could be your partner.'' The more she thought about it, the better Jill liked the idea. She could almost see herself sitting in the passenger seat, riding shotgun for Ben. She wouldn't even mind hanging out in the far back area if he didn't want anyone to see her. ''Think about it, Ben. You're off duty at the moment. I could ride along. Be your sounding board.''

She flashed what she hoped was a cajoling smile. ''Better than talking out loud to yourself, right?''

''Who said I talk out loud?''

She rolled her eyes. ''Czar, of course. He told me all your secrets.'' She tickled him under the arm. ''Please. I'm not ready to stay alone. I don't care if there is a fancy new alarm system. I'm just not ready.''

He seemed to hesitate.

''You could take me to your house. I wouldn't mind hanging out with Czar. I just don't want to be alone.''

Ben took a deep breath then let it out. ''Okay. Get your coat.''

She gave him a sloppy salute and a peck on the cheek. It wasn't as good as getting naked, but it was a start.

CHAPTER ELEVEN

BEN NEVER would have brought Jill along on this fool's errand if Amos hadn't suggested it. After leaving Jill's house, they'd stopped at the Bullion Police Department to file Czar's medical report. Amos had greeted Jill warmly and mentioned that Dorry Fishbank's mother had called a few minutes earlier to report her daughter missing.

"*Now* she's missing?" Ben had cried in exasperation. "I've been calling that woman for over a week and she keeps saying Dorry is fine."

Amos had shrugged in typical Amos fashion and given Ben permission to visit the Fishbanks to write up the report. "Why don't you take Jill along?" he'd added. "Since she and Dorry are friends, Jill might pick up something you'd miss."

Jill, of course, had jumped at the chance to be involved. Her enthusiasm hadn't lasted long, though. After about fifteen minutes of driving, she'd dozed off. Ben had moved his portable console to the floor and made a pillow for her out of the heavy sweatshirt he kept under the seat. That had sufficed until the road turned bumpy, then she'd wiggled around to find a more comfy spot for her head—his lap.

What kind of fool lets the woman he desires place her head within inches of his sexually deprived libido? Ben grimaced when another pothole caused an unfortunate contact.

His grip tightened on the steering wheel. Focus on the road, he told himself. Reaching out, he turned up the volume on the radio. Jill had selected the station. Something young. The beat stirred his pulse.

He glanced at the directions clipped to the dash. It shouldn't be much farther. *Thank God.*

The dusty road reminded him of the first back-road adventure he and Jill had undertaken. They'd been hopelessly lost. He'd been a bear and she'd been utterly delightful. Was that when he'd fallen under her spell? Or was it that first day when she'd stepped out of her little red sports car?

Ben frowned picturing the MR2 in her garage. "No driving," Whitehurst had ordered. "Just to be safe, Jill, I'm stopping your driving for a month. Head injuries are tricky, and I want to make sure you're a hundred percent."

"But how will I get to work?" Jill had protested.

The engaging doctor had blithely countered, "Who said I was letting you *go* back to work? You have a computer at your house—telecommute."

Although her parents had supported the idea, now that they were gone Ben knew he was going to have his hands full trying to keep Jill from jumping back into life full force. Perhaps that's what he admired most about her. While he'd devoted his life to keeping things static, Jill thrived on upsetting apple carts.

Joely had been telling him for years that his life was boring, too predictable. Ben had never understood—in fact, he'd been annoyed by the suggestion that something was missing from his life. But now he got it. An occasional splash of color—*like Jill's hair*—added zest to his world. New tunes—a little Ricky Martin—changed the tempo.

I need someone like Jill in my life. I need Jill.

As if hearing her name, Jill moved. As she stretched her neck, her nose accidentally brushed against his fly. Ben sucked in his gut and held his breath. Half-asleep, she sat up and dropped her chin to his shoulder. Snuggling close, she suddenly licked his cheek. A slow, languid lick that ended with a clap as her tongue popped back into her mouth.

Ben stomped on the brakes. Fortunately, he'd only been going five miles an hour. While the stop wasn't all that jarring, it got Jill's attention. She blinked owl-like and looked around. "Are we there?"

"Jill," Ben said soberly, trying to make sense of the weird emotions rushing through him. "You just licked my cheek."

She frowned. "I did?"

He nodded.

When she didn't add any comment or explanation, he asked, "Why did you lick my cheek?"

A slow blush crawled up her neck. Her eyes wouldn't meet his. "I...I...are you sure it wasn't a kiss? I'm very affectionate when I wake up from naps. And I was having this great dream."

"Were you a dog in your dream?"

She sat back as if he'd struck her. "Of course not. Why would you say that?"

"Because you licked my cheek. Just the way Czar does."

She moved to her side of the seat. "I had no idea you were so rigid. Does this mean you only like everyday, run-of-the-mill, man-on-top sex?"

Ben threw up his hands. "I can't believe we're having this conversation. I was just a little concerned about the lick. It's not that I don't like licking. I just wasn't expecting it right here. Right now."

She glanced out of the corner of her eye. A smile played

hide-and-seek with her lips. "I'm sorry. I didn't mean to scare you."

Ben threw his head back and closed his eyes. He was scared all right. Scared he might be losing his mind. He took a deep breath. "I apologize. I overreacted."

When he opened his eyes, Jill's face was one inch from his. She smiled then leaned a little bit closer. With the tip of her tongue, she outlined his lips. Her breath was warm. It smelled of French fries, which they'd picked up at the drive-through window of the burger shop on the way out of town. "Is it okay to lick if I ask first?"

Her teasing tone made him laugh. He'd have answered, but the image of her tongue on certain parts of his anatomy robbed him of breath.

Her smile slipped and she cocked her head as if straining to hear a sound. "A car's coming. We'd better pull over," she said, moving away.

Ben didn't hear anything, but he eased the Blazer to one side of the narrow path since the road curved just ahead and he couldn't see around the bend. A cloud of dust was his only warning. It was followed by a loud blast of a horn. The vehicle disappeared before Ben could get a good look.

"Maniac," Jill called over her shoulder. "What a moron! Driving that fast on a road like this." Misinterpreting Ben's look of bewilderment, Jill patted his arm and said, "Don't worry. We're almost there."

Worry? Pretty much. He just couldn't pinpoint the exact cause. There were so many possible choices.

WHILE BEN TOOK DOWN the details of Dorry's disappearance from her mother, Jill looked around. The dark paneling of the double-wide mobile home and thick drapes gave it a cavernlike feel. Every spare inch was cluttered with junk—from car parts to broken TVs.

Picturing Dorry in such a depressing environment made Jill sad. No art, no books—just a stack of yellowed *National Enquirers* beside one of the mismatched recliners that faced a huge television. A small, weasel-like man who'd been introduced as Dorry's stepfather, Roy Paten, occupied the other chair.

Where does Dorry sit when she's home? Her brothers apparently lived in the trailer across the compound. Jill had spotted three unsmiling men watching as she and Ben walked to the house.

"Are you really a friend of Doreen's?" Dorry's mother asked. Jill and Ben sat across from the woman at the messy dining-room table.

"Dorry and I went to school together," Jill said, answering the woman who eyed her suspiciously.

Although she resembled Dorry in general build, the woman looked old enough to be Dorry's grandmother. Jill could tell by the yellow stains on her fingers and withered lines around her lips that she'd been a longtime smoker. Her breath seemed to rattle going in.

"I work for the *Sentinel*. I wrote that article about Dorry a couple of months ago," Jill said. "Did you see it?"

The woman's face brightened, a crooked smile replacing her hard look. "Was that you? I bought ten copies and mailed them off to all my stupid relatives back in Oklahoma. That was real nice. You write good."

Jill reached across the table and touched the woman's hand. "Thank you."

"About Dorry, Mrs. Fishbank," Ben said, obviously anxious to stick to the purpose of their visit. Jill saw him fiddle with the cap of his pen. Ben didn't fiddle. "When did you talk to her last?"

Jill studied his profile. Forehead tense. Lips compressed

sternly. Basic cop stuff, but something was different. He seemed uncomfortable, nervous.

"It's Paten," the woman told him. "Stella Paten. Fishbank was my first husband. He cut out when Dorry was a baby. Roy 'n me been together ten years."

"Sorry. Mrs. Paten, the last time we spoke you told me your daughter was safe and sound. Has something happened to make you change your mind?" he asked.

Stella took a cigarette from a mangled pack and lit it, then dropped the shriveled match in a cantaloupe-size ashtray filled with butts. Her hand shook as she reached to pick up a small, colorful postcard from the counter behind her. "This just came in the mail."

Ben looked at both sides then passed it to Jill.

A splashy glimpse of paradise. Aquamarine water. A showy parasail with two bikini-clad women soaring in an azure sky. The notation at the bottom read: Mazatlán.

Jill turned it over. The note was brief: *Mom, Having so much fun I might never come back. Don't worry about me. Love, Dorry.*

Jill closed her eyes, trying to picture her shy friend in this mecca of bathing beauties.

"You gotta help us," Stella said, blowing out a big cloud of smoke. "Something's not right. Doreen would never abandon us—her brothers, me, her job. I don't know what we're going to do. Roy's disability barely covers the rent."

Jill looked at Ben. A cynical glint in his eyes told her what he thought of Dorry's mother's *concern* for her daughter.

Jill could see moisture collect along the red rims of Stella's eyes. "Perhaps it's just a lark," Jill said, trying to give the upset woman some kind of hope. "I know I've felt like running away before."

Dorry's mother punched out the half-smoked cigarette.

"Dorry always said she'd leave someday. I just never thought she would."

Roy Paten, who'd been staring at a car race on the muted television screen, rose and walked into the kitchen. He opened the refrigerator and took out a can of beer. "Dorry's a dreamer. Always had her nose in one of them damn love books. She used to say her prince was gonna come for her some day." His bitter laugh turned to a wicked cough.

"Does your daughter own a car?" Ben asked. "It doesn't seem likely she'd drive to Mexico, but I suppose it's possible."

Stella answered. "Roy found it parked down in her regular carpool spot. She switches off driving with a gal from the dentist's office. When Dorry's boss called asking for her, Roy hiked down the hill and there it was. Unlocked. Keys under the mat."

Jill felt Ben's inquiring look. "Stella, would you mind if I poked around in Dorry's room a minute?" she asked. "Maybe she left behind a clue of some kind."

Stella led the way down a dark hallway that smelled of cat urine and ancient tobacco. She pushed open a door and stepped back to let Jill and Ben enter.

Talk about night and day.

Neat as a sailor's bunk on inspection day, the small room was filled with light and color. The white eyelet cover on the mattress of the brass daybed was almost hidden by stuffed animals and ringlet-adorned dolls.

Jill and Ben exchanged a look of surprise. Jill walked to the five-foot-tall bookcase filled with paperback novels. Fat historicals. Contemporary novels of every size and type.

"I had no idea Dorry was such an avid reader," Jill said. She picked up the novel lying facedown on the glass-topped wicker table beside the bed; a folded piece of paper acted as a bookmark. Jill pulled it out and opened it up. "I guess one doesn't need a car to get to Mexico if one has passage on a cruise ship."

Ben stepped closer. His masculine presence seemed out of place in the girlish room, but he didn't seem bothered in the least. Focused, intense, he scanned the sheet of paper she'd found.

Her heart did a little pirouette when he looked at her and nodded. "A faxed itinerary. This ought to help." He turned to Stella. "I'd like to take this, if you don't mind. Maybe the travel agent who booked it can give us something."

Stella suddenly looked uncomfortable. "She didn't do nothing wrong, did she? I mean, I don't want to get her into trouble. We've had enough of that with the boys."

Jill took the woman's arm supportively. "Don't worry. We just want to make sure Dorry left of her own accord, not because someone threatened her or anything."

Stella frowned—as though the thought had never crossed her mind. She turned away, motioning them to follow.

At the entrance, Ben asked, "Just out of curiosity, did your daughter have enough money to purchase a ticket on a cruise ship?"

Stella's frown deepened, and she nudged them out to the front porch, which was littered with weathered boxes of all shapes and sizes, a derelict recliner and several overly ripe bags of garbage. She closed the door behind her. "I don't want Roy to hear," she said softly. "Dorry's been putting away money from each paycheck for years. She called it her *dowry*." She winced as she whispered the word. "I looked in the strongbox where she kept it and it was all gone. Every penny. Musta been almost two thousand dollars in it."

JILL WAS SURPRISINGLY QUIET on the drive back to town. Ben wasn't sure that qualified as a good thing.

"Not what you expected?" he asked.

She jerked, startled. "What? Oh, you mean Dorry's parents? No, pretty much what I thought they'd be like." She sighed. "It's not their fault, you know."

"Pardon?"

"Dorry's folks. They're doing the best they can."

Ben shrugged. He didn't want to be the one to pop her altruistic bubble. He'd known hundreds of losers like Dorry's parents. Hell, his folks weren't much better.

She gave a tug on her shoulder strap and turned to face him. "You don't agree, do you?"

It unnerved him that she could read his feelings. Nobody could do that. Except Czar. "What does it matter? I've seen hundreds of people just like that pair. They used their daughter as a steady paycheck to support their worthless lifestyle. Then one day she woke up and said, Screw this, and left. Do I feel sorry for them? Hell, no. I feel sorry for your friend. She was their victim."

Jill tilted her head, studying him. When she spoke, her voice was calm and flat—the way his usually was. "Dorry could have left at any time, Ben. She chose to stay because it was safe. Better to support a known evil than risk exposure to the unknown. Especially if the unknown might prove beyond a reasonable doubt that love doesn't prevail and dreams don't come true."

Ben took a minute to digest her words.

"Why do you hate them, Ben?" Jill asked.

Stymied, Ben looked at her. "I don't hate those people. I barely know them."

She brushed the backs of her fingers across his bare forearm. "I mean *your* parents."

He gulped as though he'd been punched in the stomach. She hastily scooted closer and put her hand on the steering wheel. The right tires howled as they hit the shoulder.

Ben brushed her hand aside and made the correction that put the Blazer safely back on the road. He knew she was waiting for his answer. His gut churned but he decided to get this little talk over with. She deserved to know the truth.

He pulled into the empty parking lot of a propane dealer and turned off the engine. "I don't hate my parents, Jill, I just don't like them."

"Why?"

"Because they were never there for me growing up." Ben used a phrase he'd heard on some talk show.

"How do you mean?"

He rolled his eyes. He should have known a journalist would want to probe deeper. "My father was an abusive drunk," Ben blurted out. "He hit my mother and threatened me and my sister—until I got bigger than him. Then he kicked me out."

Jill nodded, as if his story made sense. "And seeing the Fishbanks, I mean Patens, brought back all those bad memories."

Ben grappled for patience. "No. My parents would never live like that. They were big on appearances. Everything had to look good on the outside, even if it was rotten on the inside."

"Are they still together? Your mother and father?"

Ben couldn't prevent the bitter snicker. "Of course. She'd never leave him—what would people say? He sobered up a few years ago and is now a model citizen. Or so I've been told."

Her eyebrow rose at his snide tone. "But you don't hate them."

He smacked the heel of his hand against the steering wheel. "How could I? I haven't seen them in years."

"Does your sister see them?"

Ben frowned, recalling Joely's call about their father's

health. "She made up with them after Jenny was born. That was her choice. I don't have any reason to have anything to do with them."

"That's too bad," Jill said softly. Then, to his surprise, she changed the subject. "Could we stop at the *Sentinel* on the way home? I'd like to check my mail. Maybe Dorry sent me a card, too."

Ben stifled a sigh of relief. "Hopefully a treasure map telling you where to find the missing county-office files." He and Amos had tried to reconstruct Jill's investigation into the allegedly damaging water reports, but had discovered an entire block of years missing from the archives.

His attempt at levity failed. Ben hoped her preoccupied frown didn't have anything to do with him. His past was an open-and-shut case. History. If she were to be part of his life, she'd need to accept that.

JILL TRIED to stay focused on the list of e-mails on her screen, but it wasn't easy with everyone stopping by to give hugs of encouragement and support. A huge Welcome Back, Jill banner occupied the wall closest to the photo lab. Ben still lingered over the dozen photos of her tacked to the bulletin board along with some of her early articles.

She wished she could accept all the goodwill but something nagged at the back of her consciousness. A threat. A clue. She wasn't sure.

"Hello, Jill, good to see you," a deep voice said.

Dorry's itinerary, which Jill had just scanned into the system, slid to the floor. "Hi, Will," she said hastily, bending down to pick it up.

Will beat her to it. Their heads almost touched and Jill felt a sudden rush of vertigo. His cologne, something expensive and dramatic, made her slightly nauseous. She rocked back, and her temperamental chair buckled, nearly spilling her backward.

A strong hand on her shoulder steadied her. "That chair's worse than mine. I thought reporters had it better than civil servants." Ben's solid presence grounded her. She took a deep breath and brushed aside her foolish flight of fancy. Will was a friend, a colleague. She had no reason to feel skittish when he was near.

"What's this?" Will asked, scanning the page. Ben had agreed to let her forward a copy to her mother since Mattie knew people on almost every cruise line.

"Loose ends," Ben said, snatching the paper from Will's fingers. "Have we met?"

Jill made the introductions. She sensed Ben's watchful appraisal. She wondered if he was jealous. The idea made her smile.

Will snapped his fingers. The toothpick in the corner of his mouth wiggled like a snake's tongue. "I just had an epiphany. As long as you're both here, we could get someone to interview you. Victim with hero. Nice little PR package for both the paper and the police department. What do you say?"

He looked at Ben, obviously confident Jill would agree.

"No," Jill said.

Both men looked at her.

"I beg your pardon," Will said coolly.

Jill fought back a shiver. "We can't do it now. We're missing one of the key players—Czar," she said, thinking fast. She couldn't explain why but she felt a very strong need to leave. "I'd love to do the story as soon as he's back on his feet."

Ben nodded. "Good point. He's the real hero here. Not me."

Will shrugged. "Well, at least, let me get your statement,

Ben, about the investigation. Believe me, it hasn't been pleasant having to admit publicly that we let a stalker get that close to Jill without any of us acting on his threats." He frowned and looked at Jill. "You don't know how guilty I feel about not reporting what happened that day in the parking lot."

Ben demanded an explanation without saying a word.

Will motioned for Ben to join him at a nearby desk and the two men sat down. Jill e-mailed an attachment of Dorry's itinerary to Mattie. Hopefully, her father would check his mail while they were still in Los Angeles. Jill knew her mother would be thrilled to put her expertise to work.

As she opened a few other letters, Jill tried to tune out Will's version of her encounter with Bobby. Will's telling made it sound worse than it actually had been. "I warned Jill," he said sagely. "That guy's a born loser. He wouldn't take no for an answer when she tried to tell him she couldn't do anything more to help him."

Ben's gaze traveled to Jill. Although he spoke softly, she could hear his words. "Doesn't it strike you as counterproductive to nearly kill the one person you believe could help you?"

Will didn't answer right away. His eyes narrowed shrewdly—his reporter's nose no doubt sensing a scoop. "Are you suggesting Bobby Goetz didn't do it?"

Ben stiffened. "Not at all. Evidence looks pretty conclusive. I was just wondering about his motivation."

Will removed his toothpick and snapped it in two. "Most druggies aren't profound thinkers," he said. His smile seemed more like a sneer to Jill, who quickly looked away. She deleted a large block of old messages. In the background, she heard Will add, "Besides, who else is there? Bullion isn't exactly the crime capital of the world."

"Does Jill have any enemies that you know of? Disgruntled co-workers? Someone she might have slighted in print? She mentioned some unexplained changes to her stories."

Jill highlighted an e-mail dated the Monday after her attack. It had no message ID. In the line marked Sender, a string of numerals preceded AOL.com. While pretending to read, she listened to Will's answer. "If you mean that piece she wrote on you and your dog, I suspect that someone might have been asked by our publisher, Everett Davenport, to edit all Jill's work liberally." He lowered his voice to just above a whisper. "You probably don't know this, but Jill is persona non grata around here. When Clarice Martin, Jill's ex's new wife, worked here, she and Everett were very close, if you get my meaning."

Jill swallowed a gasp. *Clarice had been Everett's mistress? Good heavens, why didn't anyone tell me?*

Will went on. "It bothers Everett to see Jill—a constant reminder, if you get my drift. And there are plenty of sycophants who will do the head honcho's calling for the right incentive."

Jill sneaked a peek at Ben; his lips were compressed in a serious scowl. "I'd call that harassment."

Will snorted skeptically. "Welcome to the world of publishing." His cynicism made her skin crawl. She impulsively printed the e-mail message then erased the entire file. She grabbed her copy from the printer beside her desk and rose. Her vision swam, but Ben suddenly appeared at her side.

"Dizzy?"

"I got up too fast. I am feeling kinda pooped all of a sudden. Would you mind taking me home?" She nodded at Will. "Amazing, isn't it? The man not only saves my life, he plays taxi, too."

Ignoring Ben's puzzled look, she took his arm and tugged him toward the door. "Bye, everyone," she called. "See you soon."

Once outside, Jill took a deep breath. It was almost five. The sports crew would be coming in soon. Editorial would be calling it a day. She shivered. "Can we go?"

He looped his arm across her shoulders and pulled her close. "Your place or mine?" he asked, his lips brushing her crown.

She hadn't expected the offer. "Yours. Please."

BEN FIXED FOOD. It seemed a lot safer than taking her to bed. From the minute they'd walked into his house, Ben had wanted to pull her into his arms. Dog hair and all.

Czar's enthusiastic welcome had left her coated with hair.

"He's shedding worse than usual," Ben had explained. "I think he had an allergic reaction to something. Maybe the antibiotics."

Jill had looked ready to collapse. Ben had helped her to the couch in his sparsely furnished family room so he could keep an eye on her while he cooked. Czar had immediately flopped down beside her.

Ben dumped a box of spaghetti into a kettle of boiling water; he'd already doctored up a jar of store-bought pasta sauce and prepared a salad. Two heads of oven-roasted garlic drizzled in olive oil filled his kitchen with a mouthwatering aroma. The French bread was keeping warm in the oven until Jill woke up from her nap.

"Just about ready to eat?" he asked, noticing her sleepy blink.

She raised up on one elbow to look around. Czar responded with eager licks and rapid tail wagging.

Ben knew he should intercede, but he hadn't been able

to deny Czar anything since that last, harrowing episode when the dog had collapsed on the hospital floor. Torn between the two souls he cared most for in the world, Ben hadn't known how to help either one.

Fortunately, he told himself, they were both on the mend.

"Something smells yummy," Jill said. "Kentucky fried chicken?"

Ben snickered. Her teasing tone made him want to scoop her up in his arms. Instead, he played along. "That's right. I picked up a three-piece meal for you. Czar and I are having Caesar salad, pasta and garlic bread. Right, boy?"

Czar barked.

"You feed him people food?"

Ben smiled sheepishly. Ever since the gunshot incident, Czar had spurned dog food—even top-of-the-line canned stuff. He'd sit at the table and beg until Ben broke down and shared his meal with him. "It's a long story. Suffice to say, I'm cooking for three tonight."

She sat up, brushing the hair from her fingers. "I'm starved. If you don't mind, I'd like to clean up first."

"You know the way."

Instead of following her, Czar joined Ben in the kitchen. He looked at Ben with his soulful brown eyes and seemed to be conveying some deep thought. Ben dropped to a squat. "Whatcha need, boy?"

Ben tried to *hear* his friend's message, but the only thing that came to mind was Jill. And the memory of the kiss they'd shared in the hot tub. Ben had the oddest sense of standing outside his body—looking at them from Czar's point of view. *We look like a couple in love.*

"What can I do?" Jill asked, stepping around the counter.

Ben blinked to refocus. His heart gave a funny little skip.

He gave Czar a quick hug then rose. "Eat," he said, pointing to the table. "You're going to need your strength."

Her eyes grew big. "Oh, really. Why is that?"

Ben grabbed a pot holder and removed the foil-wrapped bread from the oven. "Because if I decide to ravish you later, I want to give you a chance to fight off my advances."

Her musical giggle made him smile. "What if I told you I'd surrender without a fight?"

Motioning her to sit down, he carried the bread and garlic to the table. "You? Feisty Jill Martin?" he teased, dropping a kiss on her nose.

"*Feisty?*" She touched her nose—as if remembering something that puzzled her.

"That's what Amos called you when I expressed my concern about putting you in the bite suit."

"How funny!" she said, tearing off a hunk of bread. "Penny's always called me a pushover. She said I was a wimp for not taking Peter to the cleaners when we split up."

"Why didn't you?" Ben asked, returning with the pasta and sauce. He turned off the kitchen light and sat down.

"It takes two to make a marriage work, and I'd quit trying long before the bitter end. We were headed in different directions and neither of us wanted to compromise. Why punish Peter for something I wanted?" She smeared a clove of soft, fragrant garlic on the bread. "My problem came when I found out about Clarice. My ego couldn't handle the idea that he'd found someone to replace me so quickly."

Her honesty touched him. Ben had known a lot of divorced couples—police work was brutal on marriages, but he couldn't name a single person as self-aware as Jill.

"Do you want to get married?" she asked right before taking a bite.

"Pardon?" Ben sputtered, nearly choking on his mouthful of salad.

She chewed and swallowed then smiled impishly. "Someday. Do you ever plan to marry? Or are you a confirmed bachelor? Married to your job."

Ben took his time answering. He glanced at Czar for guidance. "I never thought of myself as marriage material. My parents were pretty lousy role models."

Jill sampled the spaghetti. The unruly strands refused to stay on the fork and she wound up slurping noodles and sauce like a character in a cartoon. Twin pink dots appeared on her cheeks. "Sorry," she said, looking down. "Go on."

Ben's heart expanded in his chest. He knew he'd never felt this close to anyone before in his life. If the feeling had a name, it had to be love. Impulsively, he said, "I'd like to get married. What about you?"

She took a drink of water then sat back, as if digesting his question. "I liked being married at first." Ben couldn't prevent a tickle of jealousy, but it faded when she added, "But I'm afraid, too. What if the divorce was all my fault? Maybe I'm a jinx."

Ben reached out and took her hand. "I doubt that."

"You wouldn't be afraid to marry me?"

There was just enough mischievous twinkle in her eyes to let him know she wasn't truly agonizing over the prospect of being single the rest of her life.

"Scared spitless, but I'd do it." He brushed his lips across her knuckles. "In a heartbeat."

Their gazes met. And while things that could have been said remained unspoken, Ben knew that something important—something life altering—had been decided with a smile.

"We could hang out and watch videos after dinner," Ben said, feeling an enormous sense of peace. "Or do you want me to take you home?"

Jill squeezed his hand and said with a smile, "For some reason, I feel like I am home."

CHAPTER TWELVE

BEN REMINDED HIMSELF that the best of intentions were only as good as the end result. He'd promised himself a couple of kisses. A little innocent petting. Making love would wait until Jill was completely well.

"Jill, honey," Ben said, extricating himself from the hold she had around his neck. "This is a bad idea."

He wasn't about to jeopardize Jill's health for the sake of a romp in the hay—no matter how much his body wanted it.

The video *An American President* played in the background, but Ben hadn't seen a single scene for the past ten minutes. He'd been too busy memorizing the taste and texture of Jill's lips.

"No, it isn't," she whispered huskily. "How can you say that? It's a great idea. Make love with me, Ben. Please."

He pulled her to his chest and tightened his arms. His couch was wide enough for them to lie side by side, the overstuffed pillows of nubby, nut-brown tweed creating a cushioned haven. "I'd like nothing better than to make love with you. You can feel how much, can't you?"

She moved her hips against the evidence of his need. Her lips curved upward. "You think too much."

Ben's willpower was taking a beating. The strain showed in his voice when he said, "Jill, honey, I should take you home. What will Frank think? He might freak out if you leave him alone too long.''

She nuzzled the neckline of his shirt, deftly unbuttoning the top button. "Frank will understand. We can check on him in the morning." She undid two more and pushed aside the material to expose his nipple. She lifted her head and looked at him. Desire made her eyes stormy and mysterious. "Is licking allowed in such circumstances?"

He smiled. "Why not?"

Her wicked grin was quickly replaced by a languid look of pure seduction. Lips parted, her tongue slowly wetted her bottom lip. Never losing eye contact, she scooted down to trace tiny, maddening circles around his rigid nipple.

While her tongue worked its magic, her hands insistently tugged his shirt over his shoulders. "Off," she murmured against his chest. "I want this off."

Chuckling, he raised up and tugged the shirt free. When he leaned back to drop it over the end of the couch, Jill scooted downward. Her tongue tickled his belly button and then trailed the line of body hair back up his chest. "Much better," she whispered. "Now, if we could just do something about these damn pants."

She reached for his belt buckle, but Ben wove his fingers between hers. "Maybe we should even things up a bit a first."

Jill looked down at the oversize sweater that enveloped her like a quilt. A merry giggle bubbled up and she shook her head. "Yea gods, Mattie's Rule Forty-two: Never try to seduce a man when you're dressed like your grandmother."

She sat up, her legs dropping to the floor. Ben cocked his hips to give her more space. She smiled. "Don't move. I like that reassuring bulge against my hip—it lets me know I'm desirable."

Ben chuckled. "As if you needed reassurance. You're the most beautiful woman I've ever kissed."

"Really?"

Ben heard the tremulous question in her voice.

"Really."

She made a face. "But what about this?" she asked, tapping the yellowish bruise near her temple. Her hair was combed to hide most of the bandage, but she pushed it back. "Stitches. Staples. A little amnesia. Not exactly a turn-on."

Ben sat up and took her head in his hands, then gently pressed a kiss to the square of white gauze. "Beauty is in the eye of the beholder. And in all honesty, I hope this leaves a scar."

"Why?" she whispered hoarsely.

"So I'll never take you for granted. Because when I look at it I want to remember how close I came to losing you and how lucky I am that you're a fighter. And that you came back to me."

Jill gave a small cry and hugged him tight. "Oh, Ben, for the strong silent type you say the most amazing things."

He lowered back down to one elbow. "I get lucky from time to time."

Jill wiggled backward a couple of inches. "Speaking of lucky," she said, a mischievous gleam in her eyes, "did I ever mention that I have the catalog number for Victoria's Secret on speed dial?"

Ben's mouth went dry. "No, I'm pretty sure I would have remembered that little detail."

With a self-satisfied nod, she yanked her sweater—a massive knitted purple shroud—over her head. It sailed through the air to land with a solid thump near Czar, who rolled to his side and used it as a pillow.

"What do you think?"

In typical Jill fashion, she used her hands to direct his attention to her chest—as if Ben could possibly have prevented his eyes from staring or his tongue from hanging out of his mouth.

Her creamy white flesh was lovingly molded into an exotic snippet of beige gossamer fabric edged with bronze lace. Full and slightly upturned, her breasts filled the stretchy cups. Her nipples stood out in tantalizing relief against the sheer material. Ben had never seen anything more erotic.

"You think this is good," she said smugly, "wait till you see the panties." She pointed downward. "French cut. Basically see-through. Very sexy."

Ben wasn't sure his heart could take it. He was practically ready to embarrass himself and he still had his pants on.

Suddenly Jill threw back her head and laughed. "Oh, isn't this a hoot? I sound like someone on an infomercial." She cupped her breasts and said in a deep, staged voice, "And here, Ben, you see the C-cup model of our Evening in Venice collection. Notice the fine detail on the lace."

She moved a little closer. "Exquisite, is it not?"

Ben's gaze zeroed in on the tender touch of her slim fingers brushing against her ripe, titillated nipples. He sat up suddenly, catching her in his arms as she fell backward. His head dipped low. "I'm sold. I'll take a dozen of 'em, but I want this one, to go."

His mouth closed over one nipple. The material provided little resistance. Her hands threaded into his hair, urging him closer. He suckled deeply, pulling a low cry of wanting from her.

"Oh, Ben, I need you. I want you. Please."

Her words filled a void in his soul. He answered the best way he knew how. He stood up, taking her with him. He needed a bed for what he had in mind—a seduction they'd both remember for a lifetime.

JILL TOOK the opportunity while Ben was in the bathroom to give herself a stern lecture. She'd practically thrown herself at the poor man ever since her parents had left. In the Blazer, she'd dropped her head in his lap on purpose. She honestly didn't remember licking his cheek but wouldn't put it past her sex-starved libido. And that crazy lingerie sales pitch a minute earlier had been completely over the top.

Me—a sex goddess. Wouldn't Peter be laughing?

But despite a niggling embarrassment, Jill didn't regret a thing because she'd landed exactly where she wanted to be—in Ben's bed. The only thing she needed to remember is that desire did not equate with love. Guys needed time to assimilate their emotions. Ben wanted her—no missing the signs. But that didn't mean he wanted to make this an ever-after kind of relationship.

Jill wasn't going to fixate on tomorrow. And she'd learned that lesson the hard way. *Today is all we have, so go for it. Live life to the max.*

Having discarded her stretchy leggings, she drew her knees beneath her and rose up to peek at her image reflected in the patio door across from the bed. She'd have preferred to be ten pounds lighter, but she wasn't complaining.

"You're beautiful," Ben said, taking her by surprise. "Absolutely gorgeous."

In the reflection, she saw his naked body. He slowly approached the bed and knelt behind her. The big, sturdy mattress sunk slightly with his weight, but Jill didn't lose her balance. Entranced by the shadowy image on the glass, she kept her back to him.

He moved closer. His right hand brushed back her hair,

which had fallen across her breast. His left hand was spread wide on her belly, fingers splayed. She felt his heat behind her, and she tilted her chin.

He dipped his head and kissed her bare shoulder while his hand moved up to cup her breast. As Jill watched, his index and middle finger slipped beneath the stretchy fabric to tease her turgid nipple.

"Oh, Ben," she sighed, starting to turn.

His other hand braced her hip. "Not yet. I like the view. This way I get to touch and watch."

His fingers moved lower, inching beneath the tiny band of elasticized lace. He pulled her close so she could feel the hard length of his arousal.

Weak with desire, she watched his fingers explore the nest of burnished curls visible through the translucent material. She closed her eyes and moved her hips against his touch. She was amazed by the swiftness of her body's response.

She dived into the sensation. Free to explore—to seek the release that glittered on the edge of her consciousness. His gift was more than touch, it was permission to explode into a million tiny pieces and not worry that she wasn't pleasing him.

Limp but exhilarated, Jill leaned against him, panting. "Oh, heavens, that was amazing."

"You're amazing," he whispered, his tongue flicking against her ear.

Shivers coursed down her spine. She turned, still on her knees, to face him. "I think one of us is grossly overdressed, and I think it's me."

She ran her hands up and down the long smooth length of him from hip to shoulder. His buttocks tightened beneath her fingers. His back muscles felt like marble beneath a fluid layer of satin.

He buried his hands in her hair and gently tightened his grip, which made her scalp tingle. She tilted her chin as he lightly tugged, and he immediately plied kisses from her collarbone to her jaw. "You have a beautiful neck. Long and regal."

Jill smiled. "Mother always said I thought I was queen."

"I like your mother. And your dad."

Jill framed his face with her hands. "And my cat," she prompted.

A funny look darkened his forehead. "No. Czar likes your cat. I just tolerate Frank. And vice versa."

Thinking about Frank made her feel guilty about not going home, but how could she when her life—Frank notwithstanding—was here? She pushed the thought aside when Ben's nimble fingers slipped beneath the clasp in the middle of her back and released her bra. The pretty fabric hung from her shoulders, hiding her breasts like a misshapen rag.

He used his teeth to slip first one strap then the other from her shoulders. The bra fell to the bed. "Beautiful," he said, "but far too confining. I like this look even better."

He sank back on his calves to study her. The appreciation she read on his face eased her nervousness. She made herself keep her arms at her sides. "Touch me, please. I need to feel your hands on my skin."

His fingers moved with accuracy to her breasts. He teased her nipples until they ached for something more, then he took first one, then the other in his mouth.

"You taste so sweet," he murmured.

Jill couldn't have spoken if her life depended on it. She wanted him to move on, to give attention to the needs building deep inside her, but she had no way to ask—other than animal-like whimpers.

He ran his hands down her rib cage to her hips. With

the tiniest bit of effort, he removed her panties, then gently lowered her to the mattress.

She stretched, leaving her knees parted in invitation. Ben explored her body with his eyes, his tongue and his wicked mouth. When he moved close enough, she reached out and touched him.

Her fingers closed around him and he let out a low groan—a mixture of agony and ecstasy. "Be careful, Jill. It's been a long time for me. And you're the sexiest woman I've ever known. I'm very close to the edge."

His words were an aphrodisiac Jill had never tasted. Power. A good kind of power. "Love me?" she invited.

"No question about it," he whispered, wrapping her in his arms. He kissed her deeply, thoroughly, then turned away to retrieve a small foil packet from the bedside table. He ripped it open and quickly sheathed himself.

Jill gave herself over to his tender ministrations. She'd only been with two men in her past, and neither had been able to divine her needs, her desires, as intuitively as Ben. She'd never known a man to ask for directions, but Ben, fearless as usual, didn't hesitate to find out what made her crazy with passion.

There was only one answer, though—Ben.

JILL POLISHED OFF the last of her breakfast in bed. A first. Having a man cook for her was novel enough, but having one that carried the meal to her on a cute little tray with a cloth napkin was almost too good to be real. She'd love to lounge around all morning but she'd awakened feeling guilty about having left Frank alone all night. "Maybe you should drop me at home so I can check on Frank," she said, sipping her orange juice. "With the new alarm system you insisted on installing, he can't go in and out at will.

And Frank's not overly fond of his litter box although he's been a sport about it.''

"What do you mean, *in and out at will?*" Ben, who was standing at the closet, asked.

Jill discovered a last raspberry hiding beneath the saucer and popped it into her mouth. Chewing, she said, "I used to leave the garage window open a crack for him, but now I can't."

He shrugged on a white oxford shirt and turned to face her. "But you always locked the inside door, right?"

Jill grimaced. "Most of the time. I never worried, though. I figured it was safe because I had the garage-door opener with me and there are rosebushes under the window."

Ben's frown deepened.

"Why do you ask? I thought the police decided Bobby used the hidden key to get in."

He focused on buttoning his shirt. "It's probably nothing, but I remember seeing some cuts on Bobby's arms that he said were caused by roses. Maybe he tried that window first." He let out a breath. "Are you sure you're up for this meeting? We could reschedule."

Jill moved the tray aside and slipped out of bed. Although naked, she didn't feel overly modest—not after the amazing gymnastics they'd performed last night. "A quick shower and I'll be good to go," she promised, dashing past him.

Ben snagged a lock of hair. "Not so fast. Where's my tip?"

She turned. "As you can see, I don't have a dime on me."

His gaze traveled from toe to head in a leisurely manner. "I'd prefer more, but I'll settle for a kiss."

Jill made a face. "I haven't brushed my teeth yet."

Ben laughed. "You weren't that shy an hour ago."

She felt herself blush. The trouble with being a fair-skinned nudist, she decided, was that everyone could see when you were embarrassed. Standing on her toes, she pressed a quick—closed-mouth—kiss on his lips. "I'll be right back."

BEN SMILED as he made the bed—messy beyond words, but he wasn't complaining. Jill had been amazing. He'd been worried about letting her overexert herself, but she'd napped in childlike bliss between rounds then awakened hungry for more. He'd never known a woman so utterly void of guile, so genuine. He'd accidentally blurted out his love for her at least once, but so far she hadn't asked him to repeat the words outside the orb of passion.

What does that mean? That she's only in it for the sex?

His thoughts were interrupted by the sound of the phone ringing. He sat down on the bed and picked up the receiver.

"Hi, bro," his sister said with typical Joely energy. "How's everything? How's Czar? Is Jill up and at 'em?"

Ben pictured Jill's lush, naked body under the shower. "Um, yeah. She's in great shape."

There was a pause. "What's going on?"

"Nothing."

"Oh, come off it. Ben, I know you. Something happened."

Ben thought fast. Joely was like a bloodhound on the scent of a rabbit. "Jill and I got a lead on Dorry. Remember? Jill's missing source. And I'm taking Jill to meet with Bobby this morning. He's the guy—"

Joely interrupted him. "I know who he is. I've been paying attention. Why does she want to see him?"

Ben frowned. He wasn't certain. All he knew was that Jill had insisted on speaking to Bobby. "I need to hear it from the horse's mouth. I won't believe it otherwise," she'd told Amos.

"It's Jill being Jill."

There was a pause. "Oh my God."

Ben's heart sank. He knew that tone all too well. "What?"

"You love her."

"Joely," he said in his best big-brother cop voice, "this is private. I'm not going to discuss it with you."

Her whoop made him cringe. "I can't wait to tell the folks."

"If you mention one word of this to those people, I will never speak to you again," he said stiffly.

He heard her small gasp. "But Ben, they're your parents."

"No, Joely, they're *your* parents. As far as I'm concerned, they're gene donors. I don't want them involved in my life."

"But—"

He cut her off. "No buts, Joely. I have to go, sis. Talk to you later."

He hung up the phone and spotted Czar staring at him critically. "Give me a break. My love life is none of their business," he snapped, forgetting he had company.

Czar turned his head, and Ben knew if he looked, he'd see Jill standing behind him. "Are you going to nag me, too?" he asked without turning around.

She slipped her arms under his and hugged him fiercely. "Maybe later," she said against his collar. "Right now, I have to go see the guy who tried to kill me." She kissed his ear then backed away.

Ben rose and picked up her breakfast tray. His stomach was churning but he knew how to sublimate personal problems—work. "After the interview, I'll have to take you home then return to the office."

"You're on duty? Without Czar?"

Czar's ears perked up then he looked at Ben with accusatory eyes. Ben glanced at Jill as she pulled on the same clothes she'd worn the day before. With her hair in a ponytail and her baggy top and stretchy pants, she looked sixteen.

"Desk duty," he said. "I've got a ton of paperwork to catch up on. I'll take Czar along. He can rest in my office as well as here."

Jill finished making the bed then looked at him. "I heard a rumor that Amos hopes to train you to take over from him. Is that true?"

Ben didn't like the reporter tone of her question. Out of habit, he answered carefully. "Possibly, but that won't be for a long time. I still have to prove my worth by establishing the canine patrol." He made a wry sound. "I'm not exactly off to a great start. In our first two weeks, Czar has been shot and suffered some kind of stroke. He's spent more time on medical leave than active duty. Not great PR material."

Jill made a sound of distress and rushed to Czar. "This is all my fault, not yours, boy. Don't let them tell you otherwise. You're the best."

Czar licked her cheek.

For some reason, the image unnerved Ben. Grateful for the distraction, he added her napkin to the tray and walked to the kitchen. He was so busy loading the dishwasher, he didn't hear Jill enter the room until she said, "Would Amos's job be safer than what you do now?"

He finished wiping down the counter, then said, "It's a trade-off. Bullets for politics. I'm not sure which is more dangerous."

Jill sat down on a stool to put on her shoes. "I know what you mean. Dealing with Bud Francis is risky. He's a petty despot with friends in high places."

Ben recalled what Will Ogden had told him yesterday. Did Jill know the truth about her ex-husband's new wife? He cleared his throat. "I heard something yesterday. Gossip. I don't know if you—"

"About Clarice and Mr. Davenport?"

Ben nodded.

"I heard Will tell you." She gave a big sigh and looked at the ceiling. "Clarice is a piece of work. But she hired me when I had no experience and my only claim to publishing was a couple of articles since college." She frowned. "I can't say that the timing of her relationship with Peter didn't hurt, but given some perspective, I'm done agonizing over it. Frankly, I'm glad she and Peter are together. They deserve each other."

Ben walked to the stool and kissed her. "You've really put this behind you, haven't you?"

She linked her hands behind his waist and cuddled her cheek against his belly. "It's so much easier to move forward when you're not carrying a grudge," she said, her voice muffled by his shirt. "That one was really weighing me down."

Ben flashed to his sister's charge that his antipathy toward their parents was ruining his life, interfering with his ability to commit to long term relationships.

Jill apparently interpreted his reaction because she looked up at him and said, "Hey, I'm talking about me. You have to deal with the past in your own way. If I can help, I'd like to, but I'm not going to beat you over the head with it. Okay?"

Ben stifled his inner disquiet. He had a job to do today. "Okay."

CHAPTER THIRTEEN

"I DIDN'T DO IT, man. How many times do I gotta tell you that?"

Jill sat by herself in Ben's office and listened to the tape recording of Bobby's interrogation. Bobby's attorney had called to say he'd be late.

"Why won't nobody believe me?" the voice on the tape whined.

Jill thought the desperation seemed real—a sincerity that would have caught her attention even if she didn't have a feeling something about the case wasn't right. Could Bobby have been the one to attack her? Her intuition told her no.

Of course, unsubstantiated second sight counted for squat when the evidence appeared so damning.

She and Ben had arrived at the station thirty minutes earlier. After extracting a promise to keep everything confidential, Amos had tucked her into Ben's office with tapes and the thick file the police had accumulated on the case, then he'd taken Ben aside for a private confab.

At first glance, Jill had to agree with Amos—it looked pretty certain the police had their man.

"The only thing missing is the gun," Amos had told her.

"What about prints?" Jill had asked.

Ben and Amos had exchanged a look. "Gloves. We found a pair in a Dumpster near where Bobby hangs out. There was a stocking cap, too. Forensics has a hair and fiber match from both Bobby and the carpet in your place."

Jill felt nothing but sympathy for Amos who looked tired and stressed. She'd read a couple of *Sentinel* editorials zinging the police for not solving this case faster. Will was being his usual astringent self. And Ben had mentioned that the mayor was pressuring Amos to sweep it under the carpet so the violent nature of the attack wouldn't adversely affect sales of the new Land Barons project.

And since Dorry's files had disappeared along with her, it looked as though the development would go ahead.

Czar, who'd chosen to stay at Jill's side, made a rumbling sound in his throat. She put out a hand to pet him. "What is it, boy?"

By concentrating, she heard two men speaking just outside the door. Ben and Amos.

"What's going to happen to him?" Ben asked, his voice low and serious.

"He might plead down to aggravated assault," Amos answered. "It's mostly circumstantial evidence, but the blood and tissue on the gloves is nothing to sneeze at, and the preliminary match on the shoe print looks solid, too."

"What shoe print?"

"We took a cast from the rose bed right below her garage window. Kind of odd that we even got a print. This time of year the soil's harder than rock, but the ground had been recently turned up.

"And the print matches the boots Bobby had on when we picked him up. Heavy, metal-toed jobs. He said they were part of the charity he'd gotten after Jill's story ran in the paper. Ironic, huh?"

Ben made a sound that hardly resembled a laugh. "I just remembered something Jill said on our date. She'd been working in her garden earlier that day."

Amos sighed. "Then that pretty much places Bobby in the ballpark timewise, wouldn't you say? Let's go see if any of this stuff has jogged Jill's memory.'' There was a slight pause then Amos said, "By the way, I called her house this morning to confirm this meeting, and there wasn't an answer. Can you tell me why?''

Jill looked at Czar and made a face.

"She was with me,'' Ben said solemnly.

Amos coughed. "Police protection?''

"Something like that,'' Ben muttered.

The door opened with a bang. Ben walked to her. "Are you okay? Not too tired? We could postpone—''

Jill closed the file and turned to face the men. "Nope. I feel fit as a fiddle and ready to play.'' She gave Ben a private wink then turned to Amos. "Thank you for giving me access to this. I wish I could say it helped my memory, but all I get is shadowy images—nothing that makes sense.''

Amos consulted his watch. "Don't worry about it. We just want you to get well.''

Jill read the sincerity in his tone and appreciated it. She didn't even mind the look of speculation she caught on his face when Ben put out a hand to help her rise.

"Well gentlemen,'' she said. "Shall we get this show on the road?''

"THEN THIS GUY in a beat-up old car cruised past 'n tossed this bag at the Dumpster. It missed the mark by a mile, but the guy didn't get out or nothing. He just kept on driving, so I checked it out.''

Ben decided he hated the sound of Bobby Goetz's voice. He also hated the way Jill seemed to hang on every word. Why did she have to be so kindhearted? Her compassion made him feel like a bully just because he wanted this case solved and Jill safe from threat.

"What was in the bag?'' Jill asked.

Bobby looked at his attorney for permission to answer. The Public Defender's shrug suggested he had a dozen things he'd rather be doing. "Pair of gloves, a stocking cap and a cheap-ass windbreaker. Didn't fit so I gave it to Banjo."

"Gave?" Ben asked dryly. Inwardly, he cringed. His cynical tone reminded him of Will Ogden.

Bobby flashed him a dirty look. "I traded him for some weed. Big deal. I threw the hat away. It itched, but I kept the gloves. They were leather."

"Tell us about the car again," Amos said. "Maybe Jill will recognize it from the description."

"Black or brown...maybe dark blue. I think it was a Chevy. Or a Ford. Something American, for sure. Late seventies, maybe."

Ben couldn't prevent a skeptical snort. Jill gave him an understanding smile. "Can you tell me more about the driver, Bobby?"

The man sighed heavily. The orange jumpsuit he wore made his skin tone sallow. His hands shook as he sipped from the paper cup of coffee Amos had given him. "It was dark. There aren't many streetlights in that part of town."

Ben's patience was shot. He rose. "So you never went to Jill's house? You're a complete innocent in this matter?"

"That's right," Bobby said, sitting a little straighter. "I wouldn't hurt Jill. She was good to me when nobody else was. I like her."

"But that didn't stop you from calling her, harassing her at work. And you followed her, waiting outside the *Sentinel*, then you got in her face." Before Bobby could respond, Ben added, "Don't bother denying it, we have a witness."

"Once," Bobby cried. "I was sick of all the runaround.

I know when somebody's giving me the brush-off. I just wanted to talk to her.''

"Is that why you went to her house?"

"I didn't..." Bobby whined, leaning toward his lawyer like a rat scurrying to higher ground.

"The scratches, Bobby, remember. You told me you bumped into a rose plant. Jill has roses right outside her garage window.''

"I went to apologize.'' Bobby's head dropped in defeat.

Ben's chuckle made Jill look at him sharply.

"Apologize for what?'' she asked.

Bobby reached out, as if to touch her arm, but Ben pinned his hand to the table. The man's long, unshaven face—coarsened and aged by dissipation—turned dark red. "For botherin' you.'' He made a pleading motion. "You gotta believe me.''

Jill motioned for Czar to come to her. Ben frowned. Czar would normally never respond to someone else's hand signals—especially a funky wave like that. His stomach tensed. His worst fears about his partner's fitness for duty were being confirmed.

"Bobby,'' Jill said, "I could see where someone might panic and strike out in an effort to get out of my house without being caught, but how could you bring yourself to fire a gun at Czar? You almost killed this beautiful animal.''

Bobby threw up his hands and cried out passionately, "I wouldn't hurt no dog, Jill. I like dogs. You gotta believe me. I didn't hit you. And I ain't never fired no gun. I didn't do it.''

Ben stood back, arms crossed, and watched as Jill silently communicated with Czar. Her head waggled silently, and Czar rose and walked around the table to face the prisoner. Bobby shrank back in his chair.

Czar stepped closer. Ben moved in to grab the dog's collar if the need arose. Czar sniffed Bobby's leg, working his way upward.

"Give him your hand, Bobby," Jill demanded.

Bobby gulped visibly. "Do I have to?"

His question was directed toward his lawyer, but Amos answered. "If you want anyone to believe you didn't do it."

Bobby's hand shook, but he slowly lowered it. Czar responded by sniffing it thoroughly. Then, to Ben's surprise, Czar licked it.

Ben looked at Jill who smiled serenely. "*I* may have amnesia, but Czar doesn't. I'm just surprised you didn't think of this sooner."

Ben would have answered but he couldn't. Jill didn't know about his doubts, his fears. Trust was elemental in the field, and Ben didn't trust Czar's judgment anymore. How could he? Czar had changed; he wasn't the same dog he'd been before the shooting.

JILL WOKE UP from her nap with a smile. She'd dreamt of Ben and their night together. She'd never known a more generous, considerate lover. In fact, until his sister's call this morning, Jill would have sworn that her future with Ben was a sure thing.

But that single display of rigidity—the threat to cut all ties with Joely if she mentioned his feelings for Jill to his parents—had reminded her too much of Peter. When Peter made up his mind, nothing—at least nothing Jill could say or do—would make him change it.

Stretching, Jill rose and walked to her bathroom to freshen up. She did it quickly—not ready to confront the questions she'd see in her eyes. *Do Ben and I have a future together or not?* After filling up a water glass, she wandered down the hall to her office.

She checked her voice messages. One from Amos, three from her parents, five from Penny and two hang-ups.

She called Penny first. Chatting with her friend served as a reality check. Teething issues, local gossip and gentle probing into Jill's feelings about Ben—nothing Jill couldn't handle. Since she wasn't sure the same would apply to her mother, Jill put that call off.

Instead, she turned on her computer. As she waited for the virus check to run, Jill rocked back in her chair, her gaze absently drifting over the books in her shelves.

Wasn't it funny how Dorry hid that itinerary in her book? Just the way I do.

The simple thought hit her like a slap on the cheek. *My disk.*

She jumped to her feet and pawed through her shelves until one title sparked a memory. She yanked out the fat, hardbound copy.

"Well, hello, Margaret Mitchell. What have you got for me?"

She gave the book a shake and out dropped a white plastic disk.

"Bingo."

An hour later, she picked up the phone to call Ben. She'd already copied the pertinent files and planned to forward them to him. The dispatcher informed her that Ben was away from his desk but she'd patch Jill through to Amos.

"Amos," Jill said after a few polite formalities, "cutting to the chase, I called to tell Ben that I found my files—the ones that Dad thought were missing from my computer. I'd copied all my notes about the Land Barons story on to a disk and hid it in a novel."

"Really? So someone did clean out your computer?"

A shiver passed down her spine. "Either that or it was some kind of virus. All I know is that I found all sorts of background stuff on the company and some collateral stories about places where Land Barons had gone in promising the moon then skulked off just ahead of the posse."

"Sounds incriminating. Ben will be back from the vet's office in an hour or so, I'll send him over to pick up whatever you want to give us."

"Great, but in the meantime, could I e-mail you this stuff? I probably sound paranoid, but I'd feel better if someone else had a copy."

"A little paranoia never hurt anyone, Jill. Send it over."

"Thanks. I'll go online as soon as we hang up. I only have one line in the house and I keep forgetting to recharge my cell phone."

Amos started to hang up, but Jill stopped him. "Amos, was something wrong with Czar? Is that why Ben took him to the doctor?"

In the pause that followed, Jill's stomach turned inside out. "The dog seems fine to me, but Ben's concerned that there might be a problem." Amos's voice faltered. "Maybe even brain damage. Ben says Czar hasn't been himself since all this happened."

"Who has?" Jill cried. "That doesn't mean we're crazy."

Amos chuckled. "I agree. Look, Jill, without trying to sound nosy, I got the impression you and Ben have something going. If that's true, then you know how much Czar means to Ben. Not only does the department have a lot riding on the both of them, Czar is Ben's best friend."

"I know, Amos. But Czar's fine. I can feel it. He just needs a little time to rebuild his strength."

Amos didn't reply right away. "What makes you so sure?"

Jill felt her cheeks heat up. "I think Czar and I share some special bond. I...I can't explain it, but I *know* Czar is going to be fine."

Amos sighed. "I hope you're right. Those two depend on each other in ways the average person couldn't comprehend."

Jill blinked away the tears that suddenly filled her eyes.

"WELL, PAL, I GUESS I owe you an apology," Ben told Czar as they cruised down Main Street.

The vet had acted as if Ben was the one with the problem. "You can't expect Czar to bounce back overnight," the man had said. His tone had shamed Ben for bringing up his concerns. "Give him time. And rest. Czar needs to be home recuperating. I told you that before."

"I guess we should head home for a quick nap." Or to Jill's. Where he surely wouldn't *sleep*.

His partner's sagging demeanor sealed the decision. Since Czar was an extension of himself in many ways, Ben knew that Czar would rest more completely if Ben slept, too.

Three quick turns and he pulled into his driveway—where he found a red minivan parked.

He muttered a low epithet. "We've got company, boy," he told Czar. "Joely."

Half an hour later—small talk and children updates out of the way, his sister launched into the true purpose behind her impromptu visit. "Ben, we have to talk about Mom and Dad."

He shook his head vehemently. "Jo, I've got enough on my mind."

"I know, and I wouldn't bring this up if it weren't important. I told you about Dad's tests, right?"

Ben reached for Czar, who hadn't left his side since

they'd entered the house. "You said he was having some tests. Liver, I presume. Cirrhosis is a common side effect of being a drunk." He held up his hand to prevent her reply. "Excuse me, a reformed drunk. You can repent all you want, but the damage has been done."

Joely looked upset. "You're so hard on him. When I see you with Czar and my children, you're gentle, caring, but if I even mention Dad you go belligerent."

Ben ran his hand through his hair. "I can't help it, Joely. I only have bad memories of growing up. I don't want to care about him."

Joely reached for his hand. "That's just it, Ben. You do care. You can't help yourself. And it's tearing you up inside. Don't you see that? It's like trying to deny your feelings for Jill. I hear it every time you mention her name. You love her, Ben."

He tried to scowl, but smiled instead—Jill did that to him. "You're right. She's incredible, but thanks to my background, I know I'd make a lousy husband. She deserves better than me."

"Love isn't logical, Ben. I can't speak for someone I've never met, but I do know that you love Dad and he loves you."

He jerked his hand away.

"He's your father, Ben. He's old and sick, and you have to deal with the problems between you."

Ben started to stand, but Czar suddenly jumped up. His big paws landed squarely on Ben's diaphragm, almost knocking the wind out of him. "I can't," he said, burying his face in Czar's thick coat. "I have enough to worry about with Czar."

Joely joined him on the couch. She put her arm around his shoulder. "I'm sorry, Benjie," she whispered, using her childhood nickname for him. "I know the timing sucks, but you have to try."

Ben's gut churned. The picture of his father Ben carried in his head was of a surly drunk, one hand raised in anger. But lately, other memories had wiggled past his defenses. *Like the time we went fishing with Grandpa. Dad had been laughing then. He never laughed.*

Like me.

Joely grabbed his face and said sternly, "You can't wait forever, Ben. Didn't this near miss with Jill and Czar teach you anything? Life is fragile."

Ben closed his eyes and sighed. "Okay. I'll call."

Joely sat back. "Really? When?"

"Tonight."

"Promise?" When he nodded, she jumped to her feet and picked up her purse. "Good. My work here is done. I'd better get going."

Ben shook his head. "You're leaving? You drove all this way just to rattle my cage about Dad?"

"Of course. What are sisters for?" She gave him a mischievous grin that reminded him of someone else. "Although I could stick around if you'd like to introduce me to Jill."

Ben rose and followed her to the door. "Pushy, too. How does your husband put up with it?"

"He loves me." She threw her arms around him and hugged him fiercely. "And if Jill knows what's good for her, she'll whisk you off your feet and marry you before you can think twice." She kissed his cheek. "Love is all about risk, Ben. You're the bravest man I know, so don't look back, just go for it."

He watched her walk away. Czar suddenly squeezed between Ben and the door. Ben started to wave, then on impulse asked, "What exactly is wrong with...Dad?"

Joely's hand stilled on the minivan's door handle. "He needs a liver transplant. It's not immediate, but he was told to prepare himself for the inevitable. At first, he refused to let his doctor put his name on the list of recipients. He doesn't think he deserves one.

"Fortunately, Mom and the kids and I convinced him otherwise."

Ben sighed. "Do you remember Guy Peterson? My first partner in Santa Ignacio? He died of liver cancer at forty-three. Never took a drink in his life. I was really bitter at the time. I remember wishing it could have been Dad in that hospital bed, he deserved that fate, not Guy."

Joely returned to the stoop. She patted his shoulder supportively. "I remember. But even a transplant wouldn't have helped Guy. By the time they found it, the cancer had metastasized. But Dad's a fighter. Look at the way he beat his addiction and turned his life around." She smiled at him. "Wonders abound, Ben. Look at Czar. Nobody thought he'd survive the attack. And Jill's another living, breathing phenomenon."

Ben thought about Joely's comment an hour later when he and Czar headed to Jill's. To his surprise, he'd managed to nap but had woken up missing Jill. The real marvel, he decided, would be if Jill agreed to marry him. They'd joked about it at dinner, but once he told her the whole story about his past—his family background and many shortcomings, she'd probably hightail it for safe ground.

As he turned on Jill's street, the dispatcher notified him that Amos needed to talk to him right away. He pulled into the red zone in front of the hospital. "Patch him through."

"Ben, I just talked to Jill's mother. She called my office because Jill's line was busy. Not to worry, I talked to Jill about half an hour ago and she was going online to send me some files she ran across."

"What kind of files?"

"The ones that someone erased from her computer. She'd made a backup disk and hid it somewhere in the house."

Ben smiled. Her father knew his daughter well.

Amos went on. "Bottom line is—we know who purchased that ticket for Dorry Fishbank."

Czar put his head between the partition; his warm breath smelled of fish sandwich—the result of a stop at a drive-through window.

Ben pushed his partner's muzzle to one side. "Who?"

"Clarice Martin."

Ben looked at Czar in surprise. "Are you sure?"

"Jill's mother faxed me the credit card confirmation. She was a bit coy about how she got it, but it looks authentic."

Ben shook his head trying to process the implications. "That blows my mind. I'd say we need to pay the Martins a visit."

Amos's voice sounded almost gleeful when he said, "I'll meet you at their hotel."

JILL SCROLLED DOWN the list of new messages on her e-mail screen. She couldn't believe the junk mail that somehow found its way to her computer. When she got to an odd-looking message with no return address, her heart skipped a beat.

She highlighted it.

Dear Jill,

Just a note to let you know Mom and I are fine. We're set to board the airplane in a few minutes, but I found this cybercafé and wanted to remind you that we're thinking about you. We love you, honey, and hope

things are falling into place in your life. I have a good
feeling about Ben. He's the kind of man you can trust.

Missing you,
Dad

Jill blinked back tears and hit print. When she retrieved
the printed copy, her gaze lingered on the odd heading. It
reminded her of the message she'd retrieved from her computer at the *Sentinel.* "What did I do with that?"

She trotted downstairs and checked in the laundry room
where she'd dumped her clothes that morning on the way
out the door with Ben. The tiny scrap was folded in the
pocket of her stretchy pants.

"Hey, Franklin," she said, spotting the cat curled up on
a stack of towels. "Look what I found. A treasure map,
perhaps?"

Frank followed her into the family room. When she sat
down on the sofa, he leaped to her lap, purring for attention.

"Sorry, sweetie, I know I've been ignoring you. Just let
me read this letter then we'll talk."

She held the note out of reach of Frank's twitching tail.
It only took a few lines for her to realize the message was
from Dorry.

Dear Jill,
I know you probably think the worst about me, but
who could pass up a chance to trade those dusty old
files for a ticket to paradise? The only price was my
silence. The lady who contacted me told me I couldn't
tell anyone or call my family, but she didn't say anything about e-mail, so I decided to try one of those
online coffeehouses until it was time to board the ship.

I just want you to know that I consider you a friend.
You've always been nice to me and I would have

helped you if this opportunity hadn't come along. But don't feel too bad. At least I gave the files to someone you work with—Will Ogden. He was nice enough to give me a ride to the bus depot, and I gave him the files. He said he'd keep them safe.

Again, I just wanted you to know that I think you're a real nice person and if you ever get to Mexico come look me up.

Dorry

Jill was too stunned to move. She read the letter a second time and still couldn't make sense of it. Why would Will take the files and not say anything?

A sickening thought hit her. *They bought him off. Peter, Bud—whoever was behind this—paid Will to sit on this story.*

A wave of dizziness passed through her. Will's career would be over when this got out. And Jill knew Will's work was his life.

When she was first hired at the paper, Jill had tried to get to know all her co-workers, and she'd spent considerable time talking to Will—until she realized his cynical wit thinly disguised a deeply ingrained bitterness. Brilliant but lazy, Will seemed to feel that the *Sentinel* was just a stepping stone on his path to greatness. Unfortunately, he preferred to ride, not walk.

"If this place is so penny-ante, why don't you move to a bigger paper?" Jill once asked him. "The *Bee* or the *Chronicle* would probably jump at the chance to hire someone with your experience and background."

He'd given her a droll sneer. "They only hire J-school graduates, Jillian. My degree from Backwater State won't cut it. But a Pulitzer might. How long do you think I'll have to wait until something really newsworthy happens in this town?''

She'd understood then that Will didn't have a college degree, period. Possibly he'd faked his credentials to get hired at the paper or had found another way to get his foot in the door. But he was a skilled writer and decent editor. He'd been working at the *Sentinel* since she and Peter first moved to town. Jill remembered Peter's comment after meeting Will at some Land Barons function. ''Will Ogden has a head on his shoulders,'' Peter had said. ''He's got more vision than the rest of these local-yokels combined.''

Did that mean Peter had involved Will in his schemes? Jill had to tell Ben. But first she needed to log off so she could place a call.

She was halfway up the stairs when the doorbell rang. She checked the peephole. Her heart climbed to her throat. Will.

''Hi, Jill, can I talk to you?''

Her pulse raced and warning signals told her to keep the door locked. ''Will,'' she said, her voice weak and thready. ''I was just going to take a nap. Doctor's orders. Can you come back later? I'm so tired I can barely move.''

''It'll only take a minute,'' he cajoled. ''We just got a tip that the cops are on their way to arrest Peter and Clarice. I thought you might want to be there.''

Peter and *Clarice?*

She was tempted. This was her story. She deserved the byline, but was it worth the risk? She didn't know exactly how Will fitted into the picture, but she wasn't foolish enough to trust him.

She leaned her forehead against the door and said, ''I'd like to, Will, but I can't. I'm just too weak.''

When he didn't reply, she raised to her toes and peered through the viewing hole. He was gone.

A sudden chill as cold as death ran down her spine. She spun around. Will—dressed in his usual dapper corduroy pants and Neiman Marcus sweater—stood at the opposite end of the foyer.

"How'd you get in?"

He held up a key and smiled. His self-satisfied grin made her knees buckle. "Peter lent me his."

"My father changed the locks."

"Not the one in the garage, and darned if my opener doesn't still work, too."

Jill suddenly understood: Will was the person who had attacked her. He'd tampered with her computer and stolen the files. But he hadn't killed Dorry. That was some relief. "What do you want?"

He shrugged indolently. "A decent living. Television without commercials. A Pulitzer. But I've settled for a quick payoff."

"I have no idea what you're talking about," Jill said, going for bluster. "I'm not well and I'd like you to leave. Ben will be here any minute."

Will laughed. "Nice try, Jillian. But you must not have been listening. The police, including Dog Boy, are busy arresting your ex."

"For what?"

"For all sorts of nasty stuff like insider trading, bribery, attempted murder. Both Peter and Clarice will be singing like larks in a matter of minutes, which is why you and I are leaving."

Jill's heart turned over. "I'm not going anywhere with you."

"Yes, Jill, you are."

He lifted his hand and pointed a compact silver revolver at her. The small black hole at the end of the barrel looked deadly. *How come guns never look that scary on television?*

CHAPTER FOURTEEN

BEN KNOCKED on the hotel door with mixed emotions. The cop in him tingled with anticipation, but the thrill of solving the puzzle was offset by the knowledge of how this would impact the woman he loved.

Since Joely's visit earlier that afternoon, Ben had found it easier to admit the depth of his feelings for Jill. The real test would come when he told Jill how he felt, and he was ready to take that chance—once she'd recovered from the shock of her ex-husband's nefarious schemes.

Jimmy Fowler elbowed Ben aside and pounded his fat fist on the door. "Open up. Bullion P.D."

The door opened with silent dignity. The woman standing across from them was dressed in a white wool pantsuit, her hair knotted sleekly at the nape of her neck. Except for the red around her eyes, she looked as coldly elegant as she had the first time Ben met her.

"Officer Jacobs. We've been expecting you." She opened the door wider.

Jimmy's hand went for his gun, but Amos jostled him to one side. "Relax, boys, we're here to talk."

Ben found the expression funny—like something out of an old western. When he looked at Clarice, he could tell that the thought had crossed her mind, too. Oddly, the revelation made her more human—something he wasn't prepared to acknowledge.

Czar stepped forward, tugging on the lead Ben held.

"This is the dog that saved Jill's life," Clarice said in a thin voice.

Ben thought she looked paler than usual. "Yes. His name is Czar."

"He was hurt, but now he's well. Like Jill."

Although it lacked the proper inflection to make it a question, Ben knew she was inquiring about Jill's health. "Jill's doing great. Almost back to normal."

"Which is supposed to be a *good* thing?" a voice asked dryly.

Ben turned to see Peter Martin enter the suite from an adjoining bedroom. He sensed rather than saw Jimmy's wary response. Czar, too, flattened his ears and watched Peter's every move.

Clarice sighed. "Don't start, Peter. None of this is Jill's fault."

"It's all Jill's fault," he snapped. "She's never been content to let small things go for the sake of the bigger picture. I told you she'd be a problem, but would you believe me? No."

Ben looked at Amos and Jimmy who stood to one side, listening avidly. A common police tactic to obtain a confession was to turn two cohorts against each other. He had a feeling it wouldn't take much effort with these two.

Clarice pointed toward a conference table near the window. The executive suite was equipped with extra chairs and all the trappings of business: fax, computer hookups and two phones. "Please sit down. Our lawyer is on the way. He advised us not to say anything until he gets here. Could I offer anyone a refreshment?"

"Tainted champagne, perhaps?" Ben asked, pulling out a chair.

Clarice's step faltered; Peter caught her arm. "Dammit,

Clarice, I knew we should have rescheduled. The doctor said you need rest."

Her snicker held a fatalistic quality. "Oh, I think I'll have plenty of time for that where we're going."

Ben and Amos exchanged a look. Jimmy motioned them to the window. "Lookee there. Hatch Brumley. Only Rolls in the county."

"The lawyer?" Ben asked.

"He ain't no F. Lee Bailey but it ain't for lack of trying. I've seen him on TV representing Land Barons before. He's smooth as a good bowel movement."

Clarice made a gagging sound and excused herself.

Peter gave them an accusatory look then went to wait by the door.

His wife returned, and a few minutes later, after introductions had been made and everyone was seated, Hatch Brumley opened the discussion. "How much?" he asked.

Amos, who had been in the process of removing a pen and pad from his shirt pocket, froze. "I beg your pardon."

"How much is it going to take to let the Martins walk?"

Ben studied the man with distaste. Well-dressed, in his early fifties, Hatch Brumley disguised his extra twenty pounds through the talents of his tailor. His sparse hair, a questionable shade of tan, seemed sprouted from inflamed patches of scalp. *Hair plugs?*

Jimmy made a fist and shook it at the man. "Are you trying to bribe us? 'Cause if you are, I'd be happy to show you what you can do with the money."

Brumley chuckled indulgently. "You small-town cops always think in terms of bribes. I was referring to an exchange of information in return for immunity."

Amos reprimanded Jimmy with a look. He sat forward. "Aren't you getting a little ahead of yourself, Hatch? We came here to talk to the Martins, not charge them with any crime.''

Ben was tired of playing games. ''Did you put something in Jill's drink the night of the party, Mrs. Martin?' He looked straight at Clarice.

Her odd, pale eyes didn't blink. ''Yes.''

Brumley exploded. ''Dammit, Clarice, hold your tongue. You've just incriminated yourself. What the hell do you think I'm here for?''

She looked at him. ''To protect Land Barons's interests, of course.''

''What did you put in it?''

''A sleeping aid. Nothing poisonous or deadly. My hope was that Jill would become groggy and would be afraid to drive home. This was before I found out that she'd come with a date, but, of course, by then it was too late to take it back.''

For some reason, Ben believed her. ''Why'd you hire someone to tamper with her brakes?''

Her lawyer sputtered, but Clarice cut him off. ''I don't know what happened to her brakes. Although I might suggest that you talk to Mayor Francis. I saw him wiping something black from his hands as he was entering the men's room. And it's my understanding he's an avid collector of old cars with considerable knowledge of such things. My sole contribution to the evening's fiasco was to put a sleeping powder in Jill's champagne in hopes that she'd be too woozy to drive.''

''Why?'' Amos asked.

''To allow someone time to enter her house and extract any files she had on Land Barons from her computer. We needed to find out how damaging her research might prove to be. Plus, we wanted to know whom she'd contacted with the information.''

"How'd that person get in?" Jimmy asked. "We didn't see no forced entry."

Peter gave his wife a dirty look. "Jill gave me a key so I could pick up the remainder of my personal property in her garage."

"And you gave the key to the person you hired to kill her," Ben said.

The little bit of color in Clarice's face disappeared. Her ghostly pallor looked unhealthy. "No," she cried with surprising passion. "Jill was my friend. I would never have let someone hurt her. It was an accident. She returned too soon. When the dog came at him, he reacted poorly. He didn't mean to hurt her."

Peter and the lawyer both did their best to keep her quiet, but Clarice seemed intent on spilling her guts. Ben knew that without apprising her of her rights, her confession wouldn't be allowed in court. Amos seemed to be thinking the same thing, because he pulled out his plastic Miranda card and read the words verbatim.

"Mrs. Martin, you've just admitted your involvement with a nefarious scheme that nearly killed a woman and wounded a canine police officer. These are very serious charges. Mr. Brumley's correct. Anything you say from this point on can and will be used against you. Do you understand?"

Clarice nodded.

"Good. Then listen to counsel. I'm going to suggest that we continue this at the station."

Czar made a low groaning sound that Ben usually associated with hunger. He didn't understand it given their recent stop at the fast-food shop. He absently patted Czar's shoulder and kept his gaze trained on the couple across from him.

Clarice shook her head. "You said when you called that

you wanted to talk about Dorry's ticket. Even if you hadn't figured that out, I would have called you. I'm worried about Jill. You think you caught the right man, but you didn't. That person was a patsy."

"So, who did it?" Ben asked, his stomach knotted with tension.

Hatch Brumley pounded his fist on the table. "I object. My client can't think straight with you haranguing her. I will file charges if you ask her another question. She's been under a doctor's care for several days and isn't well."

"I'm pregnant," Clarice said in a tone that implied disbelief. Tears welled up in her eyes. "Quite against all odds, I am expecting a baby."

The depth of emotion he read in her face moved Ben. Suddenly he remembered something Jill had told him. "It was my understanding that your husband—"

"Had undergone a vasectomy? That's what he told Jill, but it was a lie."

"Why?"

Peter made an unhappy sound. "Is this necessary? I don't see why my wife's condition has anything to do with—"

Clarice looked at her husband with compassion and understanding. "Peter suffers from low sperm count. He found out when he volunteered for some kind of study in college. This was shortly after he'd met Jill, and he was afraid Jill would think less of him if she knew."

She sighed and looked at Ben. "Jill's a very trusting person. She even believed him when he told her her retirement account was safe."

Peter made a sputtering sound and turned his back to her.

Clarice smiled sadly. "I, however, am more demanding than Jill. I wanted a child and was determined to do what-

ever necessary to conceive." She took a deep breath.
"We've been seeing a fertility specialist for four months."

"Didn't I tell you this was bad timing?" Peter asked.
"At this rate, the kid will only get to see us on visiting
day."

Clarice broke into sobs.

Czar gave a low cry of his own. Ben put his hand out
and stroked his head. "It's okay, boy. We'll be done here
in a minute."

Amos cleared his throat. "Before we head to the station,
I'd like to clarify one point. If Bobby Goetz didn't attack
Jill, then who did?"

Hatch Brumley leaned on the table. "That's our bar-
gaining chip, and I refuse to let either of these people say
another word."

Amos's back stiffened. "You're obstructing justice,
Brumley. There's a violent criminal out there, and if an-
other person gets hurt because you're playing kiss and tell,
I swear I'll see you disbarred."

Czar barked. Twice.

Ben's stomach turned over. He knew that bark. Danger.
The only person who could be in danger was Jill.

He grabbed for the phone and punched in Jill's number.
A busy signal. "She can't still be online, can she?" he
asked Amos, who frowned.

Flinging the receiver, he leaned across the table, grabbing Peter Martin's prissy yellow button-down shirt by the
neck. "Tell me."

Clarice gave a small peep then reached for her husband.
"Will Ogden. Peter's been paying him to write favorable
editorials, and Will—along with Bud Francis—recruited the
members of the planning board to grease the wheels, so to
speak. Will's big payoff comes when the lots are sold, but
that won't happen if Jill tells people about the water."

JILL FLEXED HER HANDS, testing the tension on the thick, coarse rope binding her wrists. The seat belt cut across her sore shoulder and she couldn't get comfortable, but somehow Jill knew that wasn't going to be an issue for long.

"Why are you doing this, Will? What have I ever done to you?"

He drove slowly, paying heed to all traffic signs. "Oh, come off it, Jill. Nobody could be that obtuse and still be alive." He reached across the bench seats of the older sedan and flicked his middle finger against her forehead, as if disposing of a pesky bug. It didn't hurt as much as it startled her, and Jill felt tears gather in her eyes.

"And then her feelings got hurt. Oh, my, how mean of me," he said in child's tone. "Grow up, Jill."

Jill tried to draw on anger and outrage to give her focus, but fear consumed her. The only thing that helped was to picture Ben. Strong, fearless. He'd rescue her, wouldn't he?

"Peter was right," Will said snidely. "Your naiveté is such a turnoff. After you came to work at the paper, I considered having an affair with you, but you always struck me as too timid."

Jill shook her head in confusion. She knew that occasionally Peter and Will had golfed together with Bud and Mr. Davenport, but she didn't think they were friends. "You and Peter are…involved?"

Will snickered. "I'm not sure I like that connotation. We're business associates. When you and Peter first moved here, he was looking for someone to help him set up a base of operation, open doors, grease a few palms."

Jill wasn't surprised that Peter was involved in such shady dealings, but she was shocked by Will's participation. "You used the paper as a forum to promote the Land Barons's agenda?"

His lip curled up. "You make that sound like a bad thing.

I prefer to think of it as helping the indecisive masses make up their minds.''

Before Jill could respond, he laughed. "Oh, that's right—our self-righteous campaigner still believes in journalistic integrity.''

Jill felt herself blush, and it made her mad. "At least I didn't sell out.''

His smirk made her cringe. "You might have if the stakes were big enough. I was banking enough to blow this town in style until you came along and ruined things,'' he said bitterly.

"The water.''

Will shook his head. "So there's a little arsenic. What's the big deal? Everybody drinks bottled water these days. Ten years from now doctors will probably decide arsenic's good for people.''

He looked left to check for oncoming traffic then turned toward the mine. Jill's heart plummeted. Although the old shafts had been closed years earlier, there were ravines, drop-offs, hidden nooks and crannies that would take days to search.

"Aren't you overreacting?" she asked. Her voice sounded strained and frightened. "I mean, those files Dorry found were ancient. The arsenic is probably long gone by now.''

He snickered. "Nice try. But wrong. And even if that were the case, just the hint of something unhealthy lurking in the soil would drive down the value of the lots. Land Barons might be able to cut its losses and bail, but there's still the problem of insider trading and bribery.''

Jill vacillated between wanting to placate him and wanting to ask reporter-type questions. As she worked the knots at her wrists, she said, "Things can't be as bad as you think, Will. I didn't suspect you, and I was closest to the story.''

The old car chugged going up the steep grade. Will downshifted with a scowl. ''You'd have found out sooner or later and you'd have exposed the whole scheme. You play by the rules, Jill. I heard you joking about your mother's rules one day.'' His laugh made her skin crawl. ''Rules are for losers, Jillian. I thought you might have gotten the message when I messed up your precious dog and cop story.'' He looked at her. ''Actually you surprised me. I figured you'd have given up and quit long ago.''

''So now you're planning to kill me? How does that help?''

He sighed. ''Consider yourself a diversion, Jill. They'll be too busy hunting for you to look for me.''

Jill shook her head. ''Why do you hate me? What have I ever done to you?''

''Me, me, me,'' he said, his tone mocking. ''This isn't about *you,* Jill. It's never been about you. You're simply an annoying fly buzzing about the pile of manure. A simple sheep who wandered too far from the flock and has fallen prey to the Big Bad Wolf.''

''You're quite mad.''

''Mad in the sense of crazy? No. Mad as in angry? Bingo. I worked very hard to make this happen and your nosy intervention has ruined everything. If you'd have died that night, we might still have pulled it off. Clarice didn't believe me, but we could have.''

Jill froze. ''Clarice is involved?''

''Who do you think introduced her to Peter?'' He put on the blinker and slowed down to make the turn into the driveway leading to the mine. In the twilight, Jill could still see the spot where Ben had tracked her that morning after Bud had ruffled her feathers.

"Is Bud in this, too?" she asked.

"Of course. And half the planning commission. We're talking deep, deep pockets, Jillian. Yes, gloat while you can. Your suspicions were grounded. Too bad you're not going to be able to spread the news."

He said the last in a lascivious tone that made her skin crawl. Would he try to rape her before he killed her? Jill's heart sped up a notch. Her wrists were raw but she kept wiggling them, trying to work one hand free.

The bumpy motion helped her move sideways. In the back of her mind, she thought she might be able to open the door and jump for it.

Will glanced her way and yanked her closer to him with a violent, wrenching grip. "Soon enough, Jill," he said, obviously reading her mind. The pungent smell of his cologne made her gag. "It'll all be over soon. Just be patient."

A nerve in her shoulder became pinched and she wiggled back to relieve it. As she did, her fingers brushed against something solid. In the fold of material created by the sagging seat cover, a toothpick was hiding.

She curled her fingers around the treasure. One of Will's fancy toothpicks. Whole, not broken in two. It wasn't much of a weapon, but it might come in handy.

The car bounced across the dusty field to the shadowy wall of rocks that led to a spot the locals called Lover's Leap. The room-size slab of granite provided a favorite make-out spot for Bullion youth. Jill, herself, could remember kissing Noah Watson there her senior year.

Will parked the car behind a cluster of scrubby bushes. He turned off the engine and got out. Jill gripped her tiny weapon and braced herself as he walked around the car.

Instead of opening the door right away, Will leaned

against the side of the car and whistled a tune she didn't recognize. "What are you waiting for?" she cried.

"My ride," he said. "A helicopter."

"What about me? You're just leaving me here?"

He looked down. The window was open halfway. In the fading light, his face looked eerily calm, almost bored. "That's right."

Jill's stomach turned over.

He pushed off from the car and walked to the trunk. Jill used the time to frantically wiggle her hands. She felt the rope give a little. Her shoulders were killing her, especially her bruised collarbone, but she fought through the pain. *I can do this. I can.*

He slammed the trunk and strolled to the front of the car. Jill strained to see what he was carrying. A bucket? A gas can. *Oh, God.*

With lazy, looping movements, he sloshed the potent-smelling liquid over the hood of the car, working his way toward the rear. Jill let out a small scream and ducked when the fluid hit the windshield.

Lying prone, she found she had better leverage. Her hand was almost free.

"Loathsome smell," Will said, his voice coming from the window behind her.

Jill whipped around so he wouldn't see her hands. She put her face close to the window, almost gagging on the fumes. "Please, Will," she begged. "Please let me go. I won't say anything. I promise."

He ignored her. "Sorry, Jill. Too late for promises."

Jill's hand popped free, but fortunately Will had turned away, probably looking for a match. She weighed her options. She might not have a chance to escape once he lit the match, but she didn't think she could outrun him if she bolted too soon. She tried to keep him talking.

"But why kill me, Will? If you fly away now, you're just a guy who broke a few rules. Big deal. But kill me, and you're a murderer."

Jill's newly sensitized hearing picked up a sound in the distance. A helicopter. She thought she heard a siren, too, but she couldn't tell how far away it was.

Will drew a lighter from his pocket.

It was now or never.

She dived for the door and wrenched it open, falling to her hands and knees. Her wrists buckled and her chin scraped the ground, but she managed to get up and start running. Away from the car. Away from the smell and the crazy man who wanted to kill her.

BEN'S TRAINING told him to check Jill's house, even though the telephone line was busy. His adrenaline surged when he pulled into the driveway and found the garage door open.

He yanked his gun from the glove compartment and jumped from the car. Czar followed at his heels.

The inside door stood open. Frank meowed plaintively, but Jill failed to answer his repeated calls.

With Czar at his side, he checked the house, room by room, then dashed to the Blazer to call in an APB.

Czar remained in the doorway, barking frantically. Ben hurried back, wondering what he could have overlooked. He found Czar and the cat nose-to-nose at the coffee table.

"Oh, God, Czar, not with the cat again," Ben groaned. "We don't have time…"

Czar made a whining sound that came off as pure exasperation. Taking a closer look, Ben spotted a piece of paper. He picked it up. "Damn. It's him, but surely Jill wouldn't have let him in."

One look at the scar on the dog's head reminded Ben of

how desperate and determined Will Ogden was. He raced to the Blazer and called for backup. Czar occupied the passenger seat, barking impatiently. Ben started the engine but pounded the steering wheel. "They could be anywhere. Where do we start?"

Czar gave him a look that seemed to say, trust me.

Ben put the car in gear and backed out of the driveway, his tires squealing. At the stop sign leading either into town or toward the mine, Czar lunged across his lap. Ben called in his location. "I think he's taken her to the mine."

He turned on the siren. "Please, let me get there in time," he muttered. "If there *is* a Time God, I could sure use a little help here."

His pulse raced; adrenaline surged through his veins. At the turnoff to the mine, the Blazer took the corner on two wheels. Both he and Czar slammed together like on a carnival ride. He pulled the car under control and shot up the incline flying over the rise like a stunt driver.

Nothing. The field was empty.

Czar pawed at the passenger window. Ben instinctively cranked the wheel and hit the gas. Dust churned as the car bounced over rocks and ruts. Czar's barking increased the same moment Ben spotted a car. An older sedan. Blue.

Even as he made the mental description, a sudden spark of light appeared and almost instantly the car was engulfed in flame.

"No," Ben cried, jumping from the Blazer before it was fully stopped. He left the door open and felt Czar's body sail past him. Ben sank to his knees immobilized by horror and grief. "Jill."

Czar latched onto his shirtsleeve with his teeth and tugged so hard it ripped. The sound penetrated Ben's agony. He looked up in time to see Czar dash through the wind tunnel of dust that suddenly arose out of nowhere. As the noise seeped into his awareness, Ben looked up. A helicopter.

Maybe it wasn't too late.

He took his gun from the waistband of his jeans and started running. He followed the sound of Czar's barking. Under his breath he whispered a prayer. *Please, let her be okay*.

JILL DIDN'T GET as far as she'd hoped, but she hadn't counted on him grabbing her by her ponytail. The pain brought tears to her eyes, but she used it to sharpen her focus. When he tugged backward, she added her weight to the momentum to throw him off balance. They went down together. He was heavier but she squirmed like an eel, and he couldn't keep her pinned down long enough to aim his gun.

As she felt her strength sapping, Jill decided to try using her weapon. Arching her neck, she curled to the side and bit his hand. Hard. She spit out the taste of his blood. When he jerked back, her right hand was freed. She stabbed at his face with all her might. The tiny piece of wood, sharp and scented, went deep—deeper than she'd expected.

His howl of pain was satisfying but short-lived. Will retaliated with word and fist. His first blow missed her face, but the second grazed her temple.

There wasn't a third.

Instead, a growl as ferocious and frightening as she'd ever heard pierced the night. The next moment a projectile flew out of the gloom and knocked Will over.

Czar.

Jill rolled to her belly and started to sob.

"Ben," she called out, crawling to distance herself from the melee going on in the dust. "Help."

A word rang out. In German. Czar broke from the body

curled in a fetal position. "Make one move and I'll let him kill you," Ben snarled.

Will didn't move. Not so anyone could see, but Jill heard something. "Ben," she cried. "He has a gun."

Her warning was lost in the crack of a gunshot. Jill knew it hadn't come from Will, but she didn't dare look. She was almost afraid to breathe. Please, God, let it be over.

"Jill," Ben said, dropping to one knee beside her. He carefully eased her onto her back. "Are you okay, baby? Tell me you're okay."

Before she could answer, a shaggy beast covered her face with slobbering kisses. She tried to defend herself but was laughing and crying at the same time.

Ben shooed the dog aside. "Dammit, Czar, she might be hurt." He brushed her forehead with a soothing touch. "Don't move, honey. The medics will be here any minute."

Honey?

Jill ignored his command and sat up. She threw her arms around him. "I don't need doctors. I just need you. Only you."

BY THE TIME the last of the loose ends was tied up, Jill and Czar were both sound asleep in the back of the Blazer. Ben had confiscated half a dozen blankets from Jimmy and the other units that had arrived on the scene and had ordered Jill to stay put.

For once, she obeyed his command, but he didn't count on it becoming a regular habit. And that was okay, too. He liked her feisty.

Amos put a hand on Ben's shoulder and gave it a supportive squeeze. "You really earned your keep tonight, son. You and Czar. This could have turned out ugly."

Ben's stomach turned over. He knew better than anyone just how close it had been.

"Is the bastard going to live?" Ben asked, more out of habit than any true concern. Ben was just glad he'd been in the right place at the right time to put a bullet in the bastard's chest before he could do any more damage.

"Looks that way. The medics said his left lung had collapsed, but the wound wasn't life threatening."

Ben took his gun from his waistband and held it out to Amos. "You'll want this until the report gets cleared, right?"

Amos chuckled. "The report is clear. Crystal clear. And since Jimmy's on his way to arrest our esteemed mayor, I don't think we'll catch any flack about procedure."

Ben had caught bits and pieces of the Martins' confession from some of the other officers. The whole story would come out soon, but it sounded as though Peter and Clarice had cut a deal in exchange for the names and dollar figures in a bribery scandal that would rock the community of Bullion to the core.

The roar of a large white van pulling away caught Ben's attention. "Anybody figure out how Channel 47 got here so fast?"

Amos chuckled. "Talk about irony. Peter had scheduled a news conference to promote Excelsior Estates. I guess they were listening to a scanner and heard what was going down."

Ben shook his head. "A media person's dream—fire trucks, police cars, ambulance, helicopter." He looked at Jill. She slept in a childlike pose with one arm flung across Czar. "Jill would have loved the excitement."

Amos jostled his shoulder. "She'll get her chance. I heard one of the *Sentinel* reporters tell that photographer—

Jamal Whatshisname—that Jill was a shoe-in for Will's job."

Ben gave his boss a wry look. "Wonderful."

Amos shrugged. "A job's a job. You just have to make sure you never let it get in the way of family." He sighed wearily. "Speaking of which, I'm going home to my wife."

Ben watched the older man walk away. *Words of wisdom,* he thought. It had taken two near misses for the truth to finally sink in, but Ben got the message. Nothing in the world was more important to him than Jill, and he planned to make sure she knew it.

He crawled into the back of the Blazer, taking care not to jostle Jill. Czar lifted his head and looked at him. Ben ran the tip of his finger down the dog's long muzzle. "Go back to sleep."

Jill sighed and stretched. She opened her eyes. The moon had finally risen and it bathed the natural amphitheater in pale light. The smoked side windows gave the vehicle's interior a cozy feeling. "Hi," she said, turning on her side. "Are you all done? Can we go home now?"

"Yes." *But which home? Mine or yours?*

"Good," she said, then added, "Can we pick up Frank on the way? He was terribly put out not to be included last night."

Ben bit down on a smile. "Yes." He dropped down on one elbow and leaned close to give her a kiss.

Jill snuggled closer. She seemed relaxed and receptive, but Ben could tell something was on her mind.

She swallowed, then asked, "Can we call your parents and let them know you're okay? With that camera crew here, they might be upset."

Ben let out the breath he'd been holding. He probably owed this one to the Time God.

"Yes," he said, pressing a kiss to her lips.

She smiled and looped her arms around his neck. Their kiss answered every question but one.

"Will you marry me?" Ben asked, his whisper hoarse with emotion.

Jill pulled back enough to look into his eyes. Her mouth curved in a smile of such joy Ben felt it all the way to his toes.

"Yes."

Ben's eyes filled with moisture. "That's all? Just yes?"

She laced her fingers behind his head and whispered, "Jill's Rule Number One—When love is the answer, you don't need words."

EPILOGUE

AMOS TILTED BACK his head and looked at the pinkish-tinged clouds floating overhead. Perfect weather for a wedding, he thought. *Maybe Jill bribed the Weather God.*

In the past six months, Amos had gotten to know Jill Martin well. They'd even started collaborating on a book—a mystery novel with a very heroic dog in it. And Amos liked everything about Jill—including her parents. Nils and Mattie had purchased their daughter's home and were frequent visitors to Bullion, between their many adventurous jaunts. Mattie had even talked Amos into booking a cruise for his thirty-second wedding anniversary.

All this love and romance was getting to him—he was almost looking forward to the trip. Especially since Ben had taken over the department so Amos could fill in as acting mayor. It wasn't an ideal situation, but the fallout from the Land Barons debacle had local politicians on their best behavior. The disgraced Bud Francis was still in seclusion, but his wife was talking about running for the post next year.

The gentle serenade of the harp had almost lulled Amos to sleep when his wife cued him with an elbow to the ribs. He stumbled to his feet and looked toward the jungle gym where the bride was beginning her walk. While Ben had lobbied for a quick trip to Reno, Jill had insisted on Founder's Park. "It's where we met."

Ben had laughed—he did that a lot these days. "Are you

going to wear the bite suit instead of a wedding dress?'' he'd teased.

''You'll see,'' she had promised.

Amos smiled as he took in Jill's lovely gown of satin and lace. A warm ivory color, it complemented her long red hair, which was capped with a crown of flowers and flowing ribbons.

The matron of honor and her two rambunctious, rose petal–dispensing toddlers had already arrived at the flower-festooned gazebo. When Jill reached her husband-to-be's side, she rose up and gave him a quick peck on the cheek.

As the minister began to speak, Amos glanced around at the many guests. Jill's friends and co-workers, of course. Most of the Bullion P.D. had turned out as well. A tanned, attractive woman Amos hadn't been able to place at first sat two rows over, her arm linked with a distinguished-looking Hispanic gentleman. *Dorry Fishbank.*

He looked across the aisle at Ben's family. Amos understood the elder Jacobs had been undergoing treatment for cancer. Although thin and pale, the man carried himself with the same pride and grace as his son.

The vows were simple but heartfelt. And when it was time for the blessing of the rings, the best man stepped forward—tail wagging. Two simple gold bands were attached to Czar's collar with ribbons.

Ben petted his old friend lightly as he removed the ring. When it was Jill's turn, she leaned down and whispered something in Czar's ear. Amos swore he could almost see the dog beam, and there was no doubt in Amos's mind that man's best friend knew true love when he saw it.